Eirinn's Dream

"I look into your green eyes," Danny said, "and I see the fields of Ireland." He reached up and gently stroked her cheek with his fingertips. "Ah, lass, a man could get lost in your eyes."

Boldly she lifted her lips to his and tangled her fingers in the thick chestnut curls at the nape of his neck. "Kiss me again, Danny," she said as she snuggled even closer into his embrace, her full breasts pushing against the hardness of his chest. "Kiss me. I know you want to. And I want you to. I've wanted you to for the longest time . . . "

She waited as he looked down at her, his eyes registering his internal struggle. "I can't," he said. She felt a shudder run through his body. "If I ever start kissin' you, girl, I'll not be able to stop. You won't let me, and I won't want to."

"So why would we have to stop if neither of us wants to?"

"Because you're Michael McKevett's little girl, and Michael is the dearest friend I have in the world. I'll not dishonor his family. Much as I want to hold you this minute, I can't do it."

He tried to pull back from her, but she held him tightly. Eirinn was accustomed to getting what she wanted, and, looking up at his warm eyes and full lips, she decided that she wanted Daniel O'Brien, and she would have him.

"If you won't kiss me, Danny," she said, her voice husky with desire, "then I'll kiss you. And I don't think you'll push me away."

CAROUSEL
Sonja Massie

PINNACLE BOOKS
WINDSOR PUBLISHING CORP.

PINNACLE BOOKS

are published by

Windsor Publishing Corp.
475 Park Avenue South
New York, NY 10016

First printing: June, 1990

Printed in the United States of America

Prologue

The young man's trembling fingertips caressed the cold steel of the derringer buried deep in his coat pocket as he descended the theater stairs, his tread light, agile, his footfalls silent on the thick carpet.

No emotion showed on his face, a handsome face, in a pretty sort of way. Pale, melancholy. Only his sparkling black eyes betrayed his excitement. He knew how to wipe his countenance clean. He was an actor. A brilliant actor, some of his critics said. And this was the most important role of his life. He had been born to act the part of executioner. Destiny had cast him for the role, and he would play it through to the devastating conclusion.

He paused at the bottom of the stairs. In front of the narrow, white door was a chair, the guard's chair; it was empty. Fate was on his side tonight.

In the distance he could hear the actors shouting their lines, the audience's laughter, though their response was subdued tonight. The play simply wasn't that good.

A sly grin tugged at the young man's delicate mouth. Little did the crowd know that within moments they would witness one of the greatest dramas in history. And he would be the star, a comet blazing a glimmering arc across the night sky. A performance never to be forgotten.

As he opened the small door a rush of adrenalin surged through his bloodstream and rivulets of icy sweat trickled down his brow. He stepped into the musty darkness of the inner passageway and closed the door quietly behind him. Groping in the blackness, he found the small rod he had secreted there and slid it into place across the door, making sure that he would not be interrupted.

In less than a minute he had passed through the second door and was standing in the stage box within arm's reach of his victim.

As he pulled the derringer from his pocket, the enormity of what he was about to do washed over him and his knees nearly buckled. But he was a disciplined professional. Drawing a deep breath of resolve, he pointed the tiny barrel at the dark head that rose from behind the high back of the chair.

For a moment the actor was struck by the humanity of the man seated in the rocking chair. He had no horns, this Satan. Even in the dim theater light the man looked weary, haggard, with the deep lines of care permanently chiseled in his homely face.

But the young man couldn't allow himself to feel pity. Not now. This was an act of war. Many times he had played the role of Brutus and had slain Caesar. And like the Roman, this tyrant must also die.

His hand tightened around the derringer; his coat sleeve slid upward, revealing the tattooed initials, J.W.B. He pointed the barrel and with infinite care squeezed the trigger. The gun exploded. And shattered a nation.

Chapter One

Eirinn McKevett bounded down her back porch stairs, taking two steps at a time, her black curls flying, her cheeks flushed, her green eyes glittering with youthful exuberance. Then she pulled herself up short, lifted her chin and descended the remaining steps with all the dignity of a young lady who had just turned sixteen and, thereby, entered womanhood.

As she crossed the grassy lot that separated her family's home from their carousel shop she lifted the skirt of her new dress to keep it off the dew-damp grass. The satin shimmered pink and mauve in the morning sun and her spirits soared.

It felt so good to be out of mourning clothes, to feel pretty again. She hoped she wasn't being disrespectful to Stephen's memory. But she was sure her brother would understand that she wanted to look nice on her birthday.

Besides, the whole city of Boston, maybe even the whole world, was celebrating. The war was over. The North had won. The Union was preserved. And most important, at least to Eirinn McKevett, her beloved brother hadn't given his life in vain.

But the moment she threw the wide door of her father's shop open and stepped inside, she knew that something was terribly wrong. A heavy silence had replaced the familiar sounds of the shop: the constant pounding of mallets on chisels, the grinding of the saws, the rich curses in Gaelic, Italian,

Russian, and German. Eirinn looked around the shop, and for the first time since she could remember, no one was working.

Ignacio Falcone stood beside a horse that he had been carving. He still held the chisel in his hand, but his young face was ashen, and he looked as though he were going to be sick.

Sitting beside Ignacio on a ten-gallon paint drum was Josef Kistner, the shop's master painter. The old man had buried his face in his stain-blotched apron and was softly weeping.

"What is it? Iggy, what's wrong?" she asked, fear turning her throat to sanded paper. But neither Ignacio nor Josef answered her.

Forgetting to hold her new skirt out of the thick dust and wood shavings that littered the shop floor, Eirinn ran to the tiny, enclosed office in the corner.

"Ma, Da!" she shouted as she opened the door and rushed inside. The sight that greeted her eyes made her legs go weak and her heart leap against her ribs.

Her father, Michael McKevett, stood in the middle of the office, his arms wrapped around his wife, Caitlin, who was weeping, her face pressed against his broad chest. Eirinn had only seen her mother cry once, three months before, when they had received word that Eirinn's brother, Stephen, had been killed.

Caitlin McKevett was a strong woman who spent her days wiping away the tears of others, not shedding her own. Eirinn knew, without asking, that tragedy had struck again.

"Da, what's happened?" she asked.

Her eyes searched Michael's face, looking for reassurance that their lives hadn't been destroyed again. Her father was big and strong, and he had always made everything right in Eirinn's world. Until Stephen's death. Eirinn looked into eyes that

8

were the same emerald green as her own, and she saw that once again something terrible had happened, something so bad that not even Michael McKevett could make it right.

" 'Tis as though we've lost Stephen all over again," Caitlin sobbed into his shirt. "How could anyone do such a dreadful thing?"

"I don't know, love," Michael murmured, smoothing his wife's copper waves. "I don't know. God curse the scoundrel and may he die with his blood in his throat."

"Da, what—" Eirinn felt gentle fingers close firmly around her shoulders from behind.

She spun around and found herself in the arms of the other man she had loved since the day she had been born, Daniel O'Brien, her father's best friend and the shop's master carver. Danny was only twelve years older than Eirinn, but he had been a second father to her, a beloved uncle, and sometimes an older brother.

"Come with me, darlin'," Daniel said as he led her from the office back into the studio. Eirinn looked up into his face and knew that whatever was wrong she could bear to hear the news if it were spoken with Danny's soft brogue.

"Why is Mama crying?" she asked him.

He pulled her closer into the circle of his arms and slid his palm beneath her chin, cradling her face in his big hand. " 'Tis the president," he said. "Someone's shot Mr. Lincoln."

"He's shot?" She shook her head, refusing to believe his words. "But not dead. Surely you're not sayin' he's dead."

"Aye, he is at that, girl. Died this very mornin', he did. We just got the word."

Eirinn's world teetered on its axis, and she gripped Daniel's muscular arms, trying to steady herself. The president. Dead.

9

"But the war's over," she argued. "Who'd kill him now when there's peace after so long?"

Daniel sighed and brushed one of her black curls away from her forehead with a calloused forefinger. "A lad full of hate, to be sure," he replied, his amber eyes moist.

Standing on tiptoe, Eirinn threw her arms around Daniel's neck and buried her face against his broad shoulder. "Oh, Danny, I can't believe it. It's too awful to be believed."

Even through the daze of her shock, Eirinn found herself aware of Daniel's arms wrapped tightly around her waist, the warm press of his body against hers, the strength that his touch imparted. It had been a long time since Danny had hugged her, and she didn't remember it feeling like this before.

Tears fell down her cheeks and sobs knotted in her throat as she burrowed deeper into his embrace.

"Ah, lass," he murmured, his lips against her hair. "Ye must be brave. 'Tis hard enough for your dear parents. You must be strong for their sakes and dry your eyes." He pulled a kerchief from his shirt pocket and dabbed at her cheeks. "There, that's a girl," he said as she fought to stifle her sobs.

His words were those of a man spoken to a child. But when Eirinn looked up into his eyes, she saw a light that she hadn't seen before, a glimmer that reflected feelings she had harbored toward Daniel O'Brien for years. In spite of her grief she felt a thrill course through her, a rush of hope, of youthful desires that she couldn't exactly name.

"Will there be war again?" she asked, trying to keep the fear out of her voice, but not succeeding.

Daniel closed his eyes and ran his fingers through his dark chestnut waves. "Mary, Jesus, and Joseph, I hope not," he replied. "We'd never survive an-

10

other." At the alarmed look in her eyes, he quickly placed both hands on her shoulders and embraced her again. "But you're not to worry about such things, darlin'," he said. "We've troubles enough of our own without borrowin' still more."

"I'll ask you to please take your hands off my sister," said a voice behind them.

Eirinn turned to see her half-brother, Ryan, watching her and Daniel, his arms akimbo, his blue eyes blazing with indignation.

"Ah, don't be a horse's arse if ye can help it, Ryan," Daniel said, dropping his hands from Eirinn's shoulders. "I was only comfortin' her in her time of sorrow. 'Tis hard news to hear, indeed."

"If Eirinn's in need of comfort, she'll get it from her own family." Ryan took three steps and wedged his tall, thin body between them.

Daniel's eyes narrowed, and Eirinn could feel the animosity radiating from him toward her brother. It grieved her heart that these two men whom she loved so dearly were constantly at each other's throats.

"Then it's in yer hands I'll leave her," Daniel replied. "Just be sure you show her the kindness she needs."

Ryan's arm curled possessively around Eirinn's waist, and for once she resented his attention. "I always take good care of my sister. We're very close," Ryan replied, his voice heavy with unspoken emphasis.

"I don't need either of you right now," she said, unwinding herself from Ryan's embrace. "I'm going to go comfort my mother, if I'm able." She turned toward the office, then stopped and added over her shoulder, "I wish you could stop your fighting for once. I should think there's enough hate in the world today without the two of you adding more."

Eirinn watched her mother as she moved around the huge kitchen and served those seated at her table. Having put her own grief aside, Caitlin McKevett plied her guests with thickly buttered soda bread, hearty mutton soup, and enough good Irish whiskey to ease their sorrows.

Caitlin and Michael McKevett had endured the horror of the Great Hunger, the Irish famine, and Eirinn couldn't remember a time when the McKevetts' table wasn't overrun with food and drink.

"If I accomplish nothing else in this world, I'll see to it that none of mine suffer the pangs of hunger," Michael had said many times. And for years she had watched him work day and night in his carousel shop to provide a stable life for his family.

Eirinn marveled at her parents' seemingly endless energy. Trying to follow in Caitlin's footsteps was an exhausting exercise. If her mother's back ever ached — as Eirinn's was aching now — or if her legs and feet screamed for relief, it never showed on her pretty face.

"Will ye have another drop, Sean?" Caitlin asked, not waiting for an answer before she filled his glass to the brim.

Sean Sullivan, a friend of the McKevetts since before the famine, smiled up at Caitlin, his blue eyes warm with fraternal affection. Eirinn had noticed that most men smiled when they looked at her mother. After all these years and all she had endured, Caitlin McKevett was still a beautiful woman, spirited and strong.

Eirinn slid a bowl of soup under Tomas Sullivan's nose, taking care to cut a wide berth around the young man. Tomas, unlike his gentlemanly father, Sean, wasn't above trying to sneak a pat on her rear. Eirinn liked Tomas, enjoyed his humor, his fire, and she found his constant flirtation exciting, but Caitlin had warned her that he played fast and loose with young ladies, and if Michael McKevett ever caught him making bold with his only daughter, he would undoubtedly send the young man packing with two broken legs and his head in a plaster as well.

"I think we should declare war on those bloody rebels all over again," Tomas expounded, shoving a handful of Caitlin's bread into his mouth. "Our honor is at stake here."

"Hold your tongue, lad," Sean gently reproached his son. "Ye've no idea what yer sayin', so don't be sayin' it. War's a cruel and hurtful thing and it honors no man."

"And you're nothing but an old dog barking through toothless gums," Tomas returned, washing the bread down with a draught of whiskey.

Eirinn caught her breath at the young man's blatant disrespect. She would never grow accustomed to the insulting manner in which Tomas addressed his father.

Michael rose from his chair and reached across the table to clasp Tomas's shirtfront in his enormous fist. "You'll not speak to yer father in that tone, lad," Michael said, his own voice soft and low.

The giant hand clenched, pulling the shirt neck tighter, until Tomas's brown face turned three shades darker. "Sean Sullivan's as brave a man as ever walked God's green earth. 'Tis easy for a pup like yourself to think himself a hound, until he find's himself face to face with killin' and dyin'. Ye've never looked death in the eye before, like some of us at this table have. And until you do, we'll not hear any more from you about war. Are ye listenin', lad?"

Tomas nodded, his face now tinged with blue.

Releasing him, Michael settled back into his chair, and the others in the kitchen resumed their breathing.

Eirinn glanced sideways at Sean to see his reaction, but his tired face held little emotion.

Once Eirinn had asked her father why Sean seemed so empty, so listless, and Michael had told her how Sean's young wife, Judy, had died on one of the many coffin ships that sailed from Ireland to Boston during the famine. Judy had been a lovely, joyful lass, Michael said, and when Sean had lost her he had lost his heart. Eirinn thought it a shame that Sean had never found another to love.

Eirinn refilled her father's glass of ale and considered what he had said about staring death in the face. It was true, she thought, that the people she knew who had endured the famine were different from the others. Her father and mother, Sean Sullivan, Daniel O'Brien . . .

There was a gentle strength, a steadfastness about them. They radiated the quiet confidence of a people who had survived the worst that life could offer and therefore feared nothing.

The kitchen door opened and Ryan walked into the room. His gait was none too steady; Eirinn suspected that he was in his cups. She hated to see him drink so much. Some men became more gay and carefree when drunk; Ryan McKevett became morose and sullen.

"That bloody Daniel is out there carving," he said as he sat down at Michael's right hand and took a bowl of soup from Caitlin. "No respect for our fallen leader. No respect at all."

"That's not true," Michael replied, avoiding Ryan's eyes. Eirinn had noticed several years ago that Michael and Ryan always avoided eye contact when they spoke. "Daniel had great respect for the president. Some men show their grief by carving

14

. . . some by losing themselves in drink," he added pointedly.

Ryan ignored the barb and settled down to eat his soup and bread, while Eirinn watched with pride. Ryan had impeccable table manners. He worked hard at being a gentleman, from the silk scarf that peeked from his pocket to the aristocratic tone of his voice, which he had carefully wiped clean of any hint of an Irish brogue. Ryan knew a lot of important society people in Boston, and some of them forgave him for his humble Irish heritage, but only because he hid it so well.

Ryan had wanted to introduce Eirinn to some of these people, but Caitlin had strictly forbidden it. "They aren't the sort of folks a young girl needs to rub up against," she had stated firmly.

And Ryan knew better than to argue with his stepmother. Caitlin, who stood an inch taller than Ryan, had been known to slap him down on occasion, verbally *and* physically.

Eirinn walked over to her father to see if his ale glass needed refilling, but he reached out for her and pulled her down onto his knee. "You look all done in, lass," he said affectionately as he squeezed her around the waist. "You'd best be off to bed now."

Eirinn looked into his green eyes, the same shade of emerald as her own, and saw his love for her, the love that had given her strength and self-confidence every day of her life. "I'll stay up a bit longer," she said, "and help Mama. She must be tired, too."

Michael looked across the room at his wife who was stirring yet another kettle of fragrant, steaming soup on the new stove he had bought her. The weary lines on his handsome face softened as he watched her. "You mustn't worry about your mother, girl. I'll help her clean up, and then I'll be carryin' her upstairs and tuckin' her into bed beside

15

meself."

At Michael's words, Caitlin turned toward him and the look they exchanged made Eirinn wish with all her heart that she had someone to love even half as much as her parents loved each other.

"Aye, run along to bed, lass," Caitlin told her as Michael stood Eirinn on her feet, rose, and walked to the stove to lift the heavy kettle for Caitlin. "You're a growing child and you need your rest."

As Eirinn kissed her parents good night her heart sank. A child? She had turned sixteen today and no one seemed to have noticed. She had stepped across the threshold that separated her childhood from the rest of her life and no one had celebrated that crossing with her.

She left them in the kitchen and walked slowly up the stairs to her bedroom, her head down, not bothering to lift the hem of her new dress. No one had noticed her dress either.

But halfway up the stairs it occurred to Eirinn that only a child would feel the petty disappointment of a ruined birthday. The president of the United States had been murdered, and the world was mourning. A woman would swallow her hurt and think only of her slain leader, of her troubled nation.

Eirinn lifted her head, squared her shoulders, and continued up the stairs with all the dignity of the woman she had become.

Moonlight streamed through the lacy curtains that covered Eirinn's bedroom window, its silver radiance nearly as bright as an afternoon sun.

With a sigh Eirinn threw back the satin comforter. There was no point in trying to sleep on a night when the world had been turned upside down. On bare feet she walked across her bedroom floor

16

and sat on the ruffled cushions of her window seat, staring out the bay windows on the city below.

At the bottom of the hill lay Boston Harbor, still, dark, and silent, with hardly a ripple on its moonlit surface. From the decks of the ships at anchor lanterns twinkled like so many summer fireflies. The clipper ships, the mighty swans of the sea, slept, their white wings folded.

It seemed to Eirinn that the whole world was sleeping tonight . . . except for her.

Her eyes scanned the streets that were lit with the golden glow of the street lamps, but there wasn't a soul in sight.

The red, white, and blue victory bunting that had decorated the shops and homes only yesterday had been replaced by black funeral drapes.

Directly below her window was her father's shop, its windows dark, its wide doors closed. But in the back of the building one window gleamed, a tiny square of light. Eirinn felt less alone. There was at least one other person in Boston who couldn't sleep tonight. Daniel O'Brien.

Slipping a burgundy velvet dressing gown over her nightdress, Eirinn made her way quietly out of her room and down the hall. As she passed her parents' door she could hear them still talking, her father's deep bass, Caitlin's soft contralto.

Though she couldn't discern their words, there was no mistaking the intimate tone of their voices. It made her lonely just to hear them. When would she ever hear the sound of a deep, comforting, male voice in the night? She was sixteen years old, and many of the girls she knew already had families of their own.

At the foot of the stairs the giant grandfather clock chimed one o'clock as she passed. Eirinn loved that clock. When she had been only four years old she had watched Michael carve the elaborate case. Around the face were the symbols of Ireland; the Celtic harp, the shamrock, and in the center above the dial, the claddaugh, the sign of love and devotion.

Michael had allowed Eirinn the honor of tying it with a red satin bow before he had presented it to Caitlin for her Christmas present. Eirinn had known even then how very much her father had loved her mother. A gift of carving was from a man's heart. She wondered as she walked out the back door if a man would ever love her enough to give her a bit of his heart.

She walked across the field to the door of the shop and slipped quietly inside. Against the far wall was Daniel's workbench, centrally located because of his responsibilities as master carver. He stood in front of the bench, mallet in one hand, chisel in the other, carving the saddle blanket of a prancing stallion.

The steady thud of his mallet echoed through the empty shop, and he didn't hear Eirinn when she walked up behind him. She stood quietly, waiting for him to notice her. Michael had taught her long ago never to startle a man when he was carving. He could slip and cut himself badly with the razor-sharp chisel.

She watched for a long time as Daniel's skillful hands worked their magic on the wood. Even the other carvers would sometimes lay down their work to watch Daniel O'Brien carve. His tools moved quickly, extensions of his skilled hands, scooping out the thin curls of wood that dropped into the pile of shavings on the floor.

His shirt sleeves were rolled up to allow him total freedom. She watched, fascinated, as his rounded biceps knotted, stretched, and swelled with every movement.

His lower arms and hands were covered with tiny

scars, the hazards of his trade, old white scars, newer red ones. Eirinn marveled at the controlled power in those hands, the same control that she sensed in the man. Daniel never lost his temper, never added his voice to the chorus of curses in the shop, never challenged another man to fight . . . a common occurrence in a shop full of vibrant, temperamental personalities.

But there was a restlessness about Daniel O'Brien, a hot spring that simmered below the still surface. Eirinn had always felt that quality in Daniel, but especially so since the war.

Daniel and her brother, Stephen, had fought side by side, and Stephen had died in Daniel's arms. That fact had been her parents' only comfort.

Daniel had never gotten over Stephen's death. He had blamed himself for not being able to save his best friend's son. Now there was grief in Daniel's eyes to add to the unrest, and Eirinn had noticed the difference in his carving.

Before the war Daniel had created delicate horses, beautiful, dainty creatures with sweet faces and noble poses. Now his stallions had reared heads, gnashed teeth, and aggressive stances. The rose and lily drapings had given way to military themes, like this stallion, who bore a musket and saber and a flag draped across his rump.

Daniel was working on a medallion that hung over the horse's flank, a round plate with some sort of face on it.

Wiping the sweat from his forehead with his wrist, he stood up and straightened his back. She moved into the circle of light cast by the lantern above his head.

"Well, good evenin' to you, darlin'," he said, and his tired smile told her how happy he was to see her. Her heart skipped a beat, then raced to make up for lost time.

"Would it bother you if I watched for a while?" she asked. "I can't sleep tonight either."

"Yer never a bother, lass. Surely you know that." He laid down his mallet and chose a smaller chisel from the row of tools spread out on his bench. After a quick sharpening on the oiled stone he began the fine detailing on the medallion. "I came into the house earlier to see you," he said, "but yer mother said you were away to bed already."

He had come into the house specifically to see her? A faint blush of happiness crept up her cheeks. "Why did you want to see me?"

"Why, indeed?" His amber eyes twinkled as he flashed her a broad, friendly smile. Not for the first time Eirinn thought Daniel O'Brien the most handsome man she had ever seen, except maybe her father. "I've something to show you."

"Then show it to me now," she said, trying unsuccessfully not to sound like an eager child.

"Soon," he said. "Just let me finish what I'm doing here. 'Twill only take a few minutes."

Obediently Eirinn sat down on a crate beside his bench, drew her knees up to her chin, and wrapped her arms around her legs. She watched quietly as he carved, his dark chestnut locks hanging down his forehead, which glistened with perspiration, the deep scowl of concentration furrowing his brow, his eyes intent on his work.

Except for Ryan, who had never developed a knack for carving, every man Eirinn had ever loved had been a woodcarver: her father, Stephen, and Danny. They were men with hard bodies and creative minds. Men with strong but gentle hands, men whose clothes and skin carried the fresh scent of wood. They were men with dreams and the skill to sculpt their fantasies and turn those dreams into realities.

As she watched Daniel carve the medallion she

saw the face of a man slowly appearing in the wood. She gasped as recognition seized her. "It's the president."

He nodded. " 'Tis Mr. Lincoln himself." Leaning back, he surveyed his work with a critical eye, then continued. "He was on me mind all day and in me heart tonight. I'm hopin' that once he's in the wood, I can forget about him . . . at least enough to sleep."

Eirinn wished that she could carve what was in her heart. But she knew that even if she carved Daniel's handsome face a hundred times she would still think of him every night when she laid her head on her pillow. She would still wonder how it would feel to have his lips touch hers, not in his uncle's quick kiss, but in a long lover's kiss—the kind of kiss that Eirinn had seen her father give her mother a thousand times.

"There. I think he's done, at least for tonight." Daniel laid his tools on the bench and covered them lovingly with a soft cloth. Then he ran his fingers slowly over the medallion, tracing the famous, rugged profile. "Mr. Lincoln was a fine president," he said. "He deserved better than to be shot like a mad dog." He sighed and wiped his face with the kerchief that always dangled from his back pocket. "But maybe this will help keep his memory alive for the people who ride this horse."

"It's a lovely tribute, Danny," she said as she stood, walked over to him and slipped her hand into his rough palm.

"Yes, well. Come along with me, lass. I want a lady's opinion of something I've been workin' on." As he led her to the rear of the shop, she blushed with pleasure. He had called her a lady. Had he finally noticed that she had become a woman?

Against the back wall, beneath a dozen or so life-size sketches, was a carousel animal covered with a

21

blue, paint-splattered cloth. "Close yer eyes," he said, releasing her hand. She heard him pull the sheet away. "Now you can look and tell me what you think."

What she saw took her breath away. It was a glorious prancing mare, the prettiest pony she had ever seen. Even her father had never carved anything so lovely as this. "Oh, Danny, she's a wonder."

Reverently she reached out her hand and stroked the mare's velvet-smooth muzzle, the long graceful neck, and the full-blown mane knotted with tiny roses and swirling ribbons. The pony's glossy black coat contrasted sharply with the delicate pastels of the pink and mauve drapings. Gold and silver bells spangled the dainty bridle. The horse's right leg was lifted in a flirting pose. She was a delicate yet spirited creature, small of stature but full of fire.

But it was the mare's eyes that fascinated Eirinn. They were bright green, like her own. And although some carousel carvers painted their animals in outlandish, unrealistic colors, Eirinn had never known Daniel to carve or paint any animal other than lifelike.

"Her eyes," she said. "They're lovely, but they're green. Horse's eyes aren't green, Danny."

She looked up at him and saw him watching her closely, a small grin tugging at the dimples on either side of his full lips. "This is a special horse," he said. "She's Irish, this pony, and my favorite Irish lass has green eyes and black hair. I thought the pony should be colored the same."

His deep voice was soft and intimate, with a tone that she'd never heard before. She realized what he was saying; he had carved and painted this pony to look like her. Was she really that beautiful to him? The thought caused a red flush to color her cheeks.

"Here you go," he said, grasping her around the waist and lifting her onto the horse. "I've allowed

22

no one to sit on her yet, not even meself. I thought you should be the first to ride your horse."

She stared down at him from atop the pony. *"My horse?"*

"She is, indeed." He covered her hand that rested on the saddle pommel with his own. "Happy birthday, love."

"Oh, Danny. . ." A sob choked her as she thought of how bitter she had been, assuming that everyone had forgotten her birthday. She thought of the clock her father had carved for her mother and of how she had just wished that a man would carve her a gift from his heart. "I . . . don't know what to say."

He laughed. "Now there's something new under the sun, Eirinn McKevett without a word in her mouth." Carefully he lifted her down from the horse. Setting her on her feet beside him, he brushed her hair back from her face. For a moment his eyes strayed to the low-cut vee of her lace nightgown that peeked from beneath her dressing gown. "Just tell me that you like yer birthday present," he said. " 'Twill be enough."

"I love my gift," she whispered as tears of gratitude spilled down her cheeks.

"Then what's this?" he asked, touching one of the drops with his fingertip. "I've made her cry, I have. Please, don't be sad, lass."

"I'm not sad," she said with a sniff. "It's just that I thought no one remembered, and then you give me this beautiful pony. I can't believe you'd carve something so lovely for me."

His arms slid around her waist, easing her toward him. She shivered, aware of the power in those arms, conscious of the warmth of his body that pressed against hers. " 'Twas your own beauty that inspired me," he said as he bent his head and kissed one of her tears away. "You've become such a pretty

23

woman, Eirinn. I've noticed how the lads watch you when you walk through the shop. And how can I blame them when I can't keep me own eyes off you?"

Slowly he kissed the other tear away. Eirinn's heart thudded in her chest as she allowed her hands to trail up his arms to his shoulders. She could feel the swell of his muscles through the thin fabric of his shirt, and she wondered how his bare skin would feel against her palms.

His lips were only a scant inch from hers, and she caught her breath, hoping that he would kiss her. He did. But it was a quick, fraternal kiss, not the long, passionate kind that her father gave her mother, not the kiss that Eirinn was craving.

But there was a light burning in his eyes that she had never seen before as he searched her face. For what, she wasn't sure.

"I look into your green eyes," he said, "and I see the fields of Ireland." He reached up and gently stroked her cheek with his fingertips. "Ah, lass, a man could get lost in your eyes."

Boldly she lifted her lips to his and ran her fingers through the thick chestnut curls at the nape of his neck. "Kiss me again, Danny," she said as she snuggled even closer into his embrace, her full breasts pressing against the hardness of his chest. "Kiss me and touch me. I know you want to. And I want you to do it. I've wanted you to for the longest time."

She waited as he looked down at her, his eyes registering his internal struggle. "I can't," he said. She felt a shudder run through his body that suddenly felt hard and tense against hers. "If I ever start kissin' you, girl, I'll not be able to stop. You won't let me, and I won't want to."

"So why would we have to stop if neither of us wants to?"

"Because you're Michael McKevett's little girl, and Michael is the dearest friend I have in the world. I'll not dishonor his family. Much as I want to hold you this minute. I can't do it."

He tried to pull back from her, but she held him tightly. Eirinn was a determined young woman, accustomed to getting what she wanted, and looking up at his warm eyes and full lips, she decided that she wanted Daniel O'Brien, and she would have him.

"If you won't kiss me, Danny," she said, her voice husky with desire, "then I'll kiss you. And I don't think you'll push me away."

With her fingers tangled in his hair, she forced his head down to hers. In a moment her mouth covered his and she allowed herself to express her desire and affection for him in her kiss.

At first he resisted, but she knew the instant that he lost control. He groaned and began to kiss her in a way that she had never imagined. His lips parted and his tongue flicked lightly over her mouth. At first she was shocked. Who would have thought that a man kissed differently than a boy? But before she had time to contemplate this new discovery his tongue had invaded her mouth and the sensations he was evoking made her knees tremble. Weakly, she clung to his broad shoulders and returned his kiss, without finesse but with youthful enthusiasm.

His big hands moved over the velvet of her dressing gown, down her back and over her hips. Cupping her buttocks, he pulled her up and against him. She felt a hardness pressing into her that frightened and yet thrilled her. Eirinn wasn't acquainted with all the fine points of lovemaking, but she knew enough to understand that Daniel wanted her. He wanted her as much as a man could want a woman, and the thought elated her.

"You shouldn't have come out here," he said, his breath ragged as his mouth left hers to travel down her throat. "You should never have come to see me wearing this." His hands moved to the front of her gown where the deep vee revealed the sheer lace nightgown that covered her breasts. "You're so beautiful. I've been tryin' not to notice, but I've wanted to touch you for ever so long. I knew that if I ever held you, even once, I'd be lost."

He sighed and lowered his head to place another trail of kisses along her collar bone. "Stop me, Eirinn," he said as that path dipped lower into her cleavage. "You started this and you must be stoppin' it. I can't."

But she was far beyond the realm of self-control. Her own breathing was labored, as though she had run too fast, too long. All she knew was that she had wanted Daniel forever and she finally had him. He was holding her, kissing her, touching her, and it was even more wonderful than she had imagined.

Then, suddenly, he stopped and stepped away from her. "No. We aren't going to do that," he said, shaking his head as though to regain his reason. "I'm sorry. I should never, never have—"

"Danny?" She moved toward him, her arms outstretched, but he shoved her back so hard that she nearly lost her balance.

"Go away, lass. Get out of here now." He turned his back on her and lowered his voice, but she still heard him say, "Please leave. I can't bear the sight of you."

Chapter Two

Can't bear the sight of you. Eirinn couldn't believe that he had said such a thing. Gentle, kindhearted Danny was telling her that he couldn't stand to look at her, when only moments before he had kissed her, touched her as only a lover would.

"Danny, what are you saying?" She saw the raw pain and confusion in his eyes and something that looked a lot like hatred. "Do you despise me now?"

She waited for his answer, her heart feeling like a stone in her throat. If Daniel hated her her life would be over. She had always depended on his love, and it had always been there to lend her strength. But on a day when the great Lincoln had died, anything could happen.

Wearily he ran his fingers through his chestnut waves and said, "No, lass, I don't hate you. But I'm asking you now, if you love me as you say you do, leave me alone. Just turn around, walk out that door, and try to forget this ever happened. 'Tis the kindest thing you could do for me, truly."

She tried to turn away, but her feet were like lead. How could she leave now, not knowing if she had destroyed their friendship? Would he ever smile at her again? How could a few kisses that had felt so wonderful have changed everything between them?

Eirinn felt the burning sting of tears behind her lids and her pride rose to give her courage. She wasn't going to let this man see her cry. If he could throw her away without explanation after holding her in his arms, she would at least show him that she wasn't the child he thought her to be.

"I'll do as you say, Danny." She lifted her chin, squared her shoulders and walked away, but at the door she paused and turned back to him. "You're in love with me, Daniel O'Brien," she said. "I saw it in your eyes a minute ago. I felt it in your touch. And only a man who loves a woman would carve something like that for her," she added, pointing to the pony. But she was careful not to look at it. If she did, she would surely start crying.

Once again she waited for his reply, but he leaned his elbows on the bench, covered his face with his hands, and said nothing. Finally she turned and walked out the door, quietly closing it behind her. It was only after she had taken five steps that she heard the thrown mallet crash against the wall.

The morning sunlight streamed through the dust-frosted windows of the shop and cast its golden rays on Michael McKevett's latest triumph. He stood, hands on hips, surveying the most ambitious of all his flying horse machines.

Michael had designed this carousel to be turned by a horse instead of by manpower, and he had been able to build it larger and heavier than his previous wheels. The horses themselves were larger, nearly life-sized, and there were more of them, twenty-two prancing steeds instead of the usual six. And the carving was the most ornate and lifelike yet. They were, indeed, horses able to sweep you away to the Land of the Ever Young.

In the back of Michael's mind another dream glimmered, brighter and grander than the wheel before him. But there was time for that dream to become reality.

Michael had realized long ago that a journey was taken one careful step at a time. He had taken many

28

steps, traveled many roads to arrive at the place where he stood today, looking at this carousel. And there would be many more roads before his dream was complete.

But Michael was a patient man, with others and with himself. He knew that anything worthwhile took time. And, besides, he had learned long ago that it was the traveling that gave the most joy, not the arrival.

The bright sunlight dimmed slightly as Ryan stepped out of the office and crossed the shop to stand beside him. As always, Michael felt a tightening in his gut when in Ryan's presence. The wave of aversion was always followed by a tide of shame. What had Ryan ever done to him, other than be Annie McKevett's son?

Michael wished to God that he had been able to love Ryan as much as he had loved Stephen and Eirinn. The guilt was overwhelming, the greatest sorrow of Michael's life.

But Michael had never been in love with his first wife, and he had never been able to fully love her son, no matter how hard he tried. Ryan was simply too much like his mother—morose, sullen, always looking for the bad in life, and finding plenty of it.

"I must have a word with you," Ryan said, and by the tone of his voice, Michael knew that he was going to tell him something he didn't want to hear.

He sighed deeply. "What is it?"

"It's Eirinn . . . and Daniel."

Michael felt a cold hand close around his heart. This was definitely something that he didn't want to hear. "What about them?"

"I think there's something going on between those two."

Michael's chest tightened. Anger, raw and red, welled up inside him. But he couldn't direct it at Daniel or Eirinn, couldn't bring himself to think the unthinkable. Before he could stop it, the anger erupted and spewed onto Ryan. "Yer bloody daft, lad. There's no more honorable man to be found than Daniel O'Brien. He loves Eirinn dearly, 'tis true, but as the sweet child she is and nothing more."

"Well, that sweet child was alone with him in the shop last night after one o'clock. And she was in her nightclothes. I saw her leaving the shop and she was crying. This morning he won't look me in the eye. I'd say there's something going on."

Michael stepped closer to Ryan, looked down into those ice-blue eyes, and hated him through and through. "Ye'll not say such a thing, lad," he said, his voice strained and harsh. "Such gossip can bring ruin to your sister and destroy a fine man. I'll not hear such words from your mouth again. Do you understand me?"

Michael watched as Ryan fought to control his own rage. Ryan wanted to fight him, Michael could read it in his eyes, maybe even kill him, so great was their long-standing anger with each other. But Michael knew something else about Ryan. He was a coward, and he would never have the strength to raise his hand to Michael or any other man. And his weakness made Michael hate him all the more.

Then, as quickly as Ryan's rage had appeared, it vanished. His face became totally blank, as though a curtain had been pulled, concealing his emotions. He looked over at the new wheel and a slight tone of contempt crept into his voice when he said, "Do you really think you can make any money with it?"

Michael thought of Annie and of how she had hated his carving because it was the one thing that she couldn't control, the only thing that was his alone. Ryan was definitely too much like his mother for Michael to truly love him.

"If I hadn't thought this carousel would put coins in me breeches, I'd never have worked so hard on it for so long," he replied bitterly.

With a curt nod Ryan turned and walked away.

Michael watched him leave and felt the familiar sense of relief to have him gone. Then he walked over to his new carousel and laid his palm on one of the horses that Daniel had carved. Michael's big hand trailed over the horse's velvety rump. He could almost feel the movement of muscle, bone, and sinew against his palm.

Every man had to trust someone, and long ago Michael had decided to trust Daniel O'Brien. Danny would never betray him. Never. And he would never do anything to hurt Eirinn.

Oh, Michael had seen the sideways glances that Daniel had cast Eirinn's way lately. But every male between the ages of eight and eighty looked at Eirinn that way. She was a beauty, just like her mother, and Michael had become accustomed to having other men admire the women that he loved.

It didn't matter. Michael trusted Caitlin. And Eirinn. And Daniel. They were the three people he loved most in the world. A man had to trust his loved ones, or go mad.

Michael turned to leave the shop, looking back one last time at the new carousel. It was a lovely creation; he was enormously proud of it. And he knew that, despite what he had said to Ryan, he would have built this carousel even if it never put a single coin in his pocket.

A soft knock rattled Eirinn's bedroom door and she sat up on her bed, dabbing at her damp eyes with a linen handkerchief.

"Eirinn, 'tis yer father. May I come in, love?"

She blew her nose, straightened her rumpled skirts and replied, "Come in, Da."

The door opened slowly and Michael stepped into

31

the small room, filling it with his massive presence. As always, Michael McKevett looked out of place in his daughter's dainty bedroom. His huge frame overpowered the delicate French furniture, his rugged masculinity at odds with the feminine lace and ruffles that adorned the bed, chairs, and curtains. But Eirinn was always glad to welcome him into her sanctuary.

There had been a time when he had sat on this bed beside her every night and told her stories about the heros and heroines of Ireland. He had told her the tale of Princess Niav and her flying horses that swept you away to that enchanted Land of the Ever Young. He had told her how the spirits of the fairy fort back in County Kerry had given him the dream of the carousel long before she had been born.

But now Michael came to her room less and less. It seemed that as she approached womanhood, all of her favorite men had been treating her differently.

"I was wonderin' if all's well with me girl," he said, reaching out and touching her tear-damp cheek with a rough forefinger. "We scarcely heard a word from you at the table this evening, and you're usually chattering like a squirrel."

She shrugged and wadded the kerchief into a tight ball against her palm. "I'm older now. Maybe it's time I changed and didn't chatter so much."

Michael smiled, a crooked, sad smile that registered mostly in his green eyes as he surveyed his daughter's shapely figure. "Aye, you've changed in many ways. Indeed, you have. But I do hope that everything about you doesn't change. I love the sound of your voice at my table. 'Tis one of the greatest joys of me life just to hear you."

He sighed, reached over, and covered her small hand with his huge palm. "I work hard all day, looking forward to the evening when I can sit down to your mother's fine meal, look across the table at her lovely face, and hear my daughter talking and laughing at my side. 'Tis more pleasure than any one man deserves, to be sure."

"Oh, Da." A moment later she was in his lap, her arms around his neck, her face buried against his broad shoulder. The tears that she had been holding in since his knock at her door came flooding back, and soon the collar of his work shirt was wet.

He rocked her gently, murmuring soft Gaelic words that she didn't need to have translated to understand how much he loved her. "There, there," he whispered, "ye mustn't cry. What is it, lass? Tell me now."

She shook her head and burrowed deeper into his arms. "I can't say."

"Since when can't you tell such things to the father who loves you?"

Drawing a deep breath of resolve, she pulled away from the comfort that his hard chest offered. She wiped at her eyes with the sodden handkerchief. "Since I became a woman yesterday. There are things a woman must keep to herself."

He nodded, and she could see in his eyes that he was sad, but he understood. "I'll miss you comin' to me with your bumps and bruises," he said.

"You can't make this one stop hurting with a kiss, Da." *You can't make Danny love me again,* she added silently.

"Well, it's a kiss ye'll get anyway," he said, with a soft peck to her cheek. "Whether it'll heal your heart or not."

He left the bed and walked over to the carousel pony which stood in the corner beside the bay window. Something in his eyes as he looked at the horse made Eirinn uneasy. He couldn't possibly know. But then, she had always been surprised at how many things her father could see.

"Tomas and Sean carried her up here for me this morning," she offered lamely. "Danny carved

33

her for my birthday . . . because it was my sixteenth and . . ."

"Yes, I know. I saw him working on it late at night. Many nights. 'Tis probably the finest work he's done yet," he added, tracing the glimmering rows of dainty bells with his fingertips.

When he turned back to face Eirinn she saw the concern in his eyes as he studied her. She looked down at the satin comforter beneath her and plucked at its lace ruffle.

"Daniel O'Brien is a master carver," Michael said, "and a fine man. He loves you dearly."

She glanced up and saw his eyes burning with intensity. "He's been like an uncle to you," he continued, "almost like a second father."

She thought of the night before, of Daniel's mouth on hers, his hands caressing her body. She felt the blood rush to her face and her father's eyes reaching into her thoughts.

Hanging her head, she said, "Yes, Danny's been kind to me . . . like an uncle . . . or a father."

Chapter Three

As quietly as possible, Michael slipped out of his clothes and hung them on the bed post. Caitlin lay with her back to him, her breathing slow and even. If she were asleep he would be disappointed, but he would understand. She had worked hard today, as always. Sometimes he felt bad about how hard she worked, but Michael knew his wife well enough to know that she would have it no other way.

As he lifted the quilt and slid into bed beside her she rolled toward him, her arms outstretched. By the dim light of the banked fire he saw the love in her whiskey-colored eyes. This was the other great pleasure that Michael looked forward to all day. Coming to bed with Caitlin. After twenty years, the joy of her warm embrace hadn't faded.

Gratefully, he snuggled up to her softness. She cuddled against him, molding her body to his, every curve finding its familiar complement.

He buried his face in her auburn hair, which still held the scent of her fresh bread and a hint of the lavender soap from her bath.

Michael took a deep breath and sighed. It was a worried, weary sound, not the contented sigh he usually breathed this time of night. Caitlin leaned over to the small table beside the bed and lit the kerosene lamp. Turning the wick up, she studied him, concern wrinkling her pretty brow. "All right. What is it?"

"I'm worried about your daughter."

"*My* daughter, is she? What has she done now, that she's *mine* and not your own?"

"I'm not sure. Have you had a talk with her?"

"A talk?"

"Aye, you know, a mother to daughter talk . . . about men and . . . things."

Caitlin laughed and the lusty sound filled the bedroom with warmth. "Of course I have, many times. 'Tis her favorite subject these days." She chuckled again, deeper, huskier, as her hand slid slowly down his belly. He shivered with pleasure as her fingers closed around him with tender possessiveness. "Why do you ask?"

"I'm afraid she might be doin' something she shouldn't . . . with someone she shouldn't be doin' it with."

Rising up onto one elbow, Caitlin looked down at him quizzically, her sensual exploration temporarily forgotten. "Whatever do you mean, Michael?"

He took a deep breath and spoke the unthinkable. "I think she and Daniel might be . . . you know . . ."

Caitlin's delicate right eyebrow lifted ever so slightly. "And where did you get such a notion as that?"

"Ryan says she went out to see him last night in her nightgown, and today she's cryin' like a lovesick cat. And then there's that pony he carved for her. Have you ever seen such a beautiful thing in all your days? The man must be in love with her, surely, or he'd never have carved something like that for her."

Caitlin smiled, even in his worry and concern, Michael couldn't help noticing how lovely she was with the lamplight glowing like a halo in her red curls. "Well, if Danny loves her so much, whatever are you worrying about? If there's something growing between them, Danny's a good man. He'll take care of her."

Michael looked at her in surprise. "Do you mean you wouldn't mind the two of them . . . gettin' together?"

"Not at all. Eirinn loves Daniel dearly, always has. And he loves her too. Surely you've seen the way he looks at her." She leaned over and kissed his cheek. "Just the way you looked at me twenty years ago."

"But that was different."

She grinned and traced his lower lip with the tip of her finger. "Was it now? How?"

"We were suited to each other, you and I. Daniel and Eirinn are so different. He's old enough to be her father and—"

"He's only twelve years older. That's not such a vast amount."

"But he's different. He's one of us." Michael didn't need to say more. He knew that Caitlin understood him. Daniel had been born in Ireland, had endured the famine and emigrated. They were a select group, these older ones, and they were constantly aware of the difference in themselves and the rest of the world, even in their own children.

"And the war," he continued, "the war changed him too. He has a troubled spirit, Daniel has. And I don't want my daughter to have to contend with that. Life's hard enough as it is without borrowing another's troubles."

Caitlin laid her head on his chest, wrapping her arm around his waist. "Aye, but she's a strong one, our Eirinn. She could bear up under Danny's load, heavy as it is. Even help him carry it from time to time when he needs her. That's what a woman does for her man. And Eirinn's a woman now . . . in case you haven't noticed."

Michael sighed. "I've noticed." He reached over and turned out the lamp. "I still don't want her to be with Daniel. I love the lad, God knows, but he'd best stay away from me daughter. Or I'll break him in two."

Caitlin laughed softly and her hands began to caress him again. "The question is . . . will your daughter stay away from Daniel?"

The pub door opened and a gust of pungent wind brought the saline smell of the Boston Harbor into the ale-scented atmosphere. Seated on a stool at the bar, Daniel O'Brien shivered, raised the collar of his jacket around his neck, and took another long draught from his mug of ale. It wasn't a cold wind that had made him shudder, just an involuntary response to his surroundings.

The Wilted Shamrock was one of the roughest, smelliest pubs on the Boston waterfront. Habited by cutthroats, opium dealers, and prostitutes, the place had seen more than its share of knifings and run-of-the-mill affrays.

And the Wilted Shamrock was exactly where Daniel wanted to be tonight. Among these criminals Daniel felt a little less like dirt. This crowd passed judgment on no one, and tonight Daniel was condemning himself enough. He didn't need anyone else to do it for him.

"Evening, Dan," said a voice that had lost most of its femininity to the harshness of strong liquor. A redhead, whose locks were a questionable shade of pink-orange, sidled up to him and slipped her arm around his neck.

"And good evenin' to you, too, darlin'," he replied. He would have called her by name, but although he had bedded her several times her name escaped him at the moment.

She leaned over and kissed him with lips that were unnaturally red. He returned the kiss to a cheek that was too pink.

"You all alone tonight?" she asked, moving closer to him and pressing her full breast against his shoulder. The cloying smell of her rose sachet was overpowering, and Daniel found himself holding his breath. Besides, beneath the heavy scent was the unwholesome smell of an unwashed body. When he had last bedded her, this girl had been cleaner, healthier. But people deteriorated quickly here on the waterfront. In another six months, a year at best, she would be an old woman.

For some reason Daniel thought of Eirinn, of the delicate scent of lemon verbena that had clung to his hands and clothes long after he had held her the other night. But he quickly pushed the memory out of his mind. Eirinn didn't belong in a place like this . . . not even the thought of her.

"Aye, I'm alone tonight," he replied, hoisting his ale again.

She took the mug from his hand, held it to her own lips, and drank deeply. Undoubtedly she meant the gesture to be intimate, but Daniel found himself unable to drink from the cup again. He pushed it toward her and lifted his hand, silently ordering another.

"You don't have to be alone tonight," she said, draining the mug. "Buy me another and you'll have company all evening." She rubbed her breast against his shoulder and ran her hand up his thigh. "I won't even make you pay . . . except for the ale. I liked being with you. You were real — "

"To be honest, darlin', I was just sitting here enjoying me own company." He reached down and gently lifted her hand from his thigh. "But I thank you for the kind offer. Maybe some other time."

He rose from the stool to leave, but the front door opened and Michael stepped inside. Their eyes met and Daniel returned to his seat. Michael walked over to him and sat on the stool beside him. Both men watched as the girl sauntered away in the direction of some sailors in the corner.

"That lass a friend of yours?" Michael asked, his disapproval registering in a scowl.

"Not really."

"Good. She's a bit of waterfront flotsam. You can tell just by lookin' at her."

Daniel thought of the first time he had been with her. She had still been new at her trade, a bit timid, awkward and shy, almost sweet. "Ah, she's not so bad," he replied, "just misused a few too many times."

"Ye may be right." Michael tossed a few coins onto the bar and two ales appeared. "To the new carousel," he said, lifting his mug.

For the first time all day, Daniel felt a surge of joy. "To the carousel. 'Tis a beauty, indeed. Slainte'."

As they drank in silence Daniel could feel something akin to anger radiating from Michael. Obviously a matter of some importance weighed on his mind, and Daniel hoped to God it wasn't what he was afraid it was.

"That was a lovely animal you carved for Eirinn," Michael said finally, and Daniel's heart skipped a beat.

" 'Twas my pleasure to do it."

"That mare was sweet and pretty, more like the ones you used to carve . . . before the war."

A host of ghostly faces suddenly appeared in the smoke-filled air around Daniel's head, and he closed his eyes to banish them. But he quickly opened them. The faces were even more vivid behind closed lids.

"A man's carving changes as he changes," Daniel replied. "What's inside comes out through his hands. You told me that often enough yourself."

Michael studied him thoughtfully over his mug and Daniel felt uncomfortable. "That's true enough," Michael said. "And it seems you've a lot of anger inside there that's coming out in your horses lately. When do you suppose it will all be out?"

Daniel thought of the body-strewn battlefield, of the men and boys he himself had killed. He thought of Stephen, the young man with Caitlin's red hair and Michael's green eyes who had died in his arms . . . a brutal, painful, and obscene death. "I don't know if it will ever be completely out," he replied.

"Are you going to be all right, lad?" Michael asked.

Daniel turned toward him and saw the love and concern on the older man's face. It was on the tip of his tongue to give the easiest answer, "I'll be fine." But he couldn't lie to his friend, this man who had brought him, an orphaned boy, out of famished Ireland and given him a home. "I don't know, Michael. 'Tis too early to tell yet. I'll just keep carving and . . ."

"Is the Night Mare still payin' you those midnight visits?"

"She was. But I've outsmarted her. Now I stay up and carve until two."

They both laughed, but there was no humor in the sound.

Michael quickly finished his ale, then turned and placed a hand on Daniel's shoulder. "You keep carving," he said. "Carve everything that's inside. Someday you'll look in there and you'll find peace. Then you can go to sleep at ten o'clock and it'll be one of Princess Niav's enchanted horses that whisks you away to the Land of the Ever Young, not the Night Mare."

"I hope so."

"I know so." Michael's hand tightened on his shoulder. "You're a strong lad, Daniel. You always have been. You'll not let this break you." He hesitated, as though choosing his words carefully. "And while you're healin' yourself, you'll not hurt any others. You understand that this is somethin' you must work through alone. For if you were to get close to a woman right now, the darkness inside you would put out any light in her. You know what I'm speaking of, lad?"

41

Daniel couldn't look up at his friend. If he were to look into those green eyes, Michael would see it all, the guilt, the love, the lust . . . every thought, every emotion he had entertained toward this man's daughter over the past few months. So, Daniel simply nodded and said, "I understand."

Eirinn hurried along the dark waterfront street, her heavy coat wrapped tightly around her. To her right lay the harbor, its waters black and unusually smooth. The only ripples were those caused by the giant rats that swam near the piers. The stench of fish and hot tar nearly gagged her, but she hurried on, trying not to breathe, trying not to see the rats and the other ugliness that floated in the water, an integral part of Boston Harbor.

As she neared the Wilted Shamrock she saw her father leaving the pub. She ducked around a corner and pulled her bonnet low over her face with one hand. If he saw her here she would be locked in her room for a week at least. Worse yet, he would tell her how disappointed he was in her judgment, and that would be much worse, especially since she knew that he would be right. She was risking her life to come into this part of town at this time of night. But what was life without some risks? And Daniel was worth any risk.

For over a week she had tried to get him alone again, tried to speak to him for even one moment. She had to repair the damage she had done to their relationship, had to tell him how sorry she was for kissing him that night.

And if she could manage it at all, she intended to kiss him again. Long and hard. And this time she wasn't going to let him push her away.

She waited until her father had reached the end of the block before going up to the pub door. Over dinner she had heard Ryan say that he had seen Daniel drinking at the Wilted Shamrock. She only hoped that he hadn't left yet.

With a deep breath of resolve she pushed the door open and stepped inside. The foul smell of the place made the waterfront seem fragrant. Her stomach churned.

A dozen male eyes turned her way and chills swept over her. Eirinn had never felt so much like a child as she did at that moment. She was out of her element and she knew it.

Frantically she sought out Daniel who was paying the bartender and apparently ready to leave. Lifting her chin, she walked over to him and placed one hand on his arm.

"Danny, I must have a word with you."

He turned to face her. His eyes widened with astonishment, then he scowled his disapproval. "What the bloody hell do you think yer doin' here, lass?" he demanded.

"You've been avoiding me night and day since . . . since . . . my birthday, and I want to speak to you about it. I couldn't very well demand an audience in front of my father or the rest of the crew. So I came here to find you."

"Yer a fool," he said and his bluntness knifed through her. "Come along now. I'll take you home and yer father will tan your backside."

His hand tightened around her arm, but she shook it off. "I'll thank you not to speak to me as though I were a child, Danny O'Brien. I—"

"A child is what you are. No woman with half a brain would come down to a place like this alone. I should spank you right here and now meself."

Fury gave her the strength to stand up to him. "I'd like to see you try it."

She glowered up at him, defiance in every line of her pretty face. He grabbed her by the shoulders and

43

several of the men nearest them stopped their own arguments long enough to eavesdrop.

"Come along," he hissed. He pushed her toward the door with fingers so tight that they pinched.

"You don't need to shove me. I'm going," she said with all the dignity she could muster.

At the door he hesitated. She could feel his anger, seething and hot, and she wondered what he was thinking.

As though reaching a decision, he said, "Wait here for a moment. And I swear, if you move a muscle, I'll paddle you right here in front of everyone."

Then he spun on his heel and walked to the corner of the pub where a young redhead entertained a bevy of sailors. Without prelude he walked up to her, put his arm around her waist and, to Eirinn's horror, planted a long, wet kiss on her red mouth.

"I'll be back in a few minutes, love," he told the woman. "I have to take this little girl home, then I'll be right back."

Tears of rage flooded Eirinn's eyes as she turned, kicked the door open, and ran out into the night.

Chapter Four

"Damn," Daniel muttered as he fought his way through the crowd to the door. But by the time he had stepped outside, she was already nothing more than a dark figure hurrying up the hill, skirt billowing in the night wind. "Eirinn, wait!" he shouted though he knew she wouldn't hear him. And she wouldn't stop even if she did.

After a moment's frustrated contemplation he decided that it was best if she didn't know he had come after her. Better that she think he was still with the redhead.

Better for Eirinn, he thought. Then he remembered the sweet way she had touched him and kissed him on her birthday. Not necessarily better for him.

He followed her all the way home, being sure to stay several blocks behind and out of sight. Once he saw a shadowy form approach her from an alley and his heart leaped. He broke into a run, but pulled up short when he saw her dismiss the man with a vigorous wave of her arm. Daniel smiled. Eirinn McKevett wasn't someone a man wanted to cross when she was angry. She had too much of her parents' fire in her, and, apparently, even a drunken derelict recognized that.

Standing beneath the shadow of the bakery awning on the corner, Daniel watched until she disappeared safely into the house. Then he sighed and whispered, "Ah . . . Eirinn."

Longing coursed through him, piercing and hot. Why did she have to be so beautiful? Why did she have to be the daughter of his best friend? And why . . . why had she chosen to love him?

Daniel turned and started back to the pub. But he paused at the corner and turned instead toward the carousel manufactory where he slept in an attic room. He could have gone back to the pub and spent the night with the redhead. But he chose instead to sleep alone. If he couldn't have the woman he wanted, he'd prefer to have none at all. At least for tonight.

And if he were lucky, the Night Mare would stay away until the dawn.

"You shouldn't have run away from me the other night," Daniel said when Eirinn approached his workbench, a pitcher of lemonade in one hand. He couldn't help noticing that she had served every other man in the shop before him. And he had paid special notice to how long she had lingered beside Tomas Sullivan, watching him work. As though that sorry pony he was carving was anything worth looking at.

Slowly, deliberately, Danny laid his chisel on the bench and reached for a tin cup that dangled from a hook over his head. Wiping the sawdust from inside it with his handkerchief, he said, "Something dreadful could have happened to you in that neighborhood so late at night."

"Why should you care?" she said, and he could see the hurt in her green eyes.

He couldn't bear to wound her any more deeply than he already had. "I care," he said simply. He held the cup out to her and lowered his voice to a conspiratorial whisper. "I didn't tell yer father that you were runnin' around there on the waterfront."

"And I suppose you expect to be thanked for that?" She tilted the pitcher to fill his cup.

"Well, no. I don't expect to be thanked, but—"

"Then you'll not be disappointed," she said, missing the cup and pouring the sticky liquid all over his hand. "Oh, dear, now I've spilled it. And what a pity! That

46

seems to be the last of it." To emphasize her point she tilted the pitcher even further and shook out the last drops onto his dripping hand.

Daniel leaned forward, his mouth almost against her ear. He tried not to think about how nice her hair smelled and how its softness tickled his nose. "Yer a spoilt brat, Eirinn McKevett," he said. "And someday I'm going to paddle yer behind, just like I said the other night."

She threw her head back and glared up at him, her eyes blazing with green fire. "You'll not paddle me, Danny O'Brien. You'll never have the chance to touch me again. One chance is all I'll give any man."

As she spun around and walked back to the office, Daniel felt his anger melt away to be replaced by fear. Fear that she meant what she said, that he had thrown away his only hope of holding her.

"Men! They're a pain in the arse!"

Caitlin looked up from the stack of papers on her desk to see her only daughter plop onto a chair across from her. She straddled the chair backward and leaned her arms across the back in a pose adopted by most of the male shop workers.

"Ladies don't say *arse*," Caitlin reminded her. "And they certainly don't sit on a chair backward."

"You say that Ryan is a pain in the arse sometimes. And I've seen you sitting in a chair like this when you thought no one was looking. Only you were sitting on Da's lap with your skirts pulled up to your knees."

"Eirinn! That's enough." Caitlin tried to sound indignant, but it wasn't easy with her daughter grinning at her that way. The girl was too clever for her own good and much too interested in things beyond her years. "Besides, I don't claim to be a lady," she said. "I'm just a hardworking Irish peasant."

Caitlin smiled as she returned her attention to her

47

paperwork. Her statement had been one of pride, not self-deprecation. Caitlin wouldn't have traded places with any lady she knew, not if it meant giving up this work she loved, this business she and Michael had built together over the years. The pride she felt in their accomplishments was far more precious to her than any birthright or dowry.

"You're the finest lady I know," Eirinn said, and Caitlin could hear the adoration in her daughter's voice. That was something else she wouldn't have traded for the world.

"Thank you." She quickly added the final column of figures, blotted the page, and set her work aside. "There's something I want to speak to you about."

Eirinn glanced down at the floor and shuffled her feet. "What is it?"

"I saw the way Tomas Sullivan was flirtin' with you out there in the shop just now. And, what's more, I saw you flirtin' back."

"You never minded me flirting with the lads before."

"But not with Tomas. I've warned you about him. He plays fast and loose with the lasses, and I want you to stay far away from him. He's not a nice boy like Danny and the others. He—"

"Nice!" Eirinn sprang up from the chair. "You think Daniel is nice?"

Caitlin was surprised beyond words. She simply stared at her daughter and wondered what she had said to cause this reaction.

"Danny isn't nice," Eirinn said as tears flooded her eyes. "He's a . . . a . . . I don't know what you call it but he's a man who goes to bed with whores. Dirty old whores with dyed hair and rouged cheeks and painted lips and . . . and . . . I hate him. Don't you ever tell me what a nice lad Danny O'Brien is."

A moment later Eirinn was gone, slamming the door behind her. It was another two minutes before Caitlin had recovered sufficiently to make a mental

48

note. She had to tell her daughter that ladies shouldn't use the word *whore* either.

"Weren't you having a good time at your father's ceili'?" Tomas asked as he sat down beside Eirinn on a bale of hay. She had thought that no one had seen her slip away from the party in the shop to the quiet of the barn loft. She had enjoyed as much of the celebration as she could stand, enjoyed dancing with every lad in sight except the one she wanted. Every man at the ceili' had noticed her new birthday dress and the way its snug lines accented her figure. Everyone except Daniel, who had seemed preoccupied with the toe of his boot whenever she had walked by. She had been sick to death of trying to feel happy for her parents and their newly completed carousel, and she was overcome with guilt that she couldn't manage even a smile.

Her parents had watched her closely all evening with looks of concern on their faces. So she had slipped away. There was no point in ruining everyone's good time.

But Tomas had followed her here to the loft, and Eirinn wasn't sure if she was glad or irritated. He had trailed at her heels all evening, asking for every other dance, fetching her punch from the refreshment table, whispering suggestions in her ear that were naughty enough to make her blush, but innocent enough that she could hardly reprimand him.

"I wasn't feeling very well," she said, "so I decided to get a breath of fresh air."

"Here in the barn?" He sniffed and grimaced. "I'd say the air in here is well scented with horse shit, but if that's what pleases you."

She raised her chin indignantly. "No gentleman says . . . that word . . . to a lady."

He moved closer to her on the bale of hay and slid one arm around her waist. The night was chilly, and his arm felt warm, so she allowed the embrace. "But you're no lady," he said. "A lad can tell that just by looking at you. A lady wears her hair all pinned up on her head with combs and such. Not all wild and free like yours." He reached up and twined one of her curls around his forefinger. "Your hair always looks as though you've just been tumbled in the hay."

Tightening his grip around her waist, he leaned back until they both fell off the bale into the straw.

"Tomas Sullivan, what do you think you're—"

"Shhh . . ." He pressed one finger to her lips. "And a lady doesn't wear a dress cut down to here . . ." His finger left her lips, trailed down her throat to the swell of her breasts above the tight-fitted bodice. "One that shows her bosom, all pretty and white and soft."

"I'll have you know that this dress is the height of fashion right now," she said, slapping his hand away. "It's the rage in Paris. I know because I saw one like it on the cover of a French fashion magazine."

His fingertips slowly returned to her bodice as he toyed with the tiny pearl buttons. "Yes, but the ladies in Paris kick their heels up in the air when they dance and pull their skirts over their heads. And they don't even wear bloomers. Can you imagine such a thing?"

Eirinn felt her face blushing deep scarlet. He shouldn't be saying these things to her, and she shouldn't let him say them. And he certainly shouldn't be touching her this way.

But it felt nice. Very nice, really. And it didn't feel at all wicked as she suspected it should.

"You're a pretty woman, Eirinn," he was saying, his face close to her ear, his breath warm on her neck. A surge of pleasure went through her. She wasn't sure if it was from his touch or from the fact that he had called her a woman.

Before she knew what was happening, Tomas's fingers had unbuttoned several of the pearls and had slipped into the softness of her cleavage.

"Tomas, no, we shouldn't."

"No one will know. We won't do anything wrong, I promise. Just let me touch you a little. I'll make it feel good, you'll see."

Tomas's breathing had become ragged, like Daniel's had been that night, but for some reason, Eirinn didn't feel that same tingling excitement that she had felt with Danny. Even though Daniel had only touched her over her nightgown, it had sent delicious chills all over her body. Tomas's hands were stroking her bare skin, and yet there was no fire spreading through her blood, not even enough to take away the chill of the night.

Suddenly her entire bodice front was unbuttoned. Tomas seemed more deft with those tiny pearls than even she was. His hands covered her breasts and squeezed. She cried out and tried to push him away. "Stop it, Tomas. You're hurting me, and I don't want to do this."

"I'm sorry," he said, and instantly his touch became more gentle. But he showed no signs of stopping. "I'll be careful, Eirinn," he said. "This is your first time, isn't it? I thought so." He shifted his weight over her, pinning her down with his thigh. "Just be easy now and I won't hurt you."

Her first time? What was he talking about? She wanted to get away from him, away from his hands, which were pushing up her skirts and burrowing like little scurrying creatures beneath her petticoat. She felt him loosen the ties of her bloomers and panic struck her. Surely he wasn't intending to . . . ?

"Tomas, don't. I don't want to do this. Please stop. I . . ."

"You want it," he said, panting now as he fumbled with his own clothes. "You want it, or you wouldn't have come out here by yourself tonight. You knew I'd follow you out here." He wedged himself between her thighs. "You've been wanting it for a long time. And now I'm going to give it to you."

She struggled against him, but he held her tightly. At the touch of his hardness between her legs she screamed, but he pressed one hand over her mouth. "Hush," he whispered. "Someone will hear you and we'll both be in trouble. Just lie quiet now and it'll be over in a minute."

It was. A second later a piercing pain ripped through the core of her body. He moved inside her . . . two . . . three . . . four . . . five times. Then he moaned, shuddered, and rolled off her.

Eirinn lay quietly, afraid to move, afraid that he might hurt her again. Though he was no longer inside her, the pain continued to stab. She closed her eyes and saw shooting white and blue bolts of light. In the distance she heard Tomas asking her if that wasn't the best thing she had ever felt. Then she heard a board creak, heard Tomas suck in his breath, and an oath muttered by a deep voice.

She opened her eyes. Looked up. And saw Daniel.

Daniel had watched her all night, though he had tried not to, and he had seen the glances she had sent his way. He had seen the hurt in her eyes, the pain of rejection. It had torn at his heart. Why had she chosen him, of all people, to fall in love with? And why on earth, of all the women that he could have, did he want her?

If she just weren't so damned beautiful. If her hair didn't glitter blue-black in the lantern light. If her breasts weren't so creamy and full, spilling over the top of that dress her mother should never have let her wear. If only her bright smile didn't have the power to chase away the darkness that hovered over his soul.

Though she hadn't been smiling much lately. And that was his fault. She was hurting because he had hurt her.

More than anything in the world he wanted to take her in his arms and tell her that he loved her, that he

52

wanted her even more than she wanted him. But in the long run that would do her more harm than good.

She was a child. A sweet, innocent girl. How could she comprehend the dark side of him when Daniel couldn't comprehend it himself? How could he ever explain to a pampered child who had never known a moment of destitution or a single act of violence, the horrors of the famine, the atrocities of war? Horrors that he had endured, atrocities that he himself had committed.

So he didn't take her in his arms and comfort her. He didn't dance with her, speak to her, or allow himself more than a furtive glance in her direction.

But he did notice the moment she left the ceili', and he saw young Tomas Sullivan follow her like a bloodhound.

In that moment Daniel hated Tomas. He hated him for being younger, for being Eirinn's own age, for being pampered and spoiled and more suited to her than himself.

Daniel tried not to follow them. What they did together was none of his business. When he had pushed her away that night in the shop he had relinquished any rights he might have over her. But he had to follow. Some perverse part of himself, buried down there with all the other darkness, had to know.

He waited as long as he could, and when he could stand it no longer, he walked slowly from the shop to the barn with a soldier's silent tread.

It was when he approached the large, double door that he heard her. A small shriek, like a wounded animal. He charged into the barn. Once inside he heard the scuffling in the hay loft overhead. He heard Tomas's moan and the loft boards' rhythmic creaking.

The sound went through him, a rush of liquid fury that robbed him of reason. He didn't care if he had any rights to her or not. Tomas Sullivan was making love to Eirinn McKevett — and Daniel was going to kill him.

53

* * *

The instant Eirinn looked up and saw Daniel she felt a rush of conflicting emotions: shame, fear, embarrassment, and grim satisfaction. He was hurt; she could see it in his eyes. And in a remote corner of her heart she was glad that she had hurt him.

A second later every emotion except that of fear disappeared as Daniel took three steps, closing the distance between him and Tomas. He grabbed the younger man by the front of his shirt and jerked him to his feet.

"What the bloody hell do you think yer doin' there with that child?" he demanded. He didn't wait for an answer. His fist crashed into Tomas's jaw and the blow sent him reeling backward against the wall. In an instant Daniel was on him again. A second blow knocked him to his knees.

"No, please." Tomas held up his hands in a feeble defense, but did little to block the third punch, or the fourth, or the fifth . . .

Eirinn leapt to her feet, her heart in her throat. "Danny, stop. Don't! You'll kill him!" She had witnessed fights before in the shop, many of them, but never one like this. She had never seen a man so out of control as Daniel. His fists pounded Tomas's face and body, landing with terrible, liquid-sounding thuds.

Tomas's protests quickly faded into incoherent cries of pain as the beating continued.

"Danny, please stop!" Eirinn threw herself against Daniel's back, trying to pull him off his victim. But he kept throwing punch after punch, his face twisted with rage, his eyes glassy.

"Force yerself on Michael's and Caitlin's little girl, will you?" he shouted, hauling the young man to his feet by his collar. "I'll kill you for it, I will. Murder you with me bare hands."

"He didn't force me," she lied. She was angry at

Tomas for hurting her, but she didn't want to see him beaten to death before her eyes. "I let him do it."

Daniel turned toward her and for a moment she thought that maybe he hadn't heard her. But she knew the instant her words registered on him. A look of anguish crossed his face, and she was surprised at how happy that look made her feel. So, she had hurt him. Good. She thought of how he had kissed that whore in the pub and she was glad that she had the power to hurt him back.

"I let him do it. I asked him to," she added.

Daniel released his hold on Tomas, who promptly sagged into a heap against the wall, then crawled away and made his way painfully down the ladder, out of sight. But neither Eirinn nor Daniel watched his departure. Instead, they stood glaring at each other, their breath coming in harsh gasps, their hands clenched into fists at their sides.

"You *let* him . . . have his way with you!"

"That's right." She turned to walk away from him, but he stepped directly into her path.

His gaze slid from her hay-littered hair down her open bodice to her rumpled skirt. "Slut."

Eirinn caught her breath as the word sliced through her, sharp and hot. She had never heard the term before, but it was an ugly-sounding word, and the contemptuous look in his eyes as they raked her bare breasts left no doubt as to its meaning.

Choking back a sob, she pushed past him and ran down the ladder. She nearly fell down the last three rungs but didn't stop until she was out of the barn and standing in the corral. Three nervous mares skittered out of her way as she collapsed against the split log railing, her head buried in the crook of her arm. In the past thirty minutes her world had collapsed around her. She had lost her virginity, had seen the man she loved nearly kill another man with his bare hands, and had been called a terrible name—a name that she was

55

afraid accurately described her recent behavior.

She began to cry, only vaguely aware of her surroundings, of the mares whinnying in the corner of the corral, of the footsteps approaching her from behind.

Warm hands closed over her shoulders and turned her around. "Ah, Eirinn," Daniel whispered as he pulled her against his chest. "I'm sorry, darlin'. I should never have called you such a thing."

His kindness only added fuel to her grief. Her tears came with racking sobs as she buried her face against his shirt, releasing all the fear and humiliation of the nightmare she had just endured.

"Oh, Danny, it was so awful," she cried. "It didn't feel good like it's supposed to. He was rough with me, and it hurt, and I was going to make him stop, but by then he had already done it."

He held her tighter and she could feel the barely restrained fury in his crushing embrace. "I'm sorry, sweetheart," he whispered, brushing kisses on her forehead. "Yer first time should have been lovely. I'm so sorry 'twas a stupid lad like himself and not me who loved you first."

She pulled back and looked up at him questioningly. "Do you mean that, Danny?"

He nodded. "I do."

His eyes trailed down the open front of her dress and this time there was no contempt in his gaze. He reached for the lowest button and carefully slipped the tiny pearl into its buttonhole. "I would have been gentle with you," he said. "I would have loved you soft and slow, the way you deserve. When it's a woman's first time she should be with a man who loves her, who'll take his time and be easy with her. A man who can teach her about her body, who can show her that bein' loved is a fine thing, the finest on earth."

His fingers were warm against her bare breasts as he slowly worked his way up her bodice. Wrapping her arms around his neck, she allowed herself to soak in the strength that radiated from him. It was so different to touch him than to touch a boy like Tomas. So wonderfully different. Tomas only took from her. Danny's touch gave.

"You didn't want Tomas Sullivan," he said, his mouth so close to hers that she could nearly taste his lips. "You wanted me. You've wanted me all along. Just as I've wanted you." His lips brushed her cheek in a sweet, light kiss. Then he continued to close her bodice. "I'm sorry, darlin'," he said, "I'm sorry that I hurt you."

"Ye'll be sorrier than that when I'm done with you," said a voice behind them.

They jumped apart, her bodice still partially open. A dark figure stepped out of the shadows and Eirinn's heart failed for the second time that night.

Her father had seen Daniel kiss her. Perhaps he had heard what they had said. He could see her half-open bodice. And Eirinn knew that there was no way either of them could convince Michael McKevett that his best friend in the world hadn't compromised his only daughter.

Chapter Five

If Daniel lived to be a hundred years old he would never forget the look on Michael McKevett's face that night. The memory would haunt him, another ghost to visit his sleepless nights.

"Michael, this isn't what you think," he said, realizing even as he spoke the words that if he were Michael, he would kill him now and listen to explanations later.

"Don't be tellin' me what I think, man," Michael replied, his voice tight and strained. "And don't try to tell me that I didn't see what I just saw."

"Da, he was just comforting me," Eirinn said. "Truly, he was—"

"Hush, darlin'," Daniel said with one restraining hand on her shoulder. He turned to Michael, and Eirinn could see in his eyes that Daniel was afraid, but mostly he looked terribly sad. "Michael, I'd never hurt Eirinn. Surely ye know that."

Michael's face was pale, bloodless in the moonlight. Eirinn had only seen him looking like that once before . . . at Stephen's funeral three months before.

"You were kissin' her just now," he said.

"Only her cheek."

"And you'll give me yer word that you've never kissed her mouth?"

Eirinn didn't dare breathe as she waited for Daniel to lie to her father or damn them both with the truth. He did neither, but simply looked down at the ground.

"And can you swear to me that ye've not touched

her bosom, though 'tis clear to see that her dress is unbuttoned?"

Again Daniel said nothing. Eirinn could stand it no longer. "Da, you must listen. Danny didn't do anything. It was—"

"A mistake," Daniel said, cutting her off. " 'Twas a dreadful mistake. And it'll never happen again."

The two men stood, eyes locked, for several long, tense moments, with only the sound of their labored breathing to break the heavy silence. Finally, Daniel said, "I'll be goin' now."

Michael nodded once, the expression on his face reflecting more pain than anger. "I think that's what ye'd best be doin'," he replied.

Daniel turned and walked away into the darkness. Eirinn wanted to follow him, but she knew Michael would never allow that. She couldn't bear to see the grief in her father's eyes, knowing that she had caused it.

Gathering her rumpled skirts, Eirinn fled in the opposite direction.

"I wish I'd never lived to see this day, Caitlin," Michael said as they lay together in the dark room. Her arm tightened around his waist, but she said nothing. Caitlin knew that no words would ease his pain, the pain of betrayal, the sharpest a man could feel.

"Danny didn't deny it. I gave him the chance, but he couldn't. I'll give him credit for that. At least he didn't lie to me."

Caitlin sighed and reached up to stroke the soft curls that spilled over his forehead. "Ah, Michael. We don't know what passed between Eirinn and Danny. Maybe 'tis between the two of them and not for us to know. Can you think of it that way?"

Michael was silent for a long time, as though giving

her words serious thought. Then he said, "No."

She sighed. "I didn't think you could."

"And you can?"

"Aye, but I'm a woman. 'Tis different, I think, with fathers and their daughters. Besides, Danny is your best friend."

"*Was* my best friend."

He lay quietly for a long time, and Caitlin thought perhaps he had finally drifted off to sleep. Then she felt a shudder run through him. Moving closer, she molded her warm body to his.

"I couldn't hit him, Cait," he said with a voice that shook with emotion. "I wanted to, God knows. But I was so full o' rage I knew that if I ever hit the lad even once I'd not stop till I'd kilt him."

She pressed a kiss to his bare shoulder. "I know."

She felt his body shake again and she realized he was crying.

"I couldn't kill Danny," he said. "He's like me own son. I just couldn't do it."

Caitlin folded the giant who was her husband to her breast as though he were a wounded child. "I know, love," she whispered. "I know."

Daniel lay across his bed, fully clothed, knowing what he had to do but postponing the inevitable for as long as possible. His life was here with the McKevetts, in the carousel shop, carving dreams with Michael. Or at least it had been, until two hours ago. In one moment his world had fallen apart, and Daniel couldn't think of any way to put the pieces back together again.

A knock on the door set his heart thudding in his chest. It wasn't a heavy knock from a large, solid fist. It was a dainty, tentative knock, a sound that frightened him even more deeply.

"Go away," he said, knowing that she wouldn't,

60

hoping to God that she would.

The door eased open and she stood there, silhouetted in the light that shown behind her. Daniel cursed himself for the joy he felt just in seeing her. After what had happened tonight he should be sick at the sight of her, but he was too deeply, hopelessly in love with her to feel anything but adoration.

"Danny, please, I know you're angry with me, but I must talk to you. No one knows I'm here. I was careful, really."

He sat up on the bed and ran his fingers through his hair in a gesture of fatigue and resignation. "What is it? Say yer piece, lass, and then away with ye."

She started to walk toward him, but he held up a warning hand. "Stay where ye are. 'Tis but a small room and I can hear you fine from over here."

Obediently she sank onto a chair set against the far wall. He noticed that she had changed into a simple, matronly gray dress with a high collar and long sleeves. He was immensely grateful, though it did little good. She was still beautiful. And he still wanted her.

"Why wouldn't you let me tell Da the truth tonight?"

"And which truth is that, darlin'?" he asked with a sigh. "Were ye plannin' to tell him that you were rolling around in the hay with Tomas Sullivan and then a moment later you were standing in a corral kissin' yet another man? Now what would yer father be thinkin' of his only daughter if he were told a thing like that?"

He watched her face fall as the truth of what he had said found its mark. She was such a child in the ways of the world, and he loved her all the more for it. He also realized just how ill-suited they were for one another. If only he didn't love her so much.

"Ah, Danny," she said, and his heart melted to hear his name on her lips. "You took the blame for me, to spare my reputation."

"I took the blame to spare the two people I love most in the world," he said.

"You mean my parents. I know you love them dearly."

He opened his mouth to tell her that he had meant Michael and herself, but he reconsidered and said nothing.

"You thought it was better for my father if he thought that his friend had betrayed him than for him to think that his daughter was a. . . ," she hesitated, choking on the word, ". . . a slut."

Daniel stood and took one step toward her, then stopped himself. "Ye must never say that word again. 'Twas wrong of me to call you that and I'll never forgive meself for it. Yer a fine lass, Eirinn. A bit high-spirited at times, but I can't fault you for that. I understand why you did what you did tonight with Tomas, and I'll never hold it against you. Though 'twill make me sad when I think of it in the years ahead."

"Then maybe I should explain it all to Da. Perhaps he'll understand too."

Daniel smiled wryly and shook his head. "That's not too likely. I'd think it would be easier for a friend to understand than a father. Besides, the blame doesn't fall too far from home as it is. It was my fault this whole thing happened. I should never have kissed you that night on yer birthday. That was the start of it all. I should never have held you."

She stood and he was afraid, by the look in her eyes, that she was going to walk across the room and put her arms around him. If she did, he would be lost, surely, for he would never have the strength to turn her away again.

But, to his relief and disappointment, she didn't. She walked toward the door. But before she left she turned and said over her shoulder, "I'm not sorry you held me, Danny. And I'm grateful it was you who kissed me first and not Tomas."

As Daniel watched her walk out the door he felt his heart go with her. In that moment Daniel realized just how much he loved Eirinn McKevett. He loved her enough to let her go.

When Eirinn woke the next morning she wondered how she could feel so happy. The night before had been one of the worst of her life.

She had lain awake for hours, wrestling with her conscience and her fear. It wasn't fair to let Danny take responsibility for what had happened, even if he had insisted on shouldering the blame.

If only Michael had not been so terribly, deeply angry, she would have gone to him in the middle of the night and confessed. Shortly after she had heard the clock downstairs chime three, Eirinn's conscience had won the battle. She had decided that in the morning, when he had cooled down a bit, she would tell him everything and risk his wrath, which, although fearsome to behold, had never been directed toward her.

Yet even with that threat hanging over her, she had awakened feeling happy and optimistic.

As her mind retraced the events of the night she realized why she felt so good. Daniel loved her. After last night there was no doubt in her mind. She had seen it in his eyes, felt it in his touch, heard it in his words and the intimate tone of his voice. No matter what else had happened last night, Daniel loved her and all was right in Eirinn's world.

Almost all.

As she climbed out of bed and washed her face at the porcelain bowl in the marble-topped nightstand, she rehearsed what she was going to say to her father today. She couldn't go on letting Danny take the blame for what happened last night. It was her fault, hers and Tomas's. No matter what her father thought of her after hearing the truth, she had to clear Daniel. Her father and Danny had been friends too long for a misunderstanding to destroy their relationship. She was the only one who could put the matter right again.

Quickly she dressed, raked a brush through her hair, and ran down the stairs. God knows, she wasn't looking forward to this, but the sooner it was over, the better.

In the shop office she found Michael, sketching a pattern of a new horse. He didn't look up when she entered the room, and her heart dropped to the soles of her kid-leather boots. She couldn't remember a time when her father's face hadn't lit at the sight of her. She had hurt him deeply, and before she was finished with her rehearsed speech, he would think even less of her.

Sitting down in a chair several feet away from him, she arranged her skirts in what she hoped was a lady-like pose. More than anything she wanted to erase from his memory the picture of how she looked last night—her hair mussed, her clothes rumpled and open.

"Good morning, Da," she said in a small voice that quivered in spite of her resolve.

" 'Tisn't a good mornin' at all, love," he replied. " 'Tis a dark and dour one, indeed."

At least he had called her "love." He didn't hate her. She took heart. "I need to talk to you about Danny," she said, "and last night."

"There's nothin' to say. What happened, happened. We can take comfort that it won't happen again." He laid down his pencil and turned to her. His eyes were red and swollen, and if Eirinn hadn't known her father better, she would have sworn that he had spent the night crying. "Daniel's gone. He left during the night. Wrote us a note, says he's gone away with the

Fenians to invade Canada." He sighed deeply. "Daniel always was soft for a lost cause."

Daniel gone? With the Fenians? Eirinn had heard of the rebel Fenians, an American-based Irish movement whose latest scheme was to invade Canada and hold the country hostage until England granted Ireland her independence. But Eirinn's mind couldn't absorb the political implications at the moment. Her brain was paralyzed with one thought only. Daniel had left. He had left her. And she had thought he loved her.

"Are you sure he's gone?" she asked, daring to hope for the hopeless.

"He's gone all right. Took young Tomas with him, he did."

"He took Tomas?"

"Aye, well, Tomas Sullivan is a hothead, always lookin' for a fight. The Fenians will make a man of him, if he don't get kilt in the process. Though I can't imagine why Danny took him along. The two of them never did get on that well."

Eirinn knew why Daniel had taken Tomas. He had wanted to make sure that Tomas would never touch her again. She wondered what threats Daniel must have made to persuade Tomas to follow him. Probably nothing too dire. As her father had observed, Tomas could never resist a tussle. *Damn them,* she thought. *Damn them both.*

"He couldn't stay, you know," her father was saying, and she heard him as though from far away. "After what happened last night he couldn't look me in the eye, and it's just as well. I don't think I could bear the sight of him, either. I want you to know, lass, that I don't blame you for what happened. 'Twas Daniel's fault entirely. Yer just a child and himself a grown man. He should have known better. Though I'm disappointed in your judgment. I think you should have a talk with your mother about men and such things."

As Eirinn listened to her father her anger swelled to nearly bursting inside her chest. Slowly the realization sank into her frozen brain. Daniel was gone. He had run away from her. She might never see him again. The man she loved had deserted her.

God, how she hated him for leaving her. She hated Daniel O'Brien with all the violent passion of a youthful heart.

She hated him almost as much as she loved him.

And she'd be damned before she would tell her father the truth now. Let him hate Daniel too.

"Well, I'm glad they're gone. Things will run a lot smoother around here without those rusty cogs in the machinery." With genteel delicacy Ryan broke off a bit of Caitlin's soda bread and popped it into his mouth. "Daniel was too set in his ways and nit-picky about the shop's carving, and Tomas was forever stirring up fights. I say good riddance."

"Why don't you just say nothin' and shove some more food into yer face," Caitlin said, pushing a basket full of bread at him.

Ryan glared up at her, then cast a sideways glance down the table to see if Michael would reprimand Caitlin for insulting him, a grown man. But as usual, Michael made no effort to censor his outspoken wife.

"A man is entitled to his own opinion," Ryan said, "and to speak his mind at his table."

Caitlin tried, without success to hide her irritation when she replied, "This is *my* table. And, yes, you've a right to speak your mind. Once. Not three times at one meal. If anyone here agreed with you, he'd have said so the first time you expressed yerself on the subject. The rest of us are sad to see the lads gone. So shut up and eat yer food before it sprouts icicles."

He cast another indignant look in Michael's direction. "Are you going to let her speak to me like that?"

"Yes, Ryan," Michael said wearily. "Shut up and eat."

Caitlin took her place at Michael's right hand, beside Sean Sullivan. For a moment she rested her hand on Sean's arm and gave him a comforting pat. Sean seemed to have aged in the past twelve hours. Though he and his son never had a kind word between them, she could tell that it grieved him to see the lad go. "He'll be all right, Sean," she said softly. "Daniel will take care of him."

"The way he took care of Stephen?" Every eye turned toward Eirinn, who had been sitting quietly throughout dinner without a word for anyone. Until now.

Caitlin felt her breath leave her body in a gasp. That was the first time she had ever heard Eirinn criticize Daniel. And such a cruel criticism, too.

No one spoke for a long moment. Finally it was Michael who broke the heavy silence. "Ye'll never say such a thing again, lass." His voice was leaden with grief. "Ye may have reason to be angry at Daniel, but ye'll never say that again. Do ye understand?"

Eirinn hung her head. "Yes, Da."

Caitlin watched her daughter though the remainder of the meal. Their eyes met only once across the table, and what Caitlin saw there brought a coldness to her heart.

Eirinn may have learned to make love from Daniel O'Brien. But she had also learned to hate.

Chapter Six

As Eirinn sat on her bed and stared down at the calendar in her lap an icy trickle of nausea ran through her belly. Her fingertip traced the squares week by week, moving backward in time. One month, then two, until she found a five day span marked with tiny stars. Two months.

Dear God in heaven, she thought. Two months.

Her hand trembled as she laid the calendar aside on the satin comforter, out of touch, out of sight. Try as she might she couldn't stop her mind from racing forward, seven months, to January.

She closed her eyes and shuddered as yet another wave of queasiness washed over her. How long could she keep her secret? How long would it be until the whole world knew what she had done that night there in the barn with Tomas Sullivan? Actually, Eirinn didn't care if the whole world knew as long as her parents didn't find out.

Michael and Caitlin had always taught their daughter to look only to her own conscience, not the opinions of others. So, Eirinn had given no thought to what her friends or neighbors might think of her pregnancy. Her grief centered around her parents and her fear of disappointing them.

Not that they would condemn her, scold her, or banish her, as some parents did when confronted with this dilemma. Instinctively, Eirinn knew that Caitlin and Michael would stand behind her and support her with their love. But the thought that she would bring more pain into their lives when their hearts were still bleeding for their lost son had caused Eirinn many a sleepless night in the past few weeks.

Rising from the bed, she walked over to the bay window and sat on the cushions in the window seat. As she placed one hand on her abdomen, she felt a stab of resentment toward this child that had come, unbidden, into her body and taken her hostage.

Then, just as quickly, the anger was replaced by acute guilt. This was a baby, an innocent child who deserved to be loved. If it were only Danny's baby she was sure that she could love it. But Tomas's child?

All that came to mind when she thought of Tomas Sullivan was his rough hands on her body, his hardness ripping into her, the searing pain, and the shame—the hot, suffocating condemnation that perhaps she had been to blame for encouraging him.

How could she tell her mother what she had done when Caitlin had warned her time and time again to stay away from Tomas? Her parents might have understood her being with Daniel. After all, they loved Danny and knew him to be an honorable man. But Tomas Sullivan? They would never understand. And how could she expect them to when she couldn't understand herself?

I can't tell them, she thought. *I simply can't. But I must. Someday soon.*

For the first time in her life Eirinn McKevett wished that she could die.

"Eirinn, what's wrong with you? Ye'll be tellin' me now and not givin' me any more lame excuses." Caitlin dried her hands on the snowy dishtowel and sat down in her chair at the table. With a determined grip she pulled her daughter onto the chair beside her.

Alarmed, she looked into the girl's eyes and saw a depth of despair that set her mind to spinning. What could be wrong with her, so wrong that she couldn't eat or sleep? Surely she didn't miss Daniel that much. Or did she?

"I've just been feeling tired lately." Eirinn crumbled the tiny tea cake that Caitlin had shoved under her nose minutes before. In the china cup her tea had cooled to lukewarm.

" 'Tis more than that and I know it. Tell me, darlin'. Surely I can help if you'll only tell me."

Caitlin watched helplessly as her child's face crumpled and tears flooded her eyes, spilling down her pale cheeks.

"No one can help me, Mama," she sobbed, burying her face in her hands.

Caitlin left her chair and knelt beside her daughter, putting her arms around the girl's shaking shoulders. "There's nothing so bad that yer father and I can't help you with it, lass. But you must tell me what it is. At least tell me if it's Danny. Is it himself yer grievin' for?"

Eirinn shook her head. "I miss him," she admitted. "I miss him terribly, but . . ."

"But that's not why yer crying all the time and refusing to eat?"

"I can't eat," she sobbed. "It makes me sick when I do."

The thought that had been plaguing Caitlin finally demanded to be seen and considered. At first the idea frightened and hurt Caitlin; then she felt a wash of relief. Any truth was better than this confusion, any answer preferable to this dark void of not knowing.

With a mother's gentle touch Caitlin laid her hand on Eirinn's belly. "Is it a baby, love?" she said, her voice quiet and steady.

Eirinn didn't reply, but her increased sobbing gave

Caitlin her answer. Fear wrestled with joy. A baby. Her Eirinn a mother. Caitlin felt a weakness take the strength from her knees and she sank to the floor.

Looking up, she saw her daughter's eyes on her, searching, pleading for understanding and compassion. How could she give anything else?

Caitlin stood and drew Eirinn to her feet. Then she wrapped her arms around the girl and held her to her ample bosom. "Don't cry, darlin'," she said, patting those glossy black curls. "Everything will be fine. I understand what yer feelin' this very minute. I understand more than you know."

Closing her eyes, Caitlin held her only child and tried to absorb some of her grief. Caitlin was all too familiar with the fear, the pain, of being unmarried and with child.

Then she thought of Michael and her heart turned over. Michael had been furious and heartbroken just to think that Daniel had kissed Eirinn. How would he take this news?

Caitlin hugged her daughter tighter, closed her eyes, and prayed that she would find the words to help Michael understand.

" 'Twas a lovely sight, wasn't it, darlin'?" Michael said as he wrapped one burly arm around Caitlin's shoulders and pulled her against him.

They walked side by side across the lush green lawn of the Common, their shoes in their hands, their bare feet shuffling through the cool grass. "Yer new carousel is the biggest and loveliest yet," Caitlin said as she slid her hand along Michael's waist and hugged him to her. "It's proud I am of ye, Michael. So very proud, indeed."

She looked up into his green eyes and saw the childish joy shining there, joy that she brought into his life every day by telling him how much she loved

71

his carving and his wonderful flying horses. Her Michael was a child in many ways, a boy in a giant's body. Caitlin worshiped him and found it easy to express that adoration in words.

Michael wasn't so expressive, at least not verbally. But Caitlin saw the love in his eyes every time he looked at her, and she felt it in his touch. Sometimes she loved him so much that her heart ached with the intensity of her feelings, especially tonight when she knew that she was going to have to say things that would hurt him. Michael felt things more deeply than most people: love, joy, pain, and hate. Caitlin had always tried to shield him as much as possible, but tonight there was no way to spare him.

When they reached the edge of the pond she dropped onto her knees in the grass and pulled him down with her. "There's something I must tell you, Michael," she said as she settled between his knees and placed her hands on his thighs. "Somethin' that will be hard for ye to hear. 'Tis about Eirinn."

Instantly the smile disappeared from his face as he reached for her, his big hands grasping her shoulders in an aching grip. "The girl's sick. Dear Jesus, I knew it."

"No. She isn't sick. She's . . ." She saw relief flood his face and knew that it was short-lived. "She's with child."

Myriad emotions crossed his face: shock, confusion, then anger and hate. And Caitlin experienced every feeling with him.

Finally he shook his head and said, "I wouldn't have believed it. I know that he touched her. I saw it with me own eyes. I thought maybe he'd kissed her and . . . God, I never dreamed that he actually . . . I'll kill him. I'll find him, wherever he is, and I'll kill the bloody bastard."

Caitlin waited quietly, saying nothing. He didn't mean it, of course. Even if Daniel had been there on the Common with them, Michael couldn't have done more than give him a sound thrashing. Michael loved Daniel almost as much as he loved his wife and daughter. That was what made this betrayal so terrible. There was no other man on earth who could have hurt Michael so deeply, because there was no one so close to his heart.

Michael swore vehemently and brought his fist down on the grass so hard that his knuckles sank into the soft earth. "And then he goes off and leaves her to raise his child alone. The boy should be horsewhipped and hanged."

"He didn't know she was with child when he left," Caitlin offered, knowing it would do no good. Desertion was desertion in a father's eyes.

"So that's why she's been so poorly lately. I knew that something was surely wrong, and I tried to get her to tell me, but she wouldn't."

"She was ashamed, Michael. 'Tis a hard thing for a daughter to tell the father she adores. She's so afraid that you won't love her anymore."

"Not love her? Well, of course I love her. Always will. But that's not to say that I don't want to paddle her bum this very minute. I can't believe she'd do such a thing, her just a child and him a grown man. What kind of a girl does something like that? Not a good one to be sure."

"A girl in love." Caitlin moved her hands slowly up his thighs. "A girl like meself when I met you all those years ago in Ireland. Surely it hasn't been so long that ye've forgotten."

She moved closer into the vee between his spread thighs, her hands caressing his hips with slow circular motions.

"Ah . . . I haven't forgotten, lass," he said in a husky whisper.

"You and I didn't need the Church to sanction the love we had for each other. Don't you remember that night when you left for England and you came to tell me goodbye. You made love to me the whole night long, and I don't recall you calling me a bad woman because I allowed it."

His eyes softened at the memory. "That was the loveliest night of me life, darlin'. And we got little Stephen from our lovin'."

"So, maybe it was that way with Daniel and Eirinn. Maybe they had a lovely night together too. Would you begrudge them that?"

"But he left her."

"You left me that night and went away to England."

"But my life depended on it. I was running from the law."

"And Daniel was running too. From you. From the shame of what he'd done to you. You asked him to go, Michael."

He sat, quietly thinking, and she waited patiently. "I'd ask him to come back if I could," he said, "if I thought that Eirinn wanted him back."

"There's no way to find him away in Canada." She swallowed the hardness in her throat. "The lad may even be dead for all we know."

He nodded. " 'Tis true. So, we'll have to help Eirinn ourselves as best we can. You were alone when you were carryin' Stephen. At least our daughter won't be alone. We can give her that much."

Sean Sullivan's hammer struck the red-hot iron on his anvil and a glimmering shower of sparks fell to the floor where they turned to black ash. Perspiration dripped from his brow and from the thatch of blond-silver hair that dangled over his forehead. His pale skin flushed from exertion and from the glow of the forge furnace.

With a sigh of fatigue he tossed the sizzling rod

into the bath of mineral darkened water and wiped his forehead with a rag that hung from a nail on the wall.

"Yer workin' too hard, Sean," Michael said from the other end of the room where he was pumping the bellows. "We're neither one as young as we once were. 'Tis time we started takin' a bit of ease."

Sean smiled his good-natured grin. "When I see you takin' a bit o' ease, I'll do it as well."

Michael resumed blowing the bellows, and Sean watched, giving his body a moment of respite. Michael was right, he thought. They weren't getting any younger. Sometimes Sean felt much older than his forty-two years. Some days he couldn't even remember being young. He must have been young once — in Ireland. Before the famine. Before he had lost Judy on that fever-ridden ship crossing the Atlantic. But that seemed like another lifetime, and Sean felt little connection to the youth who had lived it.

He thrust another rod into Michael's newly stoked fire and waited for it to heat. His arms ached with fatigue and so did his back. Smithing had always been excruciating work, and Sean had never minded the toll it had taken on his body. But these days it took longer for the soreness to go away and too long for his muscles to recover.

It was true, he was getting older. They all were, this band of refugees from Ireland.

"I'm not the only one who's been workin' too hard these days," he commented, watching the feverish pace Michael was setting. "There's no rush on this carousel. As long as we finish before Christmas, we'll be fine. So why are you drivin' yerself like a team of mules?"

Michael pulled the rod from the flame and slammed it down on his own anvil. "I've got me reasons," he replied curtly.

"Would you like to discuss those reasons with an

old friend?" he asked, hoping Michael would open up to him. He hated to see his friend hurting and not be able to do anything about it. Sean felt that he owed Michael McKevett the world, and he jumped at any opportunity to repay that debt.

"No, but I thank you for the offer," Michael said.

The instant that Michael brought his hammer down on the rod, the forge door flew open and Ryan stomped inside, his gray eyes as cold and stormy as a Boston winter.

"Why the hell am I always the last to know what's going on in this family?" he demanded of Michael, who ignored his outburst and continued pounding.

Ryan stepped up and grabbed Michael's arm to stop his hammering. Sean held his breath as Michael stared at Ryan through narrowed eyes.

"Take your hands off me, boy. *Now.*"

Ryan immediately did as he was told.

"If ye spent a bit more time here at home instead of in gambling halls and whorehouses," Michael said through a tight jaw, "ye might find yerself better informed."

Ryan flushed with anger, but he wasn't ready to drop the subject. "I heard Eirinn and Caitlin talking in the kitchen," he said.

"Eavesdropping, just like yer mother used to do," Michael said, but his voice was so low that only Sean heard him.

"And I heard Eirinn say that she's with child. How long have you all known?"

Eirinn? Pregnant? Sean caught his breath. So, that was what was wrong with the McKevetts these days. Sean cast a sideways glance at Michael and their eyes met. Sean's heart twisted for his old friend. No wonder Michael had been working so hard these past few weeks, working as though the devil himself were driving him.

"We've known for two weeks," Michael replied.

"What is it to you?"

"Eirinn is my sister, for Christ's sake."

"Your *half*-sister. You'd think she was yer wife the way you carry on."

Ryan's face turned yet another shade darker and his fists clenched at his sides. "What are you saying?"

"I'm tellin' you 'tis no business of yer own. Stay away from Eirinn and Caitlin. They've grief enough without you addin' to it. And stay out of me own sight too for a while. I'm not in the mood to deal with you right now."

Without another word, Ryan spun on his heel and left the forge, slamming the door behind him.

Sean stood quietly and an awkward silence enveloped the room. The only sound was the roar of the furnace's steady blaze.

Finally Michael spoke. "Sometimes . . . sometimes I hate that boy. God help me, but I do."

"Some are easier to love than others," Sean offered in feeble consolation. "Your Ryan and my Tomas aren't among the easy ones, I'm sorry to say."

Michael wiped a hand wearily across his forehead and sighed. "Ah, Sean. I don't know what to do for my daughter. God, she's got herself in a devil of a fix this time. How can I make this right for her?"

Sean said nothing, but an idea began to grow in the back of his mind. He would speak to Eirinn first. Maybe there was a way for him to repay the McKevetts after all.

Chapter Seven

" 'Tis a lovely summer evening out there that's goin' to waste, Eirinn," Sean said in a quiet, almost tentative voice as he leaned across the table and touched her hand lightly. "Would you like to go for a walk through the park?"

The invitation surprised her almost as much as his touch and the intimate tone of his voice. She looked up at Caitlin who was clearing the dishes away.

Except for the three of them, everyone else had left the table and returned to the shop where Michael and the crew were discussing his plan for the next carousel. Eirinn didn't know which was the strangest, having Sean ask her for a walk or seeing him take time for something so frivolous when there was so much work to be done.

"Well, I . . . I should help with the dishes," she murmured with a questioning look at her mother.

"Go ahead, child," Caitlin returned without meeting her eyes. It seemed that no one looked her in the eyes these days. "I'll have this cleaned up in no time. Sean is right. 'Tis a shame not to enjoy a fine summer evening like this."

They walked arm in arm on the Common beneath the giant limbs of the magnificent Great Elm. The twilight breeze bore the distant sounds of strolling musicians and soapbox orators and the scent of freshly mown grass.

Sean seemed quiet, thoughtful, but Sean was always preoccupied, as though his heart and mind were elsewhere. Eirinn thought of what her father had said about Judy Sullivan and wondered if Sean's heart was lying on the bottom of the deep blue sea beside her.

He looked down at her and smiled, as though suddenly aware of her presence. "Are ye enjoyin' the evenin' air, lass?" he asked.

Returning his smile she said, "Most certainly. It was kind of you to invite me."

He shrugged and squeezed her hand that lay lightly in the crook of his arm. " 'Tis my pleasure, indeed. What man wouldn't enjoy a walk with a lovely lass such as yerself?"

Quickly she glanced up at him, trying to read his intentions on that somber face. His words were flirtatious, the words of a suitor. But this was Sean, Sean Sullivan who never gave any woman the twinkle of his eye. Whatever could he have on his mind?

"Why did you invite me along, Sean?" she asked. Eirinn never wondered for long when a simple question might inform her.

He sighed, and she thought he sounded tired, or maybe nervous. With Sean it was difficult to tell.

"I've something important to discuss with you. Do you mind if we sit a while?" Without waiting for her reply he led her to a bench, whipped out his handkerchief and dusted off the boards before seating her.

Eirinn couldn't help liking the way he was treating her, as though she were a fragile porcelain doll like the one Caitlin had given her only last Christmas. She had been a child then. Now she was carrying a baby of her own. What a difference a year could make.

Did Sean know that she was pregnant? As he sat beside her on the bench she searched his face for condemnation but saw only compassion and maybe affection.

"What is it?" she asked when he didn't speak.

He took her hand and folded it between his own. Again, the gesture was one of a lover, not a beloved, older family friend. The change made her uneasy.

"Eirinn, I've been alone for a long, long time now," he began. "Losing my darlin' Judy was the hardest thing I've ever had to endure. 'Twas worse than the famine or havin' to leave Ireland. 'Twas even worse than the war. You see, I loved my Judy dearly."

The emotion in his voice embarrassed her. It occurred to her that this was a side of Sean that he showed to very few people, and she was touched that he would share his feelings with her. But at the same time it made her uneasy because she didn't know how to respond.

"She was a lovely thing," he continued, "with warm eyes and gentle ways. And pretty black hair." He paused for a moment as his eyes ran over the sweep of curls that cascaded over Eirinn's shoulder and down her breast. "Your hair is the same color as hers, only hers was straight and soft as a China silk."

Eirinn found herself wondering whether he liked straight hair more than curly. Then she wondered why it should matter to her. It didn't matter. If it had been Daniel sitting beside her instead of Sean, then it would have mattered.

"My father told me that Judy was a beauty," she offered, knowing her words would please him and wanting to please him if she could. He was being so solicitous that she wanted to return some of his kindness. "You must miss her terribly."

"Aye, I do. And it's not good for a man to be alone. I've been alone too long." His hand tightened on hers. "I've been thinkin' of takin' a wife, Eirinn."

"A wife? That's wonderful, Sean. I didn't even know you had a sweetheart. Who is she? Is it someone we know?"

He smiled and looked down as though embarrassed. For the first time it occurred to Eirinn that Sean was handsome when he smiled. His blond hair glistened in the glow of the streetlamp overhead. The dim light muted the lines in his face, and he looked much younger. When his eyes returned to hers, Eirinn saw a gleam in those pale blue depths that she hadn't seen before.

"Ah, Eirinn, you're not making this easy for me, lass," he complained softly. "I'm askin' you to marry me, but it appears I'm doin' a poor job of it."

Her mind froze. "Marry? Me? I . . . I don't understand. Why would you want to . . ."

Suddenly it dawned on her and the realization brought a wave of shame washing over her, hot and searing. Unconsciously her hand went to her belly where the slightest of swells was a constant reminder of her condition.

"Thank you, Sean, for your kindness," she said, her tone bitter in spite of her words. "But you don't have to marry me just because I'm . . . because you're a friend of the family and . . ."

Another idea brought even a deeper flush to her cheeks. "Did my father or mother ask you to do this?"

A look of surprise and confusion crossed his face, followed by a scowl. "Of course not. They don't even know I'm askin' ye. Though I think yer mother might have guessed when I suggested we take a walk." His face softened and his calloused hand patted hers. "I'm not askin' you because I have to, lass, but because I want to. Like I said, I've been a long time alone now, and it's time I took a wife. Yer lovely, and yer kind, and—"

"And I remind you of Judy," she supplied.

"That's true enough. You do have her sweet spirit and her fire. I've watched you grow up all these years. Watched you become a fine young woman. And I can't think of anyone I'd rather have for my wife. What do you say, lass? Will you be mine?"

Her eyes searched his face in the lamplight, searched for that hot passion that had been in Daniel's eyes, for the fierce longing and desperate loving. But she saw only a quiet man's affection, not blazing, only warm.

"You don't love me, Sean."

"And I'm not the man you love. I know that, but he's a long way away, darlin'. Maybe even dead, God forbid it. And yer in a bad way here, with the little one comin' and you with no husband. Let me do this for you, Eirinn. Let me do it for you and your dear parents. I may never be able to love you the way you deserve to be loved, but I'll be good to you. I promise. And I'll love your child as though it were my own."

As though it were your own? she thought. *Dear God, Sean, what would you say if you knew it was your grandchild and not Daniel's baby after all?*

"But it doesn't seem fair to you," she said as her heart reached out to him in gratitude.

"Not fair to me?" He threw back his head and laughed, and once again it occurred to Eirinn that he was a handsome man when he smiled. "I'm an old man, Eirinn, more than twice your age. And yer the most beautiful lass in Boston, surely. Ye mustn't worry about me gettin' the short end of the deal. Just say yes and I'll be the happiest Irishman ye ever laid yer pretty green eyes upon."

She thought it over, but for less than a minute. Eirinn was practical, like her mother, and it didn't take long for her to realize that this was the only solution to her problem.

"I'll marry you, Sean. And I'll be a good wife to you if I can. But you must know . . . I'll never love you. At least, not the way Judy did."

A shadow of sadness crossed his face, but it quickly disappeared. "Ah, well, darlin', we can't have everything, can we?"

With a sigh of resignation Eirinn covered the dainty carousel mare with a soft woolen blanket, Stephen's blanket, the one he had been carrying in a bed roll when he had been shot.

She was covering the horse because she couldn't bear to look at it. The last thing she needed was a constant reminder of Daniel, of his supposed affection for her, of his desertion.

What would he say if he knew that she was carrying a child? Would he put his arms around her and comfort her as he had always done when she was a child and in trouble? Or would he cast one of those covert glances at her midriff like her friends, neighbors, and the workers in the shop?

Or worse yet, would he treat her with that polite but strained kindness that her mother and father were showing toward her?

Or perhaps he would simply ignore her, as Ryan was doing.

Ryan. She had to talk to him.

Leaving her room, she walked through the

house, across the yard, and into the shop. A light was burning in the office. *It must be Ryan,* she thought. Caitlin, Michael, and Sean had already gone to bed and none of the workers, other than Daniel, went into the office unless one of the McKevetts were within.

Quietly opening the door, she peeked inside and saw Ryan sitting at Michael's desk, a pen in hand, his golden head bent over a ledger. When she stepped into the room, he jumped, spilling several drops of ink onto the page.

"Damn." He quickly threw some sand onto the paper to blot the drips. "I wish you wouldn't sneak up on me like that, Eirinn."

"I'm sorry." She wondered at his gruffness, and it occurred to her in passing that he was acting the same way he had when they were children and he had been caught doing something naughty. "What are you doing here so late?"

Brushing the sand away and snapping the ledger closed, he said, "Da was complaining that I don't take an active interest in the family business. Just because I don't carve the way Stephen and Daniel did he assumes that I'm good for nothing."

"That's not true." She sat down on a chair beside the desk and watched as he slipped the ledger into a drawer. "Da loves you dearly and he's always thought well of you."

"He loves you and Caitlin and Daniel. And he loved Stephen. He has always thought me a worthless bum because I'm more interested in casinos than in flying horse machines, but someday he'll see. I'm going to make a name for myself in Coney Island. And not in carousels either. You wait and see if I don't."

"Of course you will, Ryan," she said, leaning across the desk and offering her hand to him.

"You're handsome and smart and you have such lovely manners. You know a lot of important people and . . ."

She noticed that he wasn't taking her hand. His eyes wouldn't meet hers as he carefully examined his manicured fingertips one by one.

"What's wrong with you lately?" she asked. "Do you despise me?" She hated to hear the trembling in her voice, hated to have anyone's opinion of her, even his, matter so much.

He looked up at her in surprise, then glanced back down at his nails. "Why should you think that?"

"Because you won't even look at me anymore."

Crossing his arms across the front of his perfectly pleated linen shirt, he gave her his full attention. But the coldness she saw in his gray eyes made her shiver. "You've hurt me, Eirinn. You've wounded me deeply."

"Hurt you? How?"

"You've disappointed me. I thought that my little sister was a good person, a clean woman in body and spirit. But now we all know what you are, don't we?"

Anger welled up in her throat, but she choked it back. "No, Ryan. Why don't you tell me what I am?"

"You're just like the whores at the casinos."

She gasped as his words sliced through her. The contempt in his voice caused her anger to boil over. "And I suppose you've taken your share of these women to bed. What's the difference between the whore and the man who beds her?"

His pale face turned another shade whiter and his thin mouth pressed into a tight slit. "That you would even ask such a question shows how far you've sunk."

Even through the haze of pain that his words inflicted, Eirinn knew with a bittersweet satisfaction that the reason he hadn't answered her question because there *was* no difference, and they both knew it. He was no better than she.

She stood and walked across the room, but when she reached the door her anger was overpowered by need and loneliness. Pausing with her hand on the door, she said, "I'm losing all the men I love, Ryan. Stephen is gone, and Danny. And even Da is acting strangely toward me. I don't think I could stand to lose you, too."

She waited for him to say something, but he had taken out his gold pocket watch and was consulting the time as though late for an important engagement.

"Ryan, please." Her pride was already in tatters. Why hold back now? "Could you please try to be happy for me tomorrow? It's my wedding day. Is it too much to ask that one person I love might be happy for me?"

He snapped the lid of the watch closed and returned it to his pocket. "If it's me you're asking," he said, "it's too much."

"I'm sorry the day wasn't all you'd hoped it would be, darlin'," Sean said as he carefully untied the black grosgrain ribbon from around his neck.

Eirinn sat tensely on the side of his bed and toyed with the sash of her dressing gown. The white satin wedding dress lay carefully draped across the rocking chair in the corner of his bedroom. Sean's tiny room was little more than an outshot on the side of the forge, but it had been decided by Sean and Michael that this cramped cubicle was to be home for the newlyweds.

86

Already Eirinn missed her own cozy, feminine bedroom with its cushioned window seat and canopy bed. She didn't want to think about tomorrow, when she would be expected to spend her day in this dark room and listen to the deafening pounding of the hammer and anvil in the forge beyond the door.

The sounds of merriment continued outside their one small window, the music of the pipe and bohran, the stomping of the dancers' feet, and voices raised in song to celebrate their union.

Her parents had spared no expense to give her a wedding party that compared with the best Irish ceili'.

But the happy sounds only made Eirinn sad. She had seen the dark circles under Caitlin's eyes and the strained joviality on Michael's face. Ryan had radiated gloom throughout the ceremony, and it had been his face that Eirinn remembered seeing over Sean's shoulder when she had repeated her vows of undying love and devotion. Only Sean had seemed happy, and she had silently thanked him for that throughout the day.

Sean loosed the first three buttons of his shirt. Eirinn looked up at him, then quickly down at the floor, trying to wipe the panic off her face. From the corner of her eye she saw him watching her carefully. With relief she noticed that, although he had finished unbuttoning his shirt, he hadn't taken it off.

"It wasn't such a bad day," she replied with a feeble attempt at good cheer. "You looked very handsome in your new jacket."

He gave her a shy smile, and Eirinn realized that it might have been many years since Sean had been told that he was handsome. When he walked over to the bed and sat down beside her, she tried not to cringe visibly. But Sean was a sensitive man who always seemed to know the feelings of those around him.

Sliding his arm around her shoulders he said, "Be easy, darlin'. I'll not force you to do somethin' tonight that ye aren't wantin' to do. I know such things are new to you."

She felt a wave of misery sweep over her and drag her even deeper into the morass that she had been wading through all day. "I'm not exactly a virgin," she said as she patted the small rise of her abdomen beneath the dressing gown. "As the world can see."

Sean's arm tightened protectively around her shoulders. "Maybe not a virgin, but ye are, indeed, a blushing bride. And the world could have seen that today if they'd only looked at your lovely face instead of your belly."

Eirinn heard the anger in his voice, the most passion that she had ever seen Sean display. And it was for her. The thought warmed her to him.

Turning her face toward his, she gave him the smallest of pecks on his cheek. He looked so pleased that she gave him another.

"Ah, love," he whispered as he pulled her into his arms. "Yer a sweet thing. I don't know what I ever did to deserve two sweet, lovely wives such as yerself and my Judy."

Eirinn felt a moment's pang of jealousy toward this woman whose memory intruded even on her wedding night. But once again, Sean seemed to know her very thoughts.

"I'll not speak her name again this evenin'," he said as his hand slowly loosened the sash of her dressing gown. "I want you to know that yer the only woman in me bed tonight, the only one in me heart and mind."

As his hands moved over her, soothing, caressing, she felt her body relax under his gentle ministrations. And later, much later, when he turned out the light, removed his own clothing, and slipped into the bed beside her, she welcomed the warmth of his touch and the consummation of their marriage vows.

It wasn't until she woke at dawn the next day that she realized what she had done. Rising up onto one elbow she looked over at the man who slept beside her, her husband. She had promised to love this man until death and to keep herself unto him only.

Tears flooded her eyes and soaked her pillow. She thought of the pretty little mare with the black mane and the bright green eyes, and the tears flowed faster.

Oh, Danny, she thought. *What have I done?*

Chapter Eight

Eirinn sat on the giant paint can that Ignacio had graciously supplied for her comfort and watched as he and Josef applied a base coat of primer to twelve prancing ponies, the elegant herd of flying horses that was to grace the next McKevett carousel.

"Aren't they lovely," she said, surveying her family's accomplishment with pride.

"Si, si, vellezze, beauties," Iggie replied as he carefully brushed on the chalk white substance. "But never beauties like Daniel's. Daniel was the master."

"Almost as good as the German carvers," Josef commented with a crooked grin. Daily arguments peppered the manufactory's atmosphere, squabbles in Italian, Gaelic, and German as to whose countrymen were building the finest carousels these days. But when push came to shove, everyone who worked at the McKevett factory agreed that theirs were the finest. At least in their not-so-humble opinions.

Eirinn placed one hand on her abdomen as the child kicked against its confines. Seven months. But it seemed at least a year. On days like today she wondered if her belly could stretch any more.

This was a healthy, active child. If only it would look like her, with dark hair and green eyes. All Eirinn asked of God was that her child be born whole . . . and not have Tomas's straight, blond hair.

"Ah, a forte bambino, a boy," Iggie commented as he watched her stomach's antics with wide eyes.

"He is strong, indeed. Would you like to feel him move?" The invitation had escaped her lips before she considered its propriety. The stunned look on both Iggie's and Josef's faces told her that she had taken her Caitlin-taught practicality too far. But she saw the burning curiosity in the young Italian's dark eyes, so she repeated the offer. "It's all right, Iggie. Here, let me show you."

Taking his hand in hers, she guided it to the top of the enormous bulge that was her belly and held his palm lightly against the curve. As though on cue the child gave a lusty kick. "Mama mia," he breathed. His eyes grew misty with emotion. "That's a miracle." Reluctantly he pulled his hand away. "Grazie," he said, and Eirinn was glad that she had put the rules of society aside and given him a gift that he would always remember with awe.

"Josef, put your hand right there and feel the bambino. He's dancing like a—" Ignacio never finished his statement. He simply stared over Eirinn's shoulder, his mouth open, his eyes fixed. Josef was doing the same.

Every sound in the shop suddenly ceased. Even Michael and Sean stopped pounding on the new gear that they had fashioned only this morning in the forge. Caitlin had been showing a prospective client their latest catalog of flying horse machines, but her voice trailed away as she too turned toward the door.

A feeling of inevitability settled over Eirinn, as heavy as the child in her belly, when she turned around to see what had arrested their attention.

She knew he would be standing there. And he was.

91

His face was a bit more gaunt, his beard a week-long stubble, and his amber eyes were bloodshot. But Eirinn had never been happier to see anyone in her life.

Caitlin was the first to break the silence. "Danny, welcome home." She ran to him and threw her arms around his neck. " 'Tis such a joy to see you safe and sound, lad."

"The joy is mine just to see yer shinin' face again," he replied, but his tone was less jovial than his words. "Warms me heart to see ye all," he added with a wistful look in Michael's direction.

Eirinn watched breathlessly as her father slowly walked across the shop. The two men stood toe to toe for a long moment. Then Michael took that final step and enfolded Daniel in a hearty embrace. The happiness on Danny's face was so intense as to resemble pain. Eirinn thought for a moment that both men were going to weep openly, but instead they greeted each other in voices choked with emotion.

"We heard the Fenians' campaign failed," Michael said, "and we were afraid you lads were ghosts, surely."

Sean had quietly walked up beside them. He placed one hand on Daniel's forearm in a gesture of supplication. The look on his face was one of pure torment. "Tomas?" he asked, a father's agony of concern expressed in that one word.

"Tomas is fit," Danny assured him. "As big a dandy as ever. He stopped off for . . . for a pint and some recreation on the waterfront before comin' on home."

"Thank God," Sean breathed, and Eirinn felt his relief. She didn't really care if Tomas was alive or dead. In fact, her life would be much simpler if he never returned. But she was happy . . . for her husband's sake.

Eagerly she watched, waited for Daniel to look her way. Yet she dreaded the moment that he would. Instinctively she had stepped back into the shadows and covered her swollen belly with her arms, as though she could somehow hide this enormous burden.

She watched as his eyes swept the room and she dared to hope that he was looking for her. He was. His search came to a halt when he saw her. She saw the joy registered in his eyes and it echoed the pure rush of happiness that flooded over her when he nodded in her direction.

With a deep breath of resolve she dropped her arms and stepped into the sunlight that filtered through the dusty windows. There was no point in hiding it any longer.

She watched as the smile and color vanished from his face. It seemed the longest moment of her life as she waited for his eyes to meet hers again. When he looked down at the floor, her heart sank. Was he going to be like all the other men she loved? Would he never look at her again?

But he did. His amber eyes lifted and looked into hers and she saw no condemnation, only affection, understanding, and sorrow. In a gesture that went straight to her heart, he held out his arms to her and in a second she was hugging him, laughing and crying at the same time. "Oh, Danny, thank God you're home. We missed you so."

In some dark corner of her mind a quiet voice cautioned her that she was hugging him too long, too tightly. But she didn't listen until a louder, audible voice said, "Yes, Dan, 'tis glad we all are to see ye." Once again Sean placed his hand on Daniel's forearm, but more firmly this time. "A lot has happened since you left," he said. "Eirinn and

I got married."

Eirinn felt the arms that held her suddenly drop away. The next thing she knew it was Sean's arm that was wound possessively around her shoulders as he pulled her tightly to his side.

Daniel's eyes slid down to her abdomen again, and she could almost hear him mentally calculating the months. He looked at her and at his old friend; his brown eyes clouded with intense sadness. "I understand," he said at last.

And Eirinn knew that he did.

"Well, I can clearly see what you've been up to these past seven months," Daniel said, his face glowing with borrowed pride as he surveyed the new carousel that was almost finished.

"And what have you been doin' with yerself?" Michael asked. "I gather you lads weren't able to take Canada hostage after all."

"No, but we lost valiantly." The sarcasm was all too apparent in his voice. "Losing with honor is what we Irish do best these days."

Daniel could feel Michael's green eyes boring into him, trying to discern his intentions. There was no point in lying to this man who knew him better than he knew himself. But for Eirinn's sake, and now for Sean's, he couldn't tell Michael the truth. It was better that everyone believe him to be the father of her child. He only hoped he wouldn't have to sacrifice his friendship with Michael. Surely God wouldn't ask him to pay so dear a price.

"Why did you come back, lad?" Michael asked.

"I want to make things right with you. Is there any way I can do that?"

When Michael didn't speak, Daniel continued. "I miss the work. I'm walkin' dead without it. Surely you understand, Michael. Can you imagine havin' to leave this?" His hand made a wide sweep, indicating the carousel, the work benches, the half-carved animals. "I know yer angry with me, and I can't blame ye, but don't turn me away. I'll do anything under the sun to make it up to you."

He watched the struggle on Michael's face, deep anger warring with years of love. He hated putting the man in this position, but he had to come back. His life, his heart was here. The woman he loved was here, even if she was another man's wife.

"There's one thing I ask," Michael said. "One thing only. If you come back, you must stay away from Eirinn. She belongs to Sean now. I gave her to him when you ran away and left her in trouble. 'Twas a noble thing he did, marrying her and her carryin' yer baby. I'll not have you come between them."

Daniel chose his words carefully and spoke them with conviction. "Next to you, Sean Sullivan is the finest man I know. I'll not betray him. Or Eirinn." Suddenly he thought of Tomas and a chill went through his blood. "If any man comes between them," he added, "it won't be meself."

The creak of the bedroom door woke Eirinn from her afternoon nap. As had been her habit for the past few months, she had retreated to her old bedroom in her parents' house for a quiet bit of midday rest away from the incessant noise of the forge. It seemed that all she did these days was sleep and eat, the child inside her requiring twice as much of both.

Without opening her eyes, she said, "Thank you, Ma. Just set it over there. I'll drink it in a minute."

When she heard no reply, she opened her eyes, expecting to see Caitlin standing at her bedside with her customary cup of afternoon tea. But it wasn't Caitlin. It was Tomas.

She gasped, sat up abruptly, and clutched the sheet to her nearly bare chest. His eyes raked boldly over her, taking in the thin chemise with its low-cut neckline.

"Well, aren't you going to give me a big hug and kiss? I hear you gave old Danny quite a greeting."

"I didn't kiss Danny," she offered in feeble defense as she wondered who had told him. Danny would never have mentioned it. The lads in the shop must have been gossiping again.

He sat down on the edge of the bed and she instinctively moved away from him. "Ah, but you and I have been much closer in the past than you and Dan have been. Haven't we, Eirinn?"

Something in his eyes made her terribly uneasy. She could smell the rank odor of liquor on his breath and she wondered if her mother could hear her downstairs if she were to yell for help.

Clumsily she slid out of bed and pulled on her dressing gown. It was faster than trying to put on her dress with all those tiny buttons and sashes, and she wanted to be dressed as quickly as possible, considering the lecherous gleam in Tomas's eyes. Had he no respect for a pregnant woman? Eirinn decided, after only a moment's consideration, that Tomas Sullivan had respect for no woman.

"Your father was happy to hear the news that you're alive and well, Tomas," she said. "Have you seen him yet?"

"No. I heard that you were up here and I came straightaway to see you." He stood and walked around to her side of the bed, effectively trapping her in the narrow space between the bed and the wall. "There's no one in the house, so we can pick up where we left off."

"Tomas, don't!" She hated the fear in her own voice. "Things are different now. I'm married to your father."

"Yes, so I heard." Anger glittered in his dark eyes. "But it's my baby you're carrying there . . ." He pointed to her belly. "And that makes you more mine than his."

"This isn't your baby," she said. A maternal, protective tone had crept into her voice, giving her words more conviction.

For a moment he looked confused and disappointed. "Then whose is it?"

"It's mine," she offered helplessly.

An unattractive smile curled his thin lips. "It's mine," he said. "But I want to know why you've let everyone here believe that it's Daniel's."

His sneer made her angry, made her want to hurt him. "I didn't want anyone to know that I had been touched by the likes of you."

He sucked in his breath and took a step toward her, his fists raised. "Who the hell do you think you are, saying something like that to me? I should knock you right through that wall."

Fear swept through her, robbing her knees of strength, but she looked him straight in the eye with a courage that she didn't know she had. The courage of a woman, not a girl, a woman carrying a child inside her body. "If you ever lay a hand on me again, Tomas Sullivan, I'll kill you. I swear it."

They stood there, eye to eye, for what seemed to Eirinn like ten years before he dropped his fists. Some of the anger left his face, but one look in his eyes told her that he had only pulled the rage inside. He was still going to make her pay.

"That's no way to talk to the father of your baby," he said, "to the man you're going to marry."

"Marry? You?" The knife of fear dug deeper. "In case you haven't heard, I'm already married."

"I heard." He shook his head in disgust. "Why did you marry an old man like Sean Sullivan?"

"Because he was kind enough to marry me without even asking who had fathered my child."

A light leapt into his dark eyes and Eirinn knew that she had said the wrong thing. "Do you mean you haven't even told him, your own husband, about us?"

"He's been good to me, Tomas, and a good father to you. I couldn't repay his kindness by hurting him."

"So, the old man doesn't even know that I've had his wife." He threw back his head and laughed. His laughter was as ugly as his smile.

"Stop calling him an old man. Sean is more of a man than you'll ever be. You may have got me with child; any boy over thirteen can do that. But he made me a woman, and I'll always be very fond of him."

"Fond of him? How sweet. I wonder how fond old Sean will be of his little wife after I tell him."

"You'll not tell him." Her voice was desperate. It was all she could do not to reach out and grab his shirt in supplication. "You can't be that cruel. You'd break his heart."

"Then divorce him and marry me."

"Why? You don't want me."

"I want the baby."

"Since when did you become paternal?"

His face flushed darkly and once again his hands clenched into fists. "I won't let my father have what's mine. I want you to tell him the truth, Eirinn, and if you won't, I swear, I will."

They heard a sound behind them, a soft footstep on the thick oriental carpet. Turning, they saw

Sean standing in the doorway with a cup of steaming tea in his hand. His expression was grim, his eyes haunted as he searched Eirinn's face. "And what is it that Tomas wants ye to tell me, darlin'?"

Michael sat at his desk, bent over a ledger. The oil in the kerosene lamp was burning low, but he hadn't noticed. His full attention was, and had been for the past hour, centered on a particular column of figures that didn't add up. He had found a similar row on the previous page, and a sinking feeling in the pit of his guts told him that the ledger was full of such inaccuracies. Some of the figures were entered with Caitlin's neat hand, some with his scrawl. Then there were others carefully printed to mimic Caitlin's. But Michael knew his wife's handwriting almost as well as he knew her compunction for accuracy. These mistakes weren't accidents. He was being robbed, and Michael knew by whom. With a violent oath he hurled the ledger across the room and stomped out of the office.

Ryan had just begun to tighten the support cables on the new carousel when he heard the office door slam. He saw Michael coming toward him and he mentally began to rehearse his excuse for not having the rest of his work done. Damn, but the man was forever on his back about something. Didn't Michael realize that there was more to life than building these cursed machines?

But the excuses fled his mind when he saw the expression on Michael's face; it was as dark as the November evening outside, and just as cold.

"Ryan, get yer arse into my office," Michael

bellowed, his deep voice reverberating off the shop walls. "And hurry up before I stomp a mud-hole in it."

Ryan followed him into the office with the slumped posture of a whipped pup. Several hundred thoughts raced through his mind. What was wrong? Had Michael found out about his gambling debts? Had one of the girls at the casino come to him for money?

Until he saw Michael pick up the ledger, Ryan hadn't even considered that Michael might have uncovered his embezzlement of the company funds. That was the one area that Ryan thought he had under control, the one scheme that had been so carefully concealed that he had thought it would never be discovered.

"What the devil did you think you were doin' here with these books?" Michael demanded, shoving the ledger under his nose.

"What are you talking about?"

Michael smacked him on the side of the head with the journal. "Don't ye dare lie to me, boy. If ye lie, I swear I'll break ye in half with me bare hands. And ye know I can do it."

Ryan felt a cold wash of fear as he considered those words. Michael's anger was seldom aroused, but Ryan had seen the damage those big hands could do when the man lost control of his temper. And he looked on the verge of losing it now.

"Yer stealin' me blind." Michael threw the ledger onto the desk and flipped it open to the center. "Look at that." He grabbed Ryan by the back of the neck like a dog and pushed his face down toward the opened page.

"I don't know what you're talking about. That's Caitlin's writing there and—"

"God dammit, lad. If it's yer own two legs ye

want to walk out of here on, ye'd best not tell me it's Caitlin's fault that I'm hundreds of dollars short here. I've checked and double checked, and I know what ye've been up to and why."

Michael released his neck and walked over to the window. For a moment Ryan considered bolting through the door and trying to escape. But if Michael wanted to find him, he would. And if he had to hunt him down, he'd be even more angry when he found him.

"Is it the gamblin' or the women or the opium?" Michael asked. "Or all three?"

Ryan chose the one that he thought would be the least of the three devils in Michael's eyes. "Women."

"Do you have one in trouble?"

Ryan thought about this one carefully before answering. That would be an easy excuse, one that Michael would have to pretend at least to sympathize with, considering Eirinn's recent dilemma. But then he would be required to produce a grandchild one day and that could prove sticky. "No. Nothing like that."

"Are you tryin' to tell me that you ran up a bill as large as that whorin'?"

Ryan studied the cracks in the wooden floor and nodded.

"Ye've some appetite, it seems. Ye could have kept a mistress in fine style for that price. Ye'd do a heap better if ye'd keep that fly of yers closed until ye find a nice girl and marry up with her."

"A nice girl like the one you married?" Ryan asked, keeping his voice low, but not low enough.

"What did you say?"

As usual when he thought of Caitlin, Ryan's blood reached its boiling point. He took a couple of steps backward, out of striking range, and said,

101

"You're a fine one to talk about the women I chose to spend my time with. How about you? Marrying an English landlord's whore, bedding her while you were still married to my mother."

Ryan paused for a moment when he saw the fire ignite in Michael's green eyes, but his anger spurred him on. "Don't you think I ever noticed that Stephen was older than me by several months? You got your whore pregnant before you sired me. If my poor mother hadn't died, you never could have married Caitlin and Stephen would have been your bastard son. Don't you think I thought about that when you loved Stephen all those years and hated me? I'm your son, your true son. Me, Ryan McKevett."

Michael's face turned a deadly shade of gray, and Ryan saw a shudder go through the giant body. Michael was going to kill him with those big hands unless he turned and ran, but for once Ryan wasn't going to run. He had come this far, spoken the words that he had wanted to speak for years. If he died now, at least he would die like a man and not like some whimpering puppy.

The silence in the room weighed down on them both as they stood there glaring at each other, hate radiating between them. Finally Michael spoke, and his voice shook with the intensity of his anger. "If ye ever . . . *ever* . . . speak of my wife in that manner again, I'll break ye in half. If ye ever call Stephen McKevett a bastard again, I'll kill ye where ye stand. That's a promise. I swear it on Ireland's precious soil. 'Tis yerself that's the bastard, not Stephen. 'Twas yer dear mother, Annie McKevett, who played the whore. She pretended to be a saint, full of modesty and pious as a Sunday morn, but she was a whiner and a tale-bearer, like yerself, and a traitor to Ireland. She wouldn't let her own hus-

102

band touch her, but she slept with another man and got herself pregnant with you."

Ryan winced as the words found their mark and stabbed deeply like well-thrown darts. "No, that can't be true."

" 'Tis true. Every word of it. Ask Daniel O'Brien. Annie was his own sister, and he was but a lad at the time, but he knew the truth about her. She was filled with hate and bitterness and blinded by her own self-righteousness. And her son is just like her. Yer hers, Ryan, hers and someone else's. Yer none of mine. Now I'll ask ye to get out of my sight before I break my promise to Caitlin. She made me swear that when the day came that I wanted to kill you . . . I wouldn't. Because she said it would break Eirinn's heart. And so it would. So get out. Now."

Ryan turned and fled. Out of the office. Out of the shop where he had spent so many miserable hours. But he knew, even as he slammed the door, that he'd be back before the night was over. He wasn't finished with Michael McKevett yet.

Chapter Nine

"What is it ye have to tell me, Eirinn?" Sean repeated his question as he set the cup of tea on the marble-topped washstand and walked over to the bed.

Eirinn tried to skirt around Tomas, but he effectively blocked her way with his body.

Sean noticed the gesture and scowled. Holding out his hand to her, he said, "Come here, darlin' and tell me what's wrong. You look like ye've heard the scream of the banshee."

Tomas moved aside and Eirinn hurried past him. As she wrapped her arms around Sean's waist, she buried her face against the front of his shirt and tried to control her shivering.

"What's wrong with me wife?" he asked Tomas with more anger in his voice than Eirinn had ever heard. "What have ye said to her that would set her to shakin' like this?"

"I was just insisting that she be honest with you, Papa."

Eirinn felt her heart stop beating. If she'd had a gun in her hand, she would have turned around and shot Tomas dead where he stood. She'd have done anything to protect Sean from the pain that his son was apparently going to inflict on him.

"Eirinn's a good woman," Sean said, "and she doesn't need lessons in honesty from you."

Tomas walked out from behind the bed. "Oh, I think she does. Has she told you who the father of her baby is?"

Eirinn felt Sean's body stiffen against hers. "I didn't ask," he replied.

"Only because you thought it was Danny's. But it's not Danny's, is it, Eirinn?"

Eirinn whirled on him, fighting back the tears that filled her eyes. "Tomas, don't. Please!"

"Tell him, God dammit, or I will."

"No. I can't."

"I think you'd better leave, Tomas," Sean said. "I'll speak to me wife about this in private. 'Tis none of yer concern."

"Ah, but it is my concern, Papa," he said with cruel deliberation. "It's my baby she's carrying there in her belly."

Eirinn looked up at Sean, and the expression she saw on his face made her wish she could die rather than hurt this gentle man.

"Yer a dirty liar," Sean said through clenched teeth. "Ye'll take those words back before I cram them down yer throat."

"It's the truth, old man. I had her before you did. Ask her yourself."

Sean turned to Eirinn with pain-filled eyes. "Is it true, darlin'? Did you let Tomas love you?"

"He didn't make love to me. Love had nothing to do with what he did to me." She choked back her sobs and held tightly to her husband's hand. "He forced me, Sean. He hurt me. I didn't want him to do it and I told him so, but he did it anyway."

"She's lying." Tomas walked over to her and grabbed her arm in a grip that made her cry out. "She asked for it. She begged me for it."

She asked for it? The words twisted inside her as her mind flashed back to that night. Had she asked for it? So many times growing up she had heard that if a girl went to a lonely place with a young man, unchaperoned, she was asking for trouble. Had it been her fault after all?

"God damn ye to hell and back," Sean hissed as he tore Tomas's hand away from Eirinn's arm. With the strength of a blacksmith, Sean threw his son against the wall. Tomas's head banged so hard that a picture of Stephen clattered to the floor.

"I should have thrashed you years ago," Sean said, his hand tight around Tomas's throat. "Ye've had it comin' and now yer gonna get it."

Sean's fist slammed into Tomas's face with a sickening liquid thud. Eirinn screamed. Tomas tried to fight back, but Sean pounded him again and again until he crumpled into a heap on the floor.

Then, as suddenly as Sean had begun the beating, he stopped. Backing away from his son, he held his hands up as though in surrender. Then he too dropped to the floor on his knees and clasped his hands to his chest.

"Jesus Christ," he gasped. He held out one hand to Eirinn, palm up. "Darlin', help me."

She rushed to him and put her arms around him, but he jerked and fell backward to the floor where he lay, writhing in pain.

"Sean! What's wrong?" Tomas hadn't laid a hand on him, and yet he was dying before her eyes. "Oh, God, Tomas! What's happened to him?"

Tomas lifted himself off the floor, shaking his head as though dazed. "It's his heart. He's having heart failure."

"Do something! Help him, for God's sake. He's your father."

Sean had stopped groaning and clutching his chest. For a blissful moment Eirinn thought he had recovered. She tried to gather him into her arms, but his body was limp.

Tomas reached over her and placed his palm on Sean's chest. Then he leaned down and put his hand on his throat, thumb pressed to his jugular. "He's dead," he said simply, as though announcing

106

the coming of a winter rain. "We killed him."

Ryan moved silently through the darkness of the shop, a black shadow among darker shadows. Moonlight streamed through the windows, muted by the perpetual wood-dust haze, bathing the newly finished carousel with a pastel patina. The horses' eyes gleamed moon silver as he glided by them. They gave him the shivers. It was as though they were watching his every move. They were Michael's creations, and they would tell their master what he had done.

Then Ryan smiled at his own fanciful imagination. When he was finished they wouldn't tell anyone anything. He would be thorough.

Straining his ears for any sound, he heard only the ship's bells in the harbor far away. Without another moment's hesitation, he hurried toward the office. Inside, on Michael's desk, was the kerosene lamp, and in Caitlin's drawer were the matches. That was all he needed.

Daniel couldn't sleep. Ghosts, disembodied spectral faces, floated in the dark room above his bed. Some of the faces were familiar, the faces of those he loved, but most were not. They were men, old and young, some wearing Union caps, some Confederate, most bareheaded. Some had their eyes closed in death, eyes that his own gun and bayonet had closed. Many of them simply stared ahead with eyes glazed by horrors their brains couldn't comprehend.

Daniel was afraid to close his own eyes, afraid because he might sleep, and when he slept those faces spoke. It was bad enough to see their eyes, but it was unbearable to hear their accusations and their screams of agony.

He thought that perhaps if Eirinn were lying there beside him, her presence might exorcise the demons, at least for one night. She was sunshine and light. But was there enough sunlight in any one woman to dispel a darkness as black as his?

No, he decided as his body gave up the fight and drifted toward sleep. His pain was too deep, the turmoil too strong. It would overpower any good in her and destroy her. Besides, she was Sean's wife now. Beyond his reach forever.

The faces opened their mouths and he heard the screams, the roar of cannon and musket. He smelled the smoke of the battlefield. Thick. Suffocating. A coughing spasm racked his lungs. He sat up gasping on the bed.

One thought jolted his sleep-drugged brain fully awake. This wasn't gunpowder smoke. It was burning wood.

"Oh, God, he can't be dead." Eirinn leaned over her husband's body, trying to shake life back into him. "Sean, please don't die."

"He's already dead, I tell you. For Christ's sake, leave him alone, Eirinn."

She looked up at Tomas, but through him, seeing nothing but her husband's limp body, his ashen face.

Stumbling to her feet, she ran to the door and down the upstairs hall. "Ma! Da! It's Sean! He's—"

"Shut up, you fool." Tomas's hand closed around her arm and nearly jerked it from its socket. "If you say another word, I swear I'll kill you."

From where she stood, teetering on the top step of the staircase, she was hardly in any position to struggle with him, and a quiet voice of reason told her that this was no time to fight.

"I have to go get help," she told him with a calmness that surprised even her. "Maybe Ma or Da can help Sean. You have to let them try."

"If you go get them now I'll have to tell them what happened in there. Is that what you want?"

Bile welled up in her stomach, but she forced it back down. "I have to get help for my husband."

"He's dead."

"Let go of my arm."

"I'll kill you if you tell them."

"Let go of me. Now."

She watched as the decision played across his face. And she knew that he was deciding whether to let her go or to push her down the stairs.

"You'll never be able to explain both of us being dead," she said, her tone steady, the words of reason.

But Tomas's decision was never made. An instant later, they heard the back door slam and Michael's deep voice boomed through the night, followed by Caitlin's cry of alarm and those of the workers.

"Fire!"

"Oh, God!"

"Jesus Christ, it's the shop! The shop's on fire!"

Two hours later they sat in a half circle on the grassy field that separated the McKevetts' house from what had once been the McKevett Carousel Manufactory.

They were a grimy, singed, tired group. Totally defeated. Not a tear fell; they were beyond tears.

"It's all gone, love," Michael said in a hollow voice as he put his arm around his wife's shoulders and pulled her against his bruised and battered ribs.

Michael had tried to run into the burning shop to rescue his carousel, and it had taken Caitlin,

109

Josef, Ignacio, half a dozen neighbors, and a well-aimed right hook from Daniel to stop him. "Everything we worked for all these years is gone."

"I know," she said, laying one hand on his thigh. "I'm so sorry, Michael. I know what that carousel meant to you."

"Everything isn't lost," Ryan said and everyone turned to look at him as though surprised that he was among them. He too was smoke-blackened, and his blond bangs were singed as well as his eyebrows. "We'll collect a handsome sum from the insurance company."

No one said anything, but even he could tell that his words were ill-spoken for the time and place.

" 'Tisn't a matter of money, Ryan," Caitlin said. "That carousel represented months of backbreaking work on the part of everyone here, excepting maybe yourself. We all put our hearts into that machine and now it's nothin' but a pile of ashes. We haven't even a shop to build another."

"What I want to know is how that fire got started," Daniel said, speaking for the first time from where he lay in the grass at Michael's and Caitlin's feet.

"Aye, we all want to know the answer to that one," Michael replied.

At Michael's knee Eirinn began to sob quietly. He pulled her into his arms and began to rock her, gently stroking her hair. "There, there, darlin'," he whispered. "Don't cry. We started with nothin' before and we'll start over again. We'll have another shop and another fine carousel, ye'll see."

Tomas watched Michael's every move from his seat on the back porch. Then he cleared his throat loudly and said, "Has anyone seen Papa?"

There was silence as everyone scanned the circle of McKevetts, their friends, and employees. "I wonder where he could be that he didn't hear the

110

commotion or see the fire."

Eirinn's weeping disintegrated into hysterical sobs. Michael held her tighter and Caitlin moved to put her arms around her as well.

As Daniel watched his eyes narrowed with suspicion. He looked over at Tomas—and back to Eirinn. Then he hoisted his tired body up from the grass. "I'll go look for Sean," he said. He slapped Tomas on the back as he passed him. Much harder than necessary. "Maybe ye'd better give me a hand, lad."

Why did it have to rain today? Daniel asked the Almighty as he stared up into the gray November sky. *Why must the rain always fall on funerals?*

He stared down into the rectangular hole in the earth that was about to receive the mortal remains of his friend, Sean Sullivan, and remembered the day he had buried his father, Kevin O'Brien. It had rained that day, too, a soft, misty Irish rain. Not an icy downpour like today.

Michael had held his hand when they had lowered Daniel's father beneath the sod and had spoken words of comfort to the boy who had become a man at the age of eight. Now Michael held the hand of his own child, Eirinn, but his words of comfort seemed to have no effect on her grief.

Daniel wanted to go to her, take her in his arms, and absorb some of her sorrow. But he wasn't sure if she would welcome his consolation. He and everyone else at the funeral was surprised at the depth and intensity of her grief. Daniel had assumed that she had married Sean out of convenience alone, but only a woman in love would be so distraught.

Yet there was a strange quality about her grieving, something that Daniel couldn't quite figure out. Once or twice he had seen Eirinn glancing over at Tomas, and if he hadn't known better he would have sworn that she looked guilty.

Tomas, on the other hand, showed no traces of shame. He was guarded and restless, as though he were eager to have the funeral over. As though he had an important appointment elsewhere. Daniel had even seen him consult his pocket watch a few times during the priest's final prayers. Hardly the picture of a grief-stricken son.

Finally the prayers were finished. Eirinn was too upset to throw the first handful of soil onto the lowered coffin, so Daniel did it, while Caitlin tossed in a bouquet of flowers. Tomas turned and disappeared in the mist of the falling rain.

Daniel could stand it no longer. As he walked over to the McKevetts he heard two of the elderly ladies who lived in the brownstone next door talking in hushed voices.

"It was his heart, they say. What a shame."

"And him still a young man with a babe on the way."

"Caitlin thinks it was the fire, you know. They believe he saw it from that upstairs window and had heart failure then and there."

The oldest of the two clucked her tongue sadly. "And just look at little Eirinn. Have you ever seen anyone grieve so hard? Danny, tell us, is there anything we can do?"

Daniel scarcely heard her. His mind was on Eirinn. Walking up to Michael, he said, "Let me try." He motioned toward Eirinn. "Please, Michael."

Something flickered in Michael's eyes and for a moment his arms tightened around his daughter. Then he stepped away from her.

Daniel needed no urging. Forgetting all about social amenities and preserving reputations, he folded her to him. To his relief, she put her arms around his waist, holding him tightly.

"Oh, Danny. He's dead and it's all my fault."

"Shhh, love. Don't talk now," he whispered in her ear. Somehow he was afraid to let her go on, at least here where others could hear.

"He was so good to me. He was bringing me a cup of tea and—"

"I know, sweetheart." He pressed his fingers to her lips. "Let me take you home now and you can tell me all about it."

He turned her around and started to walk her across the graveyard, but halfway to the gate her knees buckled. He caught her before she hit the ground.

"Oh, God!" she gasped, clutching her arms around her swollen belly. "Danny, help me!"

Michael and Caitlin rushed to their side, and Michael reached for his daughter. But Caitlin stopped him with a gentle hand on his shoulder.

As Daniel lifted Eirinn in his arms, he felt a violent shudder run through her body. She moaned, and Daniel knew the sound of agony, having heard it many times before on the battle-field.

"What is it, Eirinn?" Caitlin asked. "What's wrong?"

"It's the baby. Dear God, I think it's coming now."

Chapter Ten

It can't get worse. Surely the pain can't get any worse than this, Eirinn thought, but the next contraction proved her wrong. Just when she thought she had reached the pinnacle of human suffering, the next spasm in her belly pushed her to new heights.

Through a haze she saw her mother and the midwife hovering nearby. Then she saw a man—a doctor—and she knew she was in trouble. They never called a doctor unless someone was going to die. And the way her belly felt, as though it were ripping apart, she just hoped to God that death would come soon.

"Danny," she gasped between pains. "Where's Daniel?"

The midwife bathed her forehead with a damp cloth and said, "Hush there, sweetie. You can't have any gentlemen in here right now. It wouldn't be decent."

Eirinn groaned and tossed her head from side to side on the pillow. "Please, I want Danny."

Then she heard Caitlin say, "To hell with your rules, Mrs. Murdock. If she wants to see Daniel, I'm bringing him in."

Another spasm, like a steel band, wrapped around her and squeezed mercilessly, then another. When they were over she lay panting, sweat streaming down her face. Looking up she saw Daniel bent over her. The tears that she had fought to control for hours began to fall, but they were tears of relief.

"Ah, love," he whispered as he brushed the damp, black ringlets from her face. "Is it so very bad?"

"It's bad," she gasped. "I didn't know . . . anything . . . could hurt so much."

"But it'll be over soon," he said, stroking her cheek. "Very soon. Is there anything I can do for ye, darlin'?"

She nodded weakly. "Yes. Tomas —"

Another pain hit and her words dissolved into moans. Then there was another contraction. And another.

And when Eirinn finally opened her eyes, Daniel was gone.

As Daniel scoured the waterfront docks, taverns, and hellholes, looking for Tomas, one thought kept running through his brain, a thought that made his pulse pound with rage. She wanted Tomas. Now, in her childbirth bed, during what had to be the most traumatic experience of her life, she had asked for Tomas Sullivan.

Daniel had stood outside that bedroom door for hours, pacing the upstairs hall with Michael, wishing to God that he could just see her, touch her, and maybe somehow reassure her.

When Caitlin had summoned him, had told him that Eirinn had asked for him, his heart had leaped. She wanted him. She had asked for *him*.

But she had only wanted him to fetch Tomas for her, and of course, like a fool, here he was, searching for that bloody bastard. He couldn't tell her no. He had never been able to tell her no. If she asked him to drop dead at her feet, it was a corpse he would be. Because he was a man, she was a woman; he loved her, and that was the way of the world.

"Aye, women, they drive ye mad," he muttered to an old sailor who was propped against some barrels of herring on the dock. "But the asylum would be a lonely place without them," he added with a wry smile.

With mixed feelings he was about to give up the search when he spotted Tomas among a tight knot of men standing on one of the docks. Daniel recognized the ship anchored there, the *Morning Glory*, an immigrant ship bound for Ireland.

"That dirty little bugger," Daniel mumbled as he strode up the gangplank after Tomas who was about to disappear on board the ship.

"Tomas. Tomas Sullivan. Stay where ye stand there, lad," he called out.

Tomas turned around, and the look on his face was that of a trapped weasel, well on his way to being skinned.

"Where do you think yer off to this fine day?" Daniel asked when he caught up to him on the ship's deck.

"There's nothing to hold me here now that my father's dead," Tomas said, shifting the carpet bag in his hand from side to side.

"There's a young woman back there, bringin' a babe into the world with much sufferin' and agony. That babe's yers. I'd say that's enough to hold any man."

Tomas opened his mouth to speak, and Daniel hoped that he would deny that Eirinn's child was his. Then he could beat him to death and not even have to confess it to the priest. God would certainly understand.

"Eirinn asked for ye, boy," he said, the admission costing him dearly. "I've come to take ye back to her."

Daniel stepped closer to the young man and for

the first time he noticed the bruises and swelling around his eyes. It had been dark after the fire and during the funeral Tomas had stood in the background with his hat pulled low over his face. "Whatever happened to ye?" he asked.

"Some timbers came down on me when we were fighting the fire."

Instinctively, Daniel knew he was lying, but he had other things on his mind than whatever brawl Tomas had gotten himself into. "Are ye comin' with me or shall I tell that sweet girl that ye've deserted her entirely?"

"I have nothing to offer her, Danny. You're the one she loves, the one she's always wanted. You take care of her for me, will you?"

Daniel stared at Tomas in disbelief and loathing. If it had been his own child Eirinn was bringing into the world he would have stayed beside her, even held her in his arms until she gave birth. He couldn't imagine how a man could walk away from a woman and a child, especially if that woman was Eirinn McKevett.

"Aye, I'll take care of Eirinn. Sail away if that's what ye must do. But I tell ye now—if ye walk away from her, don't be comin' back. For if ye do, I'll kill ye. And just to make sure that ye believe me, I'll give ye a taste of me knuckles to help ye remember."

Tomas turned and tried to run, but Daniel caught him on the ship's bow and finished the beating that Sean Sullivan had begun.

"Danny? Where's Danny?" Eirinn asked. She could hear her own voice, but it sounded as though it were coming to her through a tunnel. At the far end of that dark passageway stood Caitlin and Michael. Far away. Out of reach.

The terrible spasms no longer racked her body. All she felt now was an aching emptiness. Where was Daniel? He had left her. Again.

"He went to find Tomas, child," Caitlin was saying as she patted her hand. "Don't you remember? You asked him to bring Tomas to you."

Eirinn shook her head violently. "No. I don't want him to *bring* Tomas. Want him to keep Tomas away. Away from the baby. He wants my baby."

"If it's away ye want Tomas, love," Michael said, "it's away he'll be. Don't you worry about that at all, at all."

"But . . . but Tomas said . . . he wants the baby. His baby. Tomas's baby."

Even in her dazed condition, Eirinn was aware of a long, heavy silence in the room. Then Michael said, "Tomas's baby? Eirinn, are ye tellin' us that the babe was Tomas's and not Danny's?"

She nodded and somehow felt as though an enormous weight had been lifted from her. "Not Danny's. Danny and I never . . ."

A thick blackness closed around her, narrowing the tunnel entrance to a tiny dot of light. Eirinn thought of her baby. She didn't know where he was, but suddenly she felt alone, terribly alone.

Then even the tiny dot disappeared.

Daniel came running up the stairs, taking two at a time. When he reached the upstairs hallway, he stopped, swallowed, and tried to control the fear that welled up from his stomach and filled his mouth with a bitter taste. Outside the bedroom door stood Caitlin and Michael. There were tears in Michael's eyes, and Caitlin was sobbing openly.

"Dear Jesus," Danny whispered, "she's dead. Eirinn's dead."

"No," Michael replied. "She's alive. 'Tis the child

118

that's dead. A little boy, it was. Born too early."

Daniel felt ashamed for the flood of relief that washed through him, leaving his knees weak. He should be grieving over the loss of the child, but he was so happy to hear that Eirinn was alive he didn't care if the rest of the world went to the devil.

"May I see her, Michael?" he asked gently, mindful of their sorrow. They had so been looking forward to this first grandchild. "I just have to see her with me own eyes. See that she's truly alive and well."

"Certainly ye may. She was askin' for ye."

"She was? I thought it was Tomas she was after seein'."

Caitlin shook her head as she wiped at her eyes with Michael's handkerchief. "She wasn't askin' you to fetch Tomas for her. She was wantin' ye to keep him away from her."

"Well, it's away he is. On an immigrant ship bound for old Ireland."

Michael nodded his approval. "Thank ye, Danny. I'm indebted to ye."

Daniel walked to the door and quietly opened it, but he paused when he felt Michael's big hand on his shoulder. "After ye've seen her and she's seen enough of you, will ye come down to the kitchen and have a pint with me? There's somethin' important I must speak with you about."

Daniel looked into Michael's eyes and for the first time since Michael had caught him holding Eirinn that night in the corral, Daniel felt that bond between them, the bond that had been the most precious thing in Daniel's life until Eirinn. His heart rejoiced.

"As soon as I've seen her, I'll be there straightaway."

* * *

Eirinn felt the bed depress and she opened her eyes to see Daniel sitting down beside her.

"Danny," she said and held her arms out to him.

"Mr. O'Brien, really!" The midwife bustled over to the bed, her face flushed with outrage. "It's bad enough that you're here in the lady's room, let alone that you would sit on her bed like that. I really can't allow you to—"

"Leave us be, woman," Daniel replied with a wave of his hand. "Ye've done yer work, now away with ye." To emphasize his point he dug deep into his pocket, fished out a coin, and dropped it into her palm.

The midwife's scruples seemed to have a price after all—the amount of silver in her hand. Without another word she gathered up her bundle of supplies and left the room.

Daniel turned to Eirinn and accepted her embrace, feeble though it was. "Well, that wasn't as hearty as your usual hug," he said, his amber eyes teasing away some of her pain. "But I'll wait until ye've mended for a better one."

But the comfort he offered was short-lived. A choking knot formed in her throat as she fought back the tears. "Did they tell you? My baby died."

"I know, darlin'. I'm so sorry. It must be a dreadful thing, indeed, to carry a child so long and then to lose it."

She nodded and reached for his hand. "Only two days ago I had a husband and a baby. Now I have neither. Danny, I feel so alone."

He squeezed her hand between his and smiled at her, and some of her loneliness abated. "Yer never alone, Eirinn," he said as he wrapped his arms around her shoulders and pulled her against him. "As long as Daniel O'Brien's alive, ye'll never be alone again."

"But you ran away from me before," she said. "I was going to tell my father the next morning that it was Tomas I was with that night in the barn and not you. But when I woke, you were gone."

"I'm sorry, love." His hands smoothed her tangled locks and caressed her back in a gesture that was void of sexuality but rich with affection. "Why did you let them think the child was mine? Why didn't you tell them that Tomas was his father?"

"I was ashamed of being with the likes of Tomas. And I didn't want my child to grow up thinking he'd been sired by a scoundrel like him. I didn't think either of you would ever come back. Oh, Danny, I thought I'd never see you again and it broke my heart. That's why I married Sean."

"I know, lass, I know."

Her arms stole around his waist and she laid her head on his broad chest. "Would you just hold me for a while? I'm so tired and it feels so good to have you hold me."

"I'll hold you as long as you like," he said. "Just go to sleep, love. We'll talk more when ye wake."

As he continued to stroke her hair, he hummed an Irish lullaby, and she felt a drowsiness slip over her. His body was warm against hers as she cuddled into him. Nuzzling against his shirt, she could smell the scent of his body and freshly sawed wood.

The vibrations of his chest as he sang and the solid thud of his heart lulled her, and Eirinn felt safe and loved. Feelings she had thought she would never experience again.

"Don't run away from me, Danny," she whispered.

"Never, love. Never again."

Michael watched Caitlin as she set two pints of

ale on the kitchen table, wiped her hands on a snowy dish towel, and wearily hung her apron on a hook behind the door. "Won't you join Danny and meself for a pint, darlin'?"

She cast a sideways look at Daniel and shook her head. "No, thank you. Me body feels as though Cromwell's army has tramped across it. I think it's off to bed for me. Besides, you and Danny need to be alone."

She leaned down to give Michael a kiss and he took the opportunity to slide one hand lovingly along her hip. "Ah, she's a fine one, Danny," he said as he watched her walk away. "So much sorrow has knocked upon her door, but she's still sweet and kind. God, how I do love her."

"And she loves ye right back." Danny lifted his pint. "To Caitlin McKevett."

"Aye, and to her daughter. May the good God mend her heart along with her body."

They both drained the pints before returning the empty mugs to the table. The deeper the sorrow, the drier the thirst.

"It's so glad I am that yer back home again, Danny," Michael said as he looked across the table at the closest friend he had ever had.

Michael steeled himself for what he had to say. He wanted to get through it without shedding any tears. Not that he had to hide his emotions from Danny. Daniel knew him through and through. There had never been any holding back between them, of tears, or affection, or even anger. But Michael knew that if the tears started, he would never be able to say everything he must say.

"Danny, I beg yer forgiveness," he said, clutching the empty mug in his big, callused hands. "I made a terrible mistake and—"

"Michael, don't." Daniel had only whispered the words, but Michael heard them.

Daniel stared down into his mug for a long time. When he raised his eyes, Michael was surprised to see the reflection of his own tears in those amber depths.

"I know what yer goin' to say, and I don't need to hear it."

"Maybe not. But I need to say it." They sat quietly as the clock that Michael had built chimed midnight. Then the house was silent. It had been a long, terrible day and Michael was glad it was finally over.

"I'll never forgive meself for sendin' you away," he said. "When I saw you holdin' her that night, I thought surely ye'd done somethin' to her that ye shouldn't have. And all those months when you were away and she was with child, I thought 'twas yer babe. God help me, I hated you for takin' her and then leavin' her."

He drew a deep breath and continued. "I've always loved you, Danny. Like me own flesh and blood. But I hated you, too. I felt them both at once, love and hate, and it nearly tore the heart from me."

"I'm sorry." Daniel turned the mug upside down on the table and wrapped his hands tightly around it until his fingers shook with the exertion. "Truly I am."

"Ye've nothin' to be sorry about. Ye did nothin' wrong. I just don't understand why you didn't tell me that you were innocent."

"Because I wasn't."

Michael shook his head slowly. "I don't understand."

"I kissed her once."

"Ye kissed her many a time. But there's nothin' wrong with a little—"

"'Twasn't a little kiss. 'Twas a long one. And I shouldn't have let it happen. But it was her birth-

123

day, and she was so happy and so lovely, and it happened before I knew it. And once it was happening I couldn't stop it." He paused and took a deep breath. "I'm in love with her, Michael, have been for a long time, and once she was in me arms, I couldn't push her away." He looked up at his friend with eyes that pleaded for understanding. "I know she's yer daughter, man, but look at her. Think what it must have been like for me. I'm no saint where women are concerned, never claimed to be. It would have taken Saint Patrick himself to resist such a temptation."

"That's why you left here, Danny? Because ye kissed her once?"

He nodded.

Michael was overwhelmed with relief that it had been no more. He knew that Danny was telling him the truth. And he knew what the telling cost him.

"So, what are ye plannin' to do about this love of yours?" Michael asked, though he knew the answer. There was only one answer for feelings like these. Michael had been in love once himself. Still was, for that matter, and he understood the blind, maddening force of it.

"I told her tonight that I'd never leave her again. I mean to keep me promise."

"Do ye intend to marry her?"

Danny hesitated. "She's sick now and grieving for Sean. Besides, I don't know if she'd have me."

"She'd have ye."

Michael stood, walked around the table and put his hands on Daniel's shoulders. "Tell me one thing, lad. Have ye thought about what yer goin' to do when she's sleepin' beside ye and the Night Mare comes to visit?"

Michael felt those broad shoulders sag. "Aye. I've thought about it. Eirinn shines like a sunlit morning. Maybe with her beside me the Night Mare will find someone else to torment."

Michael sighed and patted his shoulder, a gesture of compassion from a man who had been visited by that nocturnal goddess too many times himself. "Aye, that would be fine . . . if it happened just like that. But a man's problems are seldom solved by a woman. Even a woman as fine as our Eirinn."

Chapter Eleven

"Isn't Coney Island the most beautiful sight you've ever seen?" Ryan asked Michael. They stood on the pier and looked up and down the boardwalk at the bathing pavilions, restaurants, and arcades that were springing up almost overnight in this burgeoning resort.

"No. The morning sun shinin' golden on the lakes of Killarney is the loveliest sight these eyes have ever seen," he replied with a homesick ache in his deep voice.

He glanced over at Ryan. The pout that twisted the young man's handsome face made Michael want to tap him with his knuckles. Annie had always looked like that when Michael had said something that hadn't pleased her. And he had been forever saying something that had met with her disapproval.

"But it is a fine sight, indeed," he added. "All the lights do dazzle the eyes."

He was instantly rewarded with a smile from Ryan that reached all the way to those cold gray eyes.

There had been a time, only a few short weeks ago, when Michael had thought that he would never speak to Ryan again. Every time Michael thought of Ryan's insults to Caitlin he wanted to smash his fist into that haughty jaw and remove his self-righteous smirk.

But when Michael thought of how Ryan had

fought the fire beside him and Caitlin, had risked his life along with the rest of their family and friends, he felt he had to forgive him. Besides, Michael was feeling guilty that he had told Ryan about his mother's infidelity. He had promised himself that he would never tell Ryan he wasn't his true son. There had been no reason for the boy ever to know. But Michael had struck out in rage, with words instead of his fists, and the damage had been just as deep. Maybe deeper.

And Michael didn't feel good about it. This was just one more stone in the wall that separated them, a wall mortared with guilt.

There had been a change in Ryan these last few weeks. He seemed listless, preoccupied, and withdrawn. The dark circles under his eyes had become even blacker, and his skin had an unnatural pallor, even for one as fair as he. Michael wondered on the nights that Ryan never came home if he was in one of the waterfront opium dens, but he didn't ask. Some things were better left unsaid.

The only time Ryan seemed alive was when they were discussing the insurance money they were to receive any day now. Ryan had dragged Michael here to New York to see this wonder, Coney Island, telling him that it was a gold mine, the chance of a lifetime. And now that Michael had seen it with his own eyes, he had to agree.

"We'd have to start out small," Ryan was saying, his eyes bright, almost feverish. "But in time we could have the finest casino on Coney Island."

"Casino?" Michael thought the matter over carefully. "I can't see meself ownin' a gamblin' hall, takin' people's hard-earned money from them night and day."

"But it's not as though you'd be stealing from them. They enjoy gambling. The excitement. The challenge of beating the odds."

Michael shook his head sadly, wondering how much of his own money had flowed through Ryan's hands and into these casinos. "Aye, there's a fool born every minute," he said, "and every bloody one of them lives."

For once Ryan seemed too excited to take offense. "Will you just think about it? This insurance money provides a great opportunity for our family. And Coney Island is the place to invest it."

Michael looked around him at the carnival glitter and imagined a sparkling carousel spinning there in the midst of it all. Then another, and another. Flying horse machines up and down the boardwalk. And children scrambling to ride them. Children from two years old to ninety.

"Aye, Ryan," he said, "yer Coney Island is indeed a rare and wonderful place, almost like Princess Niav's Land of the Ever Young, and it does give one somethin' to think on."

"I heard about your family's shop burning to the ground." Padraic Brady stubbed out the soggy end of the cigar that he had been chewing on most of the evening and fixed Ryan with that look of warm, companionable sympathy that only those who had consumed a vast amount of liquor together could share. "A terrible thing," he clucked, "just terrible."

Ryan tilted the shot glass and tossed the amber fire down the back of his throat. It burned all the way to his stomach. Closing his eyes he drifted in the haze that the alcohol produced, a light fog that took the sharp edges off reality.

"Yes, it was a tragedy," he replied as he tucked his cards close to his vest and poured himself another glassful from the bottle that stood between him and Brady on the table. Even as he poured,

Ryan knew that it would take more whiskey than was in this bottle to take the cutting edge off his guilt.

Brady clipped the end from another cigar and lit up. "That was a shame about Sean Sullivan."

Ryan cringed, bolted the whiskey, and prayed for it to take effect soon.

As Brady puffed he peered through the smoke, closely watching a young woman who was threading her way through the crowded casino to the stage. Ryan's eyes followed his, noting the woman's black hair piled on top of her head, her generous bustline, her rosette-studded bustle and the way it swayed when she walked. Any other time Ryan might have fallen in love on the spot, but the whiskey had taken the edge off his desires.

Brady threw another three chips into the pile between them and said, "I never met Sean Sullivan but I heard that he was one of the finest blacksmiths on the coast, a great asset to your father's shop. I only wish I had a smith like him in my factory."

Ryan felt his guilt like the pointed tip of a knife gouge into his gut. Poor old Sean. God knows, he had never meant to take anyone's life with that damned fire. In fact, only moments after he had set it he had regretted the deed. But by then the fire was out of control. He had fought side by side with Michael and had risked his own life, but that knowledge did nothing to relieve his guilt. Only the whiskey did that — and opium, when he could get it. "Ah, you're doing fine with your own smiths," he said, "giving us more competition than is decent between friends."

Brady laughed and his massive jowls fluttered as though stirred by a breeze. "I never thought I'd live to hear a McKevett admit that I was giving him competition in the carousel business."

Well, I'm not really a McKevett, Ryan thought grimly as he tossed matching chips into the pot and added two more. Remembering what Michael had said about his mother, Ryan decided that it was also Michael's fault that Sean was dead. If he hadn't said those terrible things none of it would have ever happened. That thought helped even more than the whiskey, so Ryan clung to it, mulling it over and over, savoring the feel of it.

The young woman had begun her song, and after only a few bars Ryan decided that she walked better than she sang. Her voice was high and thin with a heavy vibrato that grated on his nerves. "Where did you find that little songbird?" he asked.

But Brady didn't hear the sarcasm in his tone. "Isn't she great? Sings like an angel, but between the sheets she's a little devil, if you know what I mean." Considering the leer on Brady's face, Ryan had no trouble reading his meaning.

Brady called Ryan's last bet and spread his cards on the table. Four jacks.

Suddenly the companionable warmth between them cooled at least twenty degrees, and Ryan decided that he didn't like this man at all. He was ugly, he smelled of stale cigars, and he was too damned good at poker, too consistently good to be honest. No man was that bloody lucky.

Besides, Padraic Brady was Michael's major competition in the carousel business. Some customers actually preferred Brady's gaudy, multi-jeweled, flamboyant animals to the McKevett's lifelike, intricately carved creatures. And what bothered Ryan most was that he himself was one of those people. He had been trying for years to get Daniel to break away from his staunch realism with no success.

But none of that mattered now, because the carousel shop was gone, and if Ryan had his way, it would never be rebuilt. The money would be invested in a casino, like this one, owned by Padraic Brady. Ryan would enjoy giving Brady competition in yet another business.

He watched as Brady scooped the chips into his bowler with a flourish. Yes, he would enjoy beating this man at his own game.

The girl had finished her song amid subdued applause and was leaving the casino by the back door. Ryan stood, adjusted his tie and with drunken deliberation smoothed his coat.

"Good evening, Brady," he said as he took his leave.

"It was a pleasure taking your money," Brady returned. "As always."

Discreetly Ryan followed the girl out the back door and down to the boardwalk. *A devil in bed, huh?*

He watched the sway of her bustle and thought of Brady's flapping jowls. He smoothed his hair, walked up to the young woman, laid his hand on her shoulder and said, "Excuse me, ma'am, but I had to tell you how much I enjoyed your singing tonight. You have the voice of an angel . . . and the face besides."

She smiled broadly, flashing a row of small, even teeth. Her blue eyes glittered.

Ryan held out his arm and she took it without hesitation. As he led her toward the beach, Ryan prematurely congratulated himself. Brady might have beat him at poker, but poker wasn't the only game in town.

As Ryan watched her wolf down half a chicken and a bottle of wine, he was glad that he had ordered dinner brought to his hotel room rather than eating with her in the restaurant downstairs. Her appetite was positively embarrassing.

"When was the last time you ate, sweetheart?" he asked as he reached beneath the tablecloth and placed his hand on her leg. He was surprised and pleased to feel the contours of her knee just below the thin gabardine. Apparently she was wearing no petticoats.

She blushed, but he suspected it was more from shame about her hunger than from his touch.

"I just eat a lot," she said defensively. "I may be little, but I can really put the food away . . . when it's around, that is."

He watched her lick her fingers, and once again he thanked God that he wasn't in public with her. Then she attacked an enormous slice of chocolate cake, which seemed to disappear in five bites.

"So, how long have you been a singer?" he asked, trying to sound interested. Though his interest lay more in the curve of her bosom than her vocal chords.

"All my life," she replied, running her finger along the plate to retrieve the last bit of chocolate icing. "But I'm really an actress. A Shakespearean actress."

"I see."

She sucked the chocolate from her fingertip and he watched her mouth with male fascination.

Picking up her untouched napkin, he dabbed at her lips. Despite the chicken grease and the smear of chocolate, she had a pretty, pouty mouth, and he felt his own appetite rising as he touched her.

"Thank you for the dinner," she said, her voice soft and breathy. "You're a nice man."

Her blue eyes were wide and innocent. Too innocent. They didn't match her lips or her bosom.

Ryan stood, held out his hand to her, and led her over to the bed. She hesitated only a moment

132

before sitting down beside him.

"So, tell me about Padraic Brady," he said, toying with the ribbon bow that rested between her breasts at the top of her low-cut gown.

"He's a nice man too." She watched as he untied the ribbon. The dress sprang open, revealing a dingy camisole. "What do you want to know about him?"

"How does he make his money?" Her face was lovely, heart-shaped, and blank. Ryan sighed. This wasn't going to be easy. "Does he make more money with the carousels or with the casino?"

A light of realization glimmered in her blue eyes. "Oh, I see what you mean. The casino, I think. I heard him telling one of his friends that now that he has the casino, he doesn't have to worry about whether the carousels are making a profit or not." She hesitated, eagerly searching his face. "Is that what you wanted to know?"

"That's what I wanted to know." He leaned over and placed a tender kiss on that pouty mouth. Her lips parted, inviting him inside even before he asked for entrance. Groaning, he took what she offered and more. In a moment he had pushed her back onto the bed and had filled his hands with her breasts.

To his surprise and delight, she required no seduction at all. Her small, soft hands were already removing his clothes.

Beneath the dingy linen he found exquisite, flawless white breasts and delicate pink nipples. As he dipped his head to taste one, she moaned and tangled her fingers in his hair, pressing him even closer.

"Love me," she whispered. "Please."

Ryan didn't have to be asked twice.

* * *

"That was nice," she said as she snuggled against his chest. Her tiny fingers toyed with the whorls of golden hair on his chest. "Thank you."

"It was my pleasure, indeed," Ryan said. When he relaxed and let his guard down, the Irish brogue crept into his voice, especially when he was feeling tender. And for some reason that he couldn't understand he was feeling very warm and comfortable with this girl. His right hand caressed her back as his left spread her black, silky hair across his chest. "You're a lusty lass," he added, remembering her responses to his lovemaking.

"Yes? Well, it's been a long time since I was made love to proper like."

He thought of Brady's boasting at the poker table. "Really? That's a shame. A waste of a lovely woman."

"Actually, I was with this fellow last night . . ."

"Yes?"

"But he just wasn't very interested . . . or very interesting . . . if you know what I mean."

Ryan thought of Padraic's bragging and nearly laughed aloud. So, Padraic Brady wasn't much of a lover. What a delightful tidbit to savor.

He moved his hands over her body in slow, deliberate, seductive circles. "I should think any man would be excited to have such a pretty thing as you in his bed."

She sighed. "Not so's you'd notice." Suddenly she sat up and looked down at him, a quizzical grin on her pretty face. "By the way, my name is Bernadette. What's yours?" she asked shamelessly.

"I'm Ryan McKevett." He shook her hand and she giggled. "And someday I'm going to own the finest casino on Coney Island."

"Can I sing in your casino?"

He pulled her down onto the pillow beside him and kissed her lips that were still red and swollen from his previous kisses. "If you stick with me, darlin', and help me find out what I need to know about ol' Padraic's business, you can be the star of the show."

The savory scent of Caitlin's barley soup filled the steamy kitchen, whetting the appetites of those seated around her table. Supper was long overdue, as the household had waited for Michael to return that evening from his trip to New York with Ryan.

But now that he was back, dinner still had to wait. He had news, good news that couldn't be held back any longer.

"Ye'll never believe it 'til ye see it with yer own eyes, darlin'," he said as he pulled Caitlin down onto his lap and patted her rear affectionately without regard for the others seated at the table, patiently waiting for their dinners to be served.

"There's nothing like Coney Island in all the wide world, Danny," he said. " 'Tis surely the likeness of the Land of the Ever Young. At least the closest we'll ever see. The place is everything that Ryan said it was, and more besides."

Eirinn cast a sideways glance at Daniel and saw that his face was set in grim lines. She knew that it was difficult for Danny to believe that Ryan could be right about anything.

"So, tell us your news, Michael," Ignacio said with a wistful glance toward the soup pot that bubbled on the stove.

"Yes," Josef said, "you've kept us in suspense long enough."

As Eirinn looked around the table at the animated faces and sensed their eager anticipation, she wished that she could share their interest, their curiosity, their enthusiasm. She wished that she could feel something, anything except this terrible

135

emptiness.

Since Sean's death she had been floating on the white haze of shock. She had lost too much, too quickly: Sean, the baby, the carousel shop, which had been such an important part of her life for as long as she could remember. And for some reason that she couldn't explain, her heart told her that it was all her own fault. Hers and Tomas's. And Tomas wasn't there to share this overwhelming burden of guilt.

Beneath the table Daniel reached for her hand and covered it with his own, patting it sympathetically. He had done that often these past months. Small gestures, reassuring smiles that should have comforted her. Any other time she would have been thrilled to receive this attention from Daniel. Months ago she would have reveled in his displays of affection, but now she didn't feel worthy of his love.

What would he think of her if he were to find out what had really happened that afternoon? Would he still love her if he knew that she and Tomas had caused his friend's death? She didn't think so. Danny was an honorable man, and no man of honor could excuse what had happened that afternoon.

With an effort she pulled herself up from the murky waters of depression and tried to listen to what Michael was saying. He was talking about Coney Island again, his green eyes sparkling with excitement.

" 'Tis such a grand place, Cait," he said as he squeezed her around the waist. "All it wants is a fine McKevett carousel, or two, or three. It's big enough for a dozen or more. That old Padraic Brady has one of his own installed there. Ah, Danny, ye'd weep if ye were to lay eyes on those ugly horses of his. Misshapen, sad creatures they are. And he thinks pastin' those jewels all over them makes the poor things works of art. But the people are ridin' them, day and night, and payin' five cents a head for the honor."

Daniel shook his head in disbelief.

"New York is the perfect place," Michael continued, "to rebuild our shop. With the ports there for shippin' the materials we'll need to build one machine after another."

He twisted one of Caitlin's auburn curls around his forefinger. "And there's lots of good Irish folk there, Cait. I met some people from County Kerry itself, and from Cork and Waterford. We'll feel right at home."

New York. The very words brought a flood of images to Eirinn's mind, visions of that big city, all the wonderful and terrible things she had ever heard about it.

Once again she wished that she cared, cared about anything at all.

"So, what do you say, Caitlin?" Michael asked his wife.

Unquestioning devotion shone in Caitlin's eyes as she smiled at him. "Whatever you say, Michael. I followed you all the way from Ireland to Boston. I'll gladly follow you to New York, if that's what yer wantin'."

Michael looked down the table at Josef, Ignacio, and Daniel. "And what do you say, lads? Will you come with me as well?"

Daniel turned to Eirinn and his eyes searched hers. Looking for what, she wasn't sure. He had been looking at her that way frequently these past few months.

She felt his concern and wished she could reassure him that she was fine, but Eirinn didn't know if she was fine or not. She didn't know. And worse, she didn't care.

Danny turned to Michael and squeezed Eirinn's hand under the table. "If that's what you think is best, Michael, we'll follow you. Surely you know that. As long as we can carve the horses and build yer fine machines, we'll be happy."

Carving horses? Is that what it took to be happy? Eirinn wondered if she would ever be happy again.

Chapter Twelve

As Ryan snuggled against Bernadette's warm softness between the crisp sheets, it occurred to him that there were worse ways to spend an evening than being in bed with a lovely woman, especially one so eager to please a man. He nuzzled her soft black hair and breathed the scent of her perfume—expensive perfume. Ryan knew a French fragrance when he smelled it, though he had never bought it himself.

"How can you afford that perfume on your salary?" he asked, trying to keep the jealousy and suspicion out of his voice.

She shrugged and moved a short distance away from him on the bed. "Brady gave it to me. Why?" she asked warily.

"From Brady?" He didn't know why he should be surprised, but he was. "And just what have you been doing with ol' Padraic that he'd give you French perfume in return?"

Her blue eyes widened with innocence—feigned or genuine, he couldn't tell. "Getting information for you. Isn't that what you wanted me to do with him."

"Just make sure that's all you're doing when you're in his company."

She laughed, and the sound irritated him. It had a shrill, grating quality, like her singing voice.

"You needn't worry about that," she said, "not with Paddy. I already told you about his problem.

He never even asks for . . . that. All I have to do to please him is hold his hand."

Running his fingers through her thick ebony curls, Ryan held her head firmly and brought his mouth down on hers in a bruising kiss. "You're mine, Bernadette. Just don't ever forget that." He kissed her again, even harder than before, and she whimpered from the pain.

When he finally pulled away, he saw the fear in her eyes. He smiled. Fear was a good thing to instill in a woman. It kept her in line.

"I won't forget, Ryan," she said. "I promise. I've only held his hand and asked questions. I thought that's what you wanted."

"It is. That's exactly what I want." His grimace softened. Gradually he relaxed and so did his fingers, which were still tangled in her locks. "I like your hair," he said, and he felt her let down her guard a little. "I'm glad it's black."

She raised one delicate eyebrow. "You like black hair?"

"Yes." He stared past her as though seeing something, someone in the distance. "I only wish that your eyes were green."

"I'm sorry," she said. Her blue eyes teared, but he didn't notice.

"So, what did you find out for me about Padraic Brady, my lovely little spy?" he asked.

She brightened at being called lovely. "Brady's in trouble . . . financial trouble that is."

"What do you mean he's in trouble? I thought you said that he was making a big profit from his casino."

"He is. But he invested a lot of money in a gold mine out West that turned out to be bogus. Now he needs cash for the casino. I heard him say that he's thinking of taking a partner."

"A partner? Really?" Ryan lay back on the pillow, his mind churning. Brady's partner. An interesting thought. That would be the answer to his major problem—that of not having enough capital from the insurance payoff to set up his own gambling hall. Owning half a casino was better than owning none. Besides, once he was in, it wouldn't be that difficult to get rid of Brady. One way or the other.

Excitement surged through him, concentrating in his groin. Without gentleness or finesse he rolled over onto Bernadette and took her.

"I'm doing this for you," he gasped as he quickly neared his climax. "The casino, the money, I want it all for you, sweetheart."

Bernadette said nothing but clung to him, trying desperately to match his rhythm.

His body spasmed and shuddered. Grabbing handfuls of her black hair, he exploded inside her and cried out the name that filled his mind in that moment of total release.

Later, when he regained his sense of time and place, he realized that she was lying beside him, tense and silent.

"What's wrong, sweetheart?" he asked, trying to sound concerned as he drew her against his side. He stroked her cheek once, in an attempt to demonstrate a bit of the gentleness that he had neglected to show earlier.

In the darkness he heard her sniff, then she asked. "Who's Eirinn?"

"What do you mean?"

"You called out her name just now. Who's Eirinn?"

"I hear you're in need of operating capital,"

Ryan said with a self-satisfied grin.

"Where the hell did you hear a thing like that?" Brady's jowls trembled indignantly as he shoved the pile of chips to Ryan's side of the table. Brady's poker luck hadn't been running in his favor tonight.

"It doesn't matter where I heard it. Everyone on Coney Island knows that Brady's House of Pleasures is in trouble."

Padraic's florid face blushed several shades darker. "And what if I do? Why would that matter to you? You McKevetts don't have any money now, what with your manufactory burned to the ground."

"But we'll be collecting the fire insurance any day now, and that's a tidy sum."

Brady snorted. "That's Michael McKevett's money, not yours."

"But I'm his financial adviser. I'm the one who'll decide where the money is invested." Ryan adjusted his silk tie carefully, drawing attention to the gold and diamond tack. "My father was here only this last week, and I convinced him that a casino here on Coney Island would be our best opportunity at the moment."

Leaning back in his chair, Brady folded his hands across his ample belly. "So, why buy into mine? I'd think you'd prefer to open one of your own and run me a bit of competition. That's what you McKevetts do best."

Ryan smiled slyly. "You have an established house here, a steady clientele, a good reputation. Besides, I don't have the experience and you do."

The admission cost Ryan, but he knew that he had to flatter this man, at least a little, and he knew that it would yield high dividends.

Brady silently chewed on the soggy end of his

cigar, his jowls hanging loosely like a blood-hound's.

"I have to have your answer soon," Ryan said, pushing as hard as he dared.

Brady smiled. "You don't *have* to have your answer soon. You're impatient. But I like that in a man. I'll give you my answer in the morning." He put out his cigar on one of Ryan's chips. "On second thought, I'll give you my answer now." Extending one beefy hand, he said, "You've got a deal . . . and a new business partner."

Ryan cringed when he touched Brady's chafed hand. This man repulsed him. But he looked around the dimly lit casino, at the crystal chandeliers, the thick carpeting below his feet, and the hoards of people who were spending money as though it were their last day on earth.

Ryan decided that he could tolerate Padraic Brady's cigar smoke, his flapping jowls, his crude manners, and his scaly snakeskin in exchange for half of this now. And, someday, all of it.

Padraic Brady turned out the lamp on his desk and sat in the half-light of his office. He could still hear the noise of the crowd downstairs, a happy crowd, eagerly gambling away their money. The ledger on the desk before him showed a healthy profit for the night's operations.

Brady smiled. It had been a good day. In more ways than one.

A knock on the door announced his assistant's arrival. Tim O'Day walked into the office, wearing a scowl beneath his bowler.

"Hey, boss. I gotta talk to ya."

"I'm tired. Get out of here."

"It's important."

"So, talk."

Tim closed the door securely behind him. "You ain't gonna like this, boss. But I gotta warn you about that little songbird you been hangin' around with lately."

"If you're talking about Bernadette, save your breath. I know more about her than you'll ever know," he said with a lecherous laugh.

Tim took off his bowler and twisted it miserably. "I think she's pullin' a fast one on you, boss."

Brady pushed the stogie to the corner of his mouth, where it hung limply, dribbling ash down the front of his vest. "So, spit it out."

"I don't like to be the one to tell bad tales but—"

"It *is* a dangerous pastime, but go ahead."

"Some of the boys tell me that she's two-timing you, boss."

"Really?" Brady didn't seem overly surprised.

"Yeah, they say she's been spending time with that Ryan McKevett fellow. *Night* time, that is. I just thought I should warn you. The McKevetts being your competitors with the carousels and all that."

Brady leaned back in his chair and propped his feet up on his desk. "Thank you for telling me, Tim. You're a good friend. But I already knew about that."

"You did?"

"Yeah. No problem."

"But . . . but even if you don't mind your girl being with another guy, you should think about the fact that she could be telling him your business."

"Don't worry about it, Tim." Brady stubbed out the cigar and took a fresh one from his breast pocket. "I know what Bernadette and Ryan McKevett have been doing and what she's been telling him. She's telling him exactly what I

144

want him to hear."

"Ah, Danny, there's a terrible pain in me heart," Caitlin said as she pounded the bread dough on the board in front of her. Light puffs of flour rose around them. "I just don't know what to do for me little girl to pull her out of her sorrow."

"I know, Caitlin. I'm so sorry for ye all." He stood beside her with one hand on her shoulder, trying to convey a comfort he couldn't feel. He was as worried about Eirinn as she was.

" 'Tis the deepest pain in the world for a mother," she said, "having your child's heart broken and you not able to mend it."

"I just wish there was somethin' I could do for her. But I can't make her laugh or even bring a smile to her face these days."

"Aye, 'tis a bad state she's in that the twinkle of Danny O'Brien's eye doesn't put a grin on her face. There was a time when she would have given the world to have ye lookin' at her the way ye are now. I just can't understand what's wrong with her. 'Twas a sad thing, surely, her losin' the baby and Sean together like that. But it's been months now, and it's time her heart was healin' itself, at least a little. Can't imagine what's wrong."

Daniel walked over to the stove and poured himself a cup of tea. Sitting down at the table, he wrapped his hands around the steaming cup. He stared down into the amber fluid and thought of the pain in Eirinn's eyes the day they buried Sean. Something was wrong all right. Something was very wrong.

If he could only get her to tell him where her guilt was coming from, maybe it would help her get over this sorrow that was eating her alive.

Daniel knew, perhaps better than others, that the pain of bereavement healed with the passage of time, but the wounds of guilt only festered deeper and deeper until they poisoned the entire body.

But what the hell did Eirinn McKevett-Sullivan have to feel guilty about?

As though stepping out of their conversation, Eirinn walked into the room with Michael following close behind.

"There ye are, darlin'," Michael said as he pulled out a chair for her. "Ye must start eatin' more. Yer thin as a sparrow in December."

Caitlin dusted the flour from her hands, walked over to the stove and dished up a hearty breakfast of eggs, bacon, and sausages for the three of them. Bringing the heaping plates to the table, she said, "There ye are. Eat up. Ye'll need yer strength today to be sure."

"Aye," Michael replied, " 'tis goin' to be a hard day for all of us, packing these trunks and loadin' them on the wagons. Who'd have thought we'd have accumulated so many worldly possessions since we came to America?"

Caitlin gave him an affectionate smile. "When we left old Ireland we had only the bundles in our hands."

"And the flying horses," Michael said with a note of sentiment in his voice.

"Aye." She bent and kissed his forehead lightly. "And your wonderful wheel with its flying horses."

"Are ye excited to be leavin', love?" he asked, wrapping his arm around her waist and pulling her into his embrace. "Or does it make ye sad?"

"Both," she said. "But it's a new life we have to look forward to, and we've lived so many already."

Daniel watched them with envy. When he heard them speak of past victories and sorrows, the years

146

shared together in love well lived, he wondered if Michael and Caitlin were the only people on earth blessed with such a union.

He glanced over at Eirinn, who sat head bowed over her plate that remained untouched. Would her heart ever heal enough to love openly, without reservation, as Michael and Caitlin loved each other, as Daniel had grown to love her?

The back door opened and Daniel cringed to see Ryan walk into the kitchen. He looked less dapper than usual. His straight blond hair hung limply around his face and he needed a shave. His clothes were rumpled; he had obviously slept in them on the train from New York. They had expected him three days ago.

His gray eyes glittered, and Daniel wondered what mischief he was up to that would have caused his excitement.

"I saw the trunks and the wagon outside," Ryan said as he joined them at the table. "I'm glad to see you already packing."

"Aye, well, there's no point in wasting time," Michael said as he released Caitlin and attacked his breakfast.

"You'll never believe the good news I have for you all to hear." Ryan looked around the table, but his eyes lingered on Eirinn's bent head. "Lady Luck does indeed shine on us," he added, slipping unconsciously into his Irish brogue.

"Ah, really?" Caitlin asked as she set his breakfast before him. "Did ye finally win a big haul at one of those casinos you haunt?"

"Better than that. Much better."

Daniel got a leaden feeling in the pit of his stomach, as though he had just swallowed a cannonball. Anything that was good news for Ryan McKevett was generally bad for everyone else. Intuitively he knew that this wonderful idea of Ryan's wasn't going to be received as enthusiastically as Ryan was obviously expecting.

"So tell me about the good fortune that Lady Luck has dumped in our laps this morning," Michael said with a hint of sarcasm in his voice.

But Ryan was undaunted. He picked up his fork and speared the air. "I've made a deal with Padraic Brady."

"Padraic Brady?" Caitlin's eyebrows raised two notches, registering her disapproval. "That skunk? Whatever business would you have with him?"

Ryan scowled and attempted to dismiss her with a wave of his hand. "Hold your tongue, woman, until you've heard me out."

Caitlin bristled, but said nothing as she sat down beside Michael.

Daniel smiled. He enjoyed watching the two of them quarrel. Ryan, the mangy, rebellious pup and Caitlin, the fiery she-cat. He was forever nipping at her heels while she batted at him with sheathed claws. Daniel knew—everyone knew except Ryan— that Caitlin could have slashed him if she chose.

She was a powerful woman, but basically kind. And for some reason that Daniel couldn't comprehend, she chose to make peace with Ryan. Daniel respected her for her compassion. He simply wasn't that patient.

"I'll have nothing to do with the likes of Padraic Brady," Michael said. "He knows nothin' of the beauty of the carousel. Those gaudy creatures of his are an abomination."

"No, no," Ryan interrupted. "This has nothing to do with carousels. It's about his casino—"

"A casino?" Michael's disapproval etched even deeper in his brow.

"Yes. Don't you remember when we were in New

148

York, I told you that the casinos are the way to make money on Coney Island?"

"Aye, and I also remember tellin' you that the insurance money we're gettin' will be nowhere near enough to open such an operation as that, even if I had a mind to do it. And I don't."

"I know. That's what makes this such a fine opportunity. Padraic is in bad need of money. Seems he lost some money in gold mines out West and he needs a partner. We discussed the price, and I made a fine bargain with him. As soon as we get the money from the insurance, we're in. I convinced him to wait for us. It's all set. We shook on it. I can't believe how smoothly it worked out."

Daniel could hold his silence no longer. "You shook hands on Michael's money?" Irritation prickled along the back of his neck and raised his hackles.

But Michael didn't need defending by Daniel or anyone else. "Well, that's unfortunate for you that you shook hands, boy," Michael said as he popped a sausage into his mouth. "Ye should have discussed the matter with me first, before ye made pledges that ye'll not be able to live up to."

"But we *did* discuss it. Remember? You agreed that Coney Island was a wonderful opportunity."

"Opportunity? Yes. For the flying horses."

"Why the hell is it always the damned flying horses?"

Michael frowned. "Watch yer language in front of the ladies."

Ryan ignored the admonition. "You can't see a godsend when it's right under your nose." He threw his napkin onto the table.

Daniel felt Eirinn flinch beside him, her face white and drawn. "Ryan, don't," she said, speaking her first words since coming to the table. "Please

149

don't be angry. It's a fine idea, I'm sure. But you know Da. He wants nothing to do with casinos and the likes of that. If he's not building his horses, he's not happy. Just look at how miserable we've all been since the shop burned down."

Ryan stood and slammed his fist down on the table. Again Eirinn jumped and Daniel had had enough. Standing up, he placed his hands protectively on her shoulders. He saw that Ryan noted the gesture, and he took grim satisfaction in the man's irritation.

"It's because of him, isn't it?" Ryan said to Michael, stabbing a thumb toward Daniel. "He's the reason why you're set on this. It's always the horses with the two of you. The horses. And the carving. You listen to him before you listen to your own son."

Your own son. The words hung in the room, heavy, pregnant. Daniel looked from Michael to Ryan, and he knew in that moment that somehow Ryan had found out he wasn't Michael's natural son.

It was a secret they had kept all these years. Michael, Caitlin, and Daniel. But now Ryan knew. Everyone in the room knew except Eirinn.

And if Daniel had anything to do with it, she'd never know. She had already lost Stephen. Ryan was the only brother she had left. She couldn't lose him now, not on the heels of so many other losses.

"Ryan," Daniel said, keeping his voice low and even. "I'll be askin' ye to step outside with me now."

Ryan looked from Caitlin to Michael and down at Eirinn. No one spoke. Tension filled the air, and Daniel thought that if Ryan didn't move toward the door soon, he would surely help him along with the toe of his boot applied to the seat of his pants.

"Come along now," he said in an authoritative voice that left no room for argument. "Outside. Now."

"So, how long have you known?" Daniel asked Ryan as they crossed the field that separated the house from the ruins of the carousel shop.

"How long have I known that I wasn't Michael's son?" Ryan smiled his usual bitter smile that never lit his gray eyes. "I've known all my life. From the day I was born I knew that Michael didn't love me."

"That's a lie, surely, and I'll not be listenin' to it. Michael cares for you deeply. Always has."

"Not like he loved Stephen. Not like he loves you. Can you imagine how that made me feel? Knowing that the man who was supposed to be my father cared more about his bastard son and his best friend than he did about me?"

For a moment Daniel felt sorry that he couldn't muster a speck of pity for this man who was obviously in pain. But Ryan pitied himself adequately. He didn't need the sympathy of others, and Daniel wasn't in the mood to give him any.

"Don't ye go tellin' me what a bad person Michael McKevett is," Daniel said, " 'cause I'll not listen to it. Ye haven't made it easy for him to love you with yer whinin' and yer troublemakin' and yer damned laziness. If ye'd ever acted like a son he might have found it in his heart to treat you as one."

"But I'm not his son, never was, and that explains a lot. He hated my mother and he hates me because I'm her son."

Daniel sighed wearily. "Michael doesn't hate you, lad. But if he can't love you as much as you need

151

him to, you can be sure that it breaks his heart."

Ryan turned on his heel and started to walk away, but Daniel grabbed him by the shoulder.

"Hold up there. I'm not finished yet. There's one thing ye must promise me."

Ryan shook his hand away. "I'll promise you nothing."

"Ye must swear that ye'll never mention this to Eirinn, or even speak of it in her hearing. She loves you dearly and 'twould kill her to know that yer not truly her brother."

The light that glittered in Ryan's gray eyes frightened Daniel. Sometimes he thought this man had no conscience at all. And a man without a conscience was dangerous. Daniel had seen what such a man was capable of during the war. In war or peace a man like Ryan McKevett destroyed everyone around him.

"I don't think it's Eirinn you're so worried about," Ryan said. "It's yourself."

"Meself? What are ye talkin' about?"

Ryan smiled slyly. "You know how close Eirinn and I are," he said, and the suggestive tone in his voice made Daniel want to smash his fist into his jaw.

"I know that she loves you . . . as a sister loves her brother. And I know that you've always felt a strange attachment to her. There's a sickness in you, and somehow ye've turned it toward Eirinn. But I tell ye now, if you ever hurt her, you'll pay the price. I'll take it out of your hide meself."

"I'll never hurt Eirinn. She certainly doesn't need you to defend her from me. But the day may come when she'll have to know I'm not her brother."

Rage, hot and red, surged through Daniel's bloodstream, just as it had on the battlefield seconds before he had killed. "That day had better not come for a long, long time," he said through gritted teeth. "Because the day you break Eirinn's heart with that news is the day I kill you."

February must be the dreariest month of the year, Daniel thought as he walked through the old cemetery. *That's why God in His mercy made it the shortest.*

The setting sun cast a feeble glow in the gray sky above. The houses at the edge of the cemetery were gray, as were the bare trees and the tombstones. The only contrast was a spot of black in the distance, a tiny form swathed in widow's weeds kneeling between two gravestones, one large and ornate, the other small.

"Ah, Eirinn," Danny murmured. As he walked toward her he thought of how lovely she had been on her birthday, less than a year ago, wearing that rose satin dress. Her green eyes had been sparkling then, as bright as an Irish spring morning.

Would he ever see that carefree young girl again? Something deep inside Daniel, an intuition based upon personal experience, told him that she was gone forever. Eirinn might find peace with herself someday, might even be happy again. But her spirit had been touched by tragedy and it would never be so light again. His little girl was gone, and he would miss her. His Eirinn was a woman now.

"I thought I'd find you here, love," he said as he walked up beside her. With an arm around her waist he lifted her from where she knelt in the damp grass.

As she looked up at him, he was relieved to see that her eyes were dry. Dry, but empty. "I had to say goodbye before we left Boston," she said. She glanced from the large stone to the smaller one. "I had to say goodbye to them both."

"I know, darlin'." Daniel saw the bouquet of roses on Sean's grave and a hardness knotted in his throat. But when he saw the tiny bud on the baby's grave, tears flooded his eyes. "You loved Sean more than any of us thought you did," he said, grasping her hand in his.

"Not enough," she said. "He was a kind and gentle man, a good friend. He deserved better than me."

A shudder ran through her and Daniel pulled her into his arms. She buried her face in the front of his coat while he stroked her hair. "Don't say that, love. You were a fine wife to Sean. I'm sure ye brought him a world of happiness."

He had intended for his words to comfort her, but instead she burst into tears. Her arms went around his waist, and she clung to him, sobbing.

As Daniel held her he decided that enough was enough. She was going to tell him what this was all about. One way or the other.

"Come with me, darlin'," he said as he led her over to a small wrought iron bench beneath a willow. He gently seated her, pulled a handkerchief from his pocket, and wiped the tears from her face. God, but she was pale and gaunt. If she didn't stop this she was going to die. Daniel had the terrible feeling that was exactly what she intended. Too many times Daniel had seen healthy people die simply because they no longer wanted to live. He was determined that wasn't going to happen to the woman he loved.

"Eirinn, I know it was hard for you to lose Sean the way you did, and the wee one too. But there's somethin' wrong with the way yer grievin' for him. There's somethin' eating away at you, and you must tell someone about it. Ye must tell me. Now."

Fear widened her green eyes and she tried to move away from him on the bench, but his arms around her waist held her close.

"Eirinn, there's nothin' in the world that you could tell me that would shock me. These eyes have seen it all and made me old before me time. I've seen every cruel and hateful thing under the sun, everything that people can do to one another. I'll not condemn ye, darlin'. Tell me about it."

In a gesture of trust that went straight to his heart, she held out her hand to him. He quickly took it in his and pressed the icy palm to his warm mouth.

"Sean didn't die because of the fire," she said, her voice trembling and tight. "We killed him. Tomas and I."

"Go on," he coaxed, squeezing her hand.

"Tomas came up to my room that afternoon. He threatened me that if I didn't divorce Sean and marry him, he would tell everyone that the baby was his. He wanted Sean to know that he was the child's father."

Daniel fought down his rising temper and forced himself to remain calm. "But you refused?"

"Of course I did. Sean was a good husband to me, loving and sweet. I couldn't hurt him by telling him about Tomas and me. But Sean walked into the room and he heard us talking. Tomas told him—"

Her voice broke and she began to sob again. Daniel pressed a kiss against her hair. "Tomas told him that the two of you had been lovers?"

"Yes, but I told Sean that we hadn't made love. I told him how Tomas forced me and—"

"Tomas *forced* you?" Daniel's mouth went dry and his heart thudded against his ribs. "Why didn't ye tell me that before? I'd have killed the bloody

155

bastard that night."

"That's why I didn't tell you. Besides, Tomas said that it was my fault for being alone with him in the barn. And I believed him."

Daniel wished with all his heart that he could go back to that day on the docks and finish that beating he had given Tomas as a going away gift. In his present state of mind he would gladly have cut him into pieces and fed him to the sharks.

"I don't have to ask what happened when ye told Sean Sullivan what Tomas had done to you," he said. "He surely beat Tomas to a pulp. That's why the lad was sportin' those bumps and bruises at the funeral."

"Sean started to fight him, but then his heart seized up and. . . ," she buried her face in her hands, ". . . he died. There was nothing I could do to save him. And Tomas said that if I told anyone what had happened he would kill me and the baby."

"That's why you asked me to keep him away from you when the babe was bein' born?"

She nodded.

"Ah, Eirinn." He took her in his arms and gently rocked her. "Thank ye for tellin' me, love. I see why yer pain wouldn't depart. But ye've been feelin' guilty for no reason at all."

"We killed him."

"*Tomas* killed him. Tomas raped you, and then, because of his cruelty, his father died. That has nothing to do with you. Like I told ye before, love, you were a good wife and you gave Sean a lot of happiness in the last year of his life. Ye've no reason to feel poorly toward him."

She looked up at him and he could see in her eyes that she wanted desperately to believe him. "Do you think Sean would have forgiven me if he'd lived?"

"I think that wherever Sean Sullivan is right this minute, he's lovin' you, lass. Forgivin' and lovin' you, and beggin' you to be happy."

"Really?"

He kissed her cheek, and then, because it felt like the right thing to do, he kissed the other one, then her lips. "Sean was my friend for more years than you've been alive. I knew him well. And I'm sure."

She said nothing, but as they sat there, side by side, hand in hand, her tears finally subsided. The sun sank lower in the sky, which didn't seem quite so gray now. And the wind wasn't so cold.

Finally she wiped her eyes with his handkerchief and stood. "Will you wait for me here, Danny?" she asked, and her voice sounded stronger than it had for months. "I have to go say goodbye to my husband and baby."

"I'll be here, darlin'," he said. "Take as long as ye need."

Chapter Thirteen

"Are ye proud of yer family, Caitlin?" Michael asked, as they stood in the center of the new manufactory and gazed in awe at the latest McKevett carousel. It had taken them a year to transform the old Brooklyn livery into a functioning shop and to produce a new flying horse machine.

As always, the latest carousel was finer, more ornate, and functionally more efficient than its predecessors. Michael never allowed his family and employees to forget that they were striving for perfection, a goal that once aspired to, rose again out of reach.

"So very proud, indeed," Caitlin replied, "of all of you. Yer carvin' is a wonder, Danny. Ye just get better with every horse. And you're good with the other carvers too. Ye know how to get the best from them by settin' a fine example for them to follow. Michael and I know full well what our advantage is over our competition. 'Tis Daniel O'Brien himself."

Daniel blushed at her praise. Caitlin was kind and generous with her compliments. Daniel knew that she never flattered, and that made her words mean even more.

"Look at Eirinn," she said, nodding at her daughter, who stood beside the carousel. In her hand Eirinn held the McKevetts' catalog, which she was showing to a prospective client. Mr. Reinhart owned a number of amusement rides on Coney Island, and Eirinn was rapidly convincing him that he needed at least one carousel, perhaps two, to complete his collection.

"Do ye think there's any chance of him gettin' away with any coins in his breeches?" Danny asked with a chuckle.

"From the determined look in Eirinn's eyes, I'd say he's lost the battle already. And if I know my daughter, she'll have him thinkin' he convinced her."

"Aye, if she keeps sellin' the wheels like she's been, I'll be chasin' me tail just tryin' to get them all carved." His eyes sparkled at the thought of having more orders than he and his crew could fill. "Ye taught her well, Caitlin. She's the shinin' image of her mother."

Caitlin smiled, and Daniel noticed for the first time that there were fine lines at the corners of her eyes. They were getting older, this weary band of refugees. Not even Caitlin's beauty would last forever.

Daniel looked over at Michael who was showing Ryan how to adjust the support cables that were attached to the center pole. Daniel envied Michael for having this woman to share his life. Not that Daniel wanted Caitlin. He wanted her daughter. And he had waited about as long as his heart would allow.

"Eirinn is stronger now," he said, sure that Caitlin would know what he meant.

"Aye. I don't stay awake at night worrying about her anymore. Moving here to New York was good for her spirit. 'Tis a lively city, full of vinegar, like herself." She laid one hand affectionately on Daniel's forearm. "Besides, she has some fine friends whose love has supported her through the dark times. She's much stronger now. Thank ye, Danny. I owe ye."

"You owe me nothin'," he said. "I love Eirinn

dearly. Helpin' her is the best thing I can do with me time, along with carvin'. If I've helped her at all, 'twas me own pleasure, surely. Besides, I have my own reasons for wantin' to see her strong and happy."

Caitlin's tired face lit with a smile that made her look twenty years younger, and her whiskey-colored eyes sparkled. "Does that mean ye'll be askin' for her hand soon?" she said, and Danny was pleased to hear the hopefulness in her voice.

He nodded. "I've only been waitin' for her to be finished with her grief. And I think she's as done as a person ever gets. What do you think?"

Caitlin looked at Eirinn who was holding a clipboard while her customer enthusiastically signed an order form. "Aye, Danny. She's ready."

The oars dipped into the water as the rowboat glided across the smooth surface of the lake. The evening sun streamed golden shafts of light through the trees, and their new spring leaves glimmered green-gold like a million peridots.

Eirinn sighed and leaned back on the cushions that Daniel had provided for her comfort in the bow of the boat. "I l-o-v-e the park," she said as she lifted her face to the warm sun and closed her eyes, soaking in its heat and radiance. "And I love spring."

"I love being with you."

Eirinn opened her eyes with a start and searched Daniel's face, surprised at the intimate tone of his voice. He smiled at her, then busied himself by pulling the oars into the boat and dropping an anchor, securing them to the center of the lake. A faint blush crept up his freshly shaven cheeks, and Eirinn wondered why he suddenly seemed shy and ill at ease.

MORE PASSION AND ADVENTURE AWAIT... YOUR TRIP TO A BIG ADVENTUROUS WORLD BEGINS WHEN YOU ACCEPT YOUR FIRST 4 NOVELS ABSOLUTELY *FREE*
(AN $18.00 VALUE)

Accept your Free gift and start to experience more of the passion and adventure you like in a historical romance novel. Each Zebra novel is filled with proud men, spirited women and tempestuous love that you'll remember long after you turn the last page.

Zebra Historical Romances are the finest novels of their kind. They are written by authors who really know how to weave tales of romance and adventure in the historical settings you love. You'll feel like you've actually gone back in time with the thrilling stories that each Zebra novel offers.

GET YOUR FREE GIFT WITH THE START OF YOUR HOME SUBSCRIPTION

Our readers tell us that these books sell out very fast in book stores and often they miss the newest titles. So Zebra has made arrangements for you to receive the four newest novels published each month.

You'll be guaranteed that you'll never miss a title, and home delivery is so convenient. And to show you just how easy it is to get Zebra Historical Romances, we'll send you your first 4 books absolutely FREE! Our gift to you just for trying our home subscription service.

BIG SAVINGS AND FREE HOME DELIVERY

Each month, you'll receive the four newest titles as soon as they are published. You'll probably receive them even before the bookstores do. What's more, you may preview these exciting novels free for 10 days. If you like them as much as we think you will, just pay the low preferred subscriber's price of just $3.75 each. *You'll save $3.00 each month off the publisher's price.* AND, your savings are even greater because there are never any shipping, handling or other hidden charges—FREE Home Delivery. Of course you can return any shipment within 10 days for full credit, no questions asked. There is no minimum number of books you must buy.

4 FREE BOOKS

TO GET YOUR 4 FREE BOOKS WORTH $18.00 —MAIL IN THE FREE BOOK CERTIFICATE T O D A Y

Fill in the Free Book Certificate below, and we'll send your FREE BOOKS to you as soon as we receive it.

If the certificate is missing below, write to: Zebra Home Subscription Service, Inc., P.O. Box 5214, 120 Brighton Road, Clifton, New Jersey 07015-5214.

FREE BOOK CERTIFICATE

4 FREE BOOKS

ZEBRA HOME SUBSCRIPTION SERVICE, INC.

YES! Please start my subscription to Zebra Historical Romances and send me my first 4 books absolutely FREE. I understand that each month I may preview four new Zebra Historical Romances free for 10 days. If I'm not satisfied with them, I may return the four books within 10 days and owe nothing. Otherwise, I will pay the low preferred subscriber's price of just $3.75 each; a total of $15.00, *a savings off the publisher's price of $3.00.* I may return any shipment and I may cancel this subscription at any time. There is no obligation to buy any shipment and there are no shipping, handling or other hidden charges. **Regardless of what I decide, the four free books are mine to keep.**

NAME	
ADDRESS	APT
CITY	STATE ZIP
TELEPHONE	
( )	
SIGNATURE	(if under 18, parent or guardian must sign)

Terms, offer and prices subject to change without notice. Subscription subject to acceptance by Zebra Books. Zebra Books reserves the right to reject any order or cancel any subscription.   ZBMSO2

His behavior was certainly strange today. First of all, he had invited her for a picnic in the park, something he had never done before. Then he had rented this boat, which was odd, indeed, because when she had asked him to take her for a boat ride before, he had made all kinds of excuses. She suspected it had something to do with the long, traumatic voyage he had made from Ireland to America when he had been a child.

"Would you like a glass of wine?" he asked, reaching into the basket he had brought along.

"Wine? Since when are you drinking wine instead of Guinness?"

"Ah, spring is in the air, I'm in a wee boat with a lovely lady, and I can drink Guinness anytime. This afternoon is special."

She watched his strong hands as he uncorked the bottle and poured the red fluid into two glasses that he pulled from the basket. For the first time in many months she allowed herself to fantasize what it would be like to have those hands caress her.

Danny hadn't touched her, at least not with a lover's touch, in a long time. He had been kind to her, wonderful in fact, these past few months. But she missed seeing that gleam in his eye, the light that warmed her and caused her to think dark, forbidden, exciting thoughts about what the two of them could do together.

When he handed her the glass their fingers brushed and a tingle went into her hand and up her arm. It was silly, of course, she thought, this acute awareness of a man she saw every day. But this wasn't just any man. This was Daniel O'Brien, and for a thousand reasons she loved him. If only he returned her affections.

He had loved her, wanted her at one time. She would never forget the passion in his kiss that night in the barn. But he had left her, and when he had returned from Canada their relationship had changed. After Sean's death he had been gentle and attentive, but only as a friend or beloved uncle. Always her friend, never her lover.

Eirinn cast the thoughts from her mind, dark clouds that darkened her bright mood. It was a glorious spring evening, she was in his company, and that would have to be enough.

"What are ye thinkin', love?" he asked as he settled on the bench beside her. His hard, muscular thigh pressed against hers, and she wondered if he was aware of the contact as she. Probably not.

"I was thinking about how kind you've been to me since Sean's death. I don't know what I'd have done without you."

He shrugged. "You needed a friend to stand by yer side. 'Twas my pleasure and honor to be standin' there. Ye'd do the same for me if it 'twas meself in need."

Carefully she slid her hand into his warm palm. "I would, Danny. If you ever needed me, I'd be there for you."

His smile turned grim. "Even when the Night Mare comes ridin' through me dreams?"

"What do you mean?"

"Hasn't yer father told you the story of the Night Mare?"

She shook her head.

"Aye, well, Michael prefers the lovely stories, like the tale of Princess Niav, to the dark myths." He drew a deep breath. "The Night Mare is an ancient Celtic goddess. She rides through a man's dreams with an owl on her shoulder and a wolf and a wild boar at her heels. And Death rides with her."

Eirinn hardly dared to breathe as she listened. Daniel had never spoken to her like this. Instinctively, she knew that his heart was open to her in a

He lifted her hand and pressed it to his lips. The evening sun shone on his chestnut hair, lighting it with fiery highlights that matched the hot gleam in his eyes. "I love you." His fingertip trailed from her chin down her throat to the lace edge of her bodice that was stretched tight across her full bosom. "And I want you. I want to spend every day of me life lookin' into those lovely green eyes of yers. I want to spend every night makin' love to you and holdin' yer soft body next to mine."

An arrow of desire, sharp and hot, shot through her, taking the breath from her lungs and the strength from her limbs.

"I want to live with you for the rest of me days. As they say in old Ireland, 'Come live in me heart and pay no rent.' Do you love me, Eirinn?"

She bit her bottom lip to keep it from trembling. "You know I do, Danny. I've always loved you."

"Do ye love me enough to marry me?"

"Oh, Danny," she whispered as she wrapped her arms around his neck, her fingers tangling in his sun-warmed curls. Too overcome with her own emotions to look him in the eye, she buried her face against his neck. Breathing deeply, she inhaled the spicy aroma of his shaving soap mixed with the smell of freshly sawed wood and the subtle male scent of his body.

His big hands moved down her back to her waist as he pulled her even more tightly against him. She heard the quickening of his breath when his hands slid around her midriff and slowly upward to cup the undersides of her breasts.

"Say ye'll be mine, darlin'," he said. "I want to hear ye say the words."

"I'm yours, Danny. I've always been yours." She gasped softly as his palms cupped her breasts and gently squeezed. The sensation raced through her body, robbing her of all thoughts except the aching

165

emptiness inside, a void that only he could fill. "Take me, Danny," she murmured, her lips against his.

He moaned and kissed her, hard and deep. They were both breathless before he pulled away. "Ah, lass, don't make such an offer as that," he said in a ragged voice. "Not in a public place. I'll lose hold of me senses and we'll both be arrested, sure."

"Then take me home with you, Danny," she said, surprising even herself with her boldness. "I want to be alone with you."

Daniel's amber eyes swept over her and she saw his desire, his joy reflected there. "There's nothing I want more than to be alone with ye, love," he said. "But first we must ask yer father's blessing to our marriage." She felt a shudder run through his body, and he added, "Dear Mary, Jesus and Joseph, let it be soon. I surely can't wait much longer."

" 'Tis glad I am that ye gave Danny and Eirinn yer blessing to be wed," Caitlin said as she pulled the pins from her hair and tossed them onto the dresser.

From the bed Michael watched her, his eyes dark with desire. Every night he watched as she undressed and, because she knew it gave him pleasure, she took as long as possible, her entire routine a calculated seduction.

"They're both headstrong as O'Riley's mule. They'd do it whether I gave me blessing or not," he said, but there was no bitterness in his voice.

She chuckled. "That's true enough. But they both love ye dearly, and it made them happy to have you say amen."

"But did ye see the look on Ryan's face when he heard the news?"

She picked up the silver brush he had given her for their tenth anniversary and ran it through her waves, which glowed like russet satin in the lamplight. Michael's eyes followed every stroke. "Aye, he looked as though he just swallowed a mouthful of nettles."

"I wish he weren't so possessive of Eirinn. 'Tisn't natural, the way he thinks of her as his own property."

Caitlin said nothing. She had strong feelings on the subject and some thoughts she had kept to herself for years. It had occurred to her several years ago that the day might come when Ryan would try to do something to Eirinn that mustn't be done between family members. And Caitlin had already decided that when that day came she wouldn't even tell Michael about it. She would simply take the musket from under her bed and put Ryan in his grave.

Slowly she unbuttoned her dress and let the fabric slip to the floor. Then she removed the thin chemise, her petticoat and bloomers, until she stood naked, her ivory skin glowing in the semi-darkness.

There would be no more talk about the day's events. There never was after this point in her ritual. With the grace of a queen, not an Irish peasant, she walked to the bed and slipped between the sheets. Michael's arms were open as always, ready to fold her to him. She shivered when their bodies touched. No matter how many nights, how many years, they had done this, the pleasure of his bare skin against hers never diminished.

He moaned softly and pressed his lips to her throat. "I love ye, lass," he whispered.

"Ah, yer just tellin' me that so I'll let ye have yer way with me," she teased as her hands kneaded his firm hips and pulled him tight against her.

"And what way is that, darlin'?" he asked.

She felt him growing hard, pressing into her softness. "Anyway ye like, Michael. Anyway at all, at all."

Ryan took the gold pocket watch from his vest and opened the lid. Two o'clock in the morning. Everyone was in bed—except him. And Ryan McKevett sorely wished they were all in hell. Damn them. Damn them all.

He should have been asleep too. But Michael had scolded him for not finishing his work that day and had insisted that he not stop until he had tightened and adjusted all of the support cables that were attached to the center pole.

As he looked up at the half-finished job he debated about whether to stay, complete the assembly, and obey his master like a schoolboy or whether to walk away from it all and face Michael's wrath in the morning.

He thought of Eirinn and Daniel together. He thought of them standing before the priest and swearing to love and honor each other until death. Once before he had seen Eirinn married to another man, and that had been almost more than he could bear. But at least Sean Sullivan had been his friend, and an old man besides. Daniel was his enemy, always had been. And every time Ryan thought of what Daniel would be doing to Eirinn on their wedding night he wanted to kill him. Anything to keep him from touching Eirinn.

Then the thought struck him—Daniel might have already had her.

Ryan threw down his tools. To hell with the support cables. To bloody hell with it all. He was going to bed.

168

An hour later, Ryan was lying on his bed, a small pipe, stylet, and a velvet pouch half full of black powder lying on the table beside him. He floated in a pink haze where there were no support cables and no Daniel O'Briens.

But Eirinn was there. He could see her just ahead through the fog. Her filmy nightgown drifted around her body, revealing and then concealing.

He held out his arms to her. "Come to me," he whispered.

She ran to him, her face shining with pleasure at seeing him. He gathered her into his arms and held her, savoring the rounded softness of her body pressed against his.

He couldn't wait. He had waited for her so long.

His hands moved beneath the thin fabric and touched skin that was the softest he had ever felt. "Oh, Eirinn. I love you. Let me show you how much."

She gasped and moved away, shaking her head. "No. Ryan, what's wrong with you? You can't touch me like that. You're my brother."

She turned and ran. He tried to follow, but his legs were leaden.

"Eirinn, you don't understand. It's all right if I touch you. You don't understand. I'm not really your brother."

But she had disappeared into the pink haze, and although he searched for her all night, he couldn't find her again.

When Daniel heard the creak of the shop door he knew it was Eirinn. He felt her presence even before he laid his chisel and hammer on the bench and turned to face her. He had known Eirinn all

169

her life. He had held her in his arms the day she had been born. But he never got over the thrill of being in the same room with her.

"Good evenin', love," he said as he walked across the sawdust-strewn floor to meet her halfway.

"Ah, Danny, I couldn't sleep," she said as she cuddled into his arms and laid her head on his chest. "I just kept thinking how happy Ma and Da were when you asked for my hand tonight."

Daniel pressed his lips to her hair and closed his eyes, picturing the look on Michael's face when he had asked his blessing on their marriage. Michael had been happy it was true, but Daniel had still detected a hint of Michael's old misgivings.

But as Daniel pressed Eirinn closer, he put Michael and his doubts out of his mind.

Her body was so warm and pliant as she snuggled against him. The desires of the afternoon came flooding back, hot and overwhelming in their intensity. He had wanted her so badly for so long. And she was going to be his wife. It was a dream come true that Daniel could hardly allow himself to believe.

Eirinn pulled back slightly to look up into his eyes. "There was another reason why I couldn't sleep tonight," she said, her voice low and breathy. The sound went through him and concentrated in his groin.

"And what reason was that, darlin'?" he asked, knowing her answer. The devils that had chased her sleep had visited his bedroom tonight, too, and had driven him downstairs to the shop to try to carve his frustrations away.

"I kept thinking about this afternoon in the park," she said, "and how good it felt to have you touch me."

Daniel moaned deep in his throat, the sound of a man who was fighting a losing battle. "And me fingers haven't forgotten the feel of you just yet, either," he said.

"Touch me again, Danny," she said, pressing her soft breasts against the hardness of his chest. "Please, touch me."

Daniel smiled to himself. This lass had no shame at all. She didn't seem to know the meaning of self-restraint. And he was so very grateful.

"Yer father gave his blessing to our *marriage,*" he said. "I'm sure he'd not be pleased at the thought of us coming together beforehand."

Her hands moved up his chest, sending waves of need through his body that left his knees weak.

"This isn't between you and my father, Daniel," she said as her fingertip found the sensitive hollow at the base of his throat. "Everyone's in bed and asleep. I know. I checked before I left the house."

"What are you sayin', love?" he asked, his own voice as breathless as hers.

She raised her eyes to his and the fire he saw in those green eyes added to the inferno that was already blazing though him. "I want to be with you tonight, Daniel. I've married you already in my heart. I don't need a priest to tell me that I'm yours."

He said nothing for a long moment as he studied her face, looking for any signs of doubt or misgivings. He didn't see any.

"Are ye sure, Eirinn?" he asked. "Be sure, love." Her gaze never wavered. "I'm sure."

Without another thought of Michael, Caitlin, or tomorrow, Daniel took her by the hand and led her up the stairs to his room.

"You were wearin' this same robe that night when you came to me on yer sixteenth birthday," Daniel said as his hands ran down her burgundy velvet sleeves.

Eirinn shivered at his touch, slow and gentle despite the urgency that she saw in his eyes. "You remember what I was wearing that night?" she asked.

He nodded and smiled. "I remember everything about that night. I remember the way yer eyes sparkled in the lantern light, the softness of yer lips when you kissed me. If I live to be a hundred years old and combing my great grandchildren's hair, I'll never forget that fine evenin'."

His hands moved over her shoulders, sweeping the robe back and down her arms. It fell into a soft heap on the brightly colored rag rug.

"You must have thought me a silly child that night, coming to you that way," she said, aware of the pain in her voice. His rejection still hurt after all these years.

"Not at all, at all," he said. With deft movements of his agile fingers he untied the blue bits of ribbon that fastened the front of her gauze nightgown. "I thought you were a lovely lass, a woman full-grown and full of spirit. God forgive me for the thoughts I entertained about you that night . . . and every night after," he added.

Eirinn closed her eyes as his warm hands moved over her shoulders again, and a moment later the gown joined the robe at her feet. She felt a sudden unexpected rush of modesty. Daniel had never seen her naked before, at least, not since she was a baby.

She heard him draw a deep breath, and she opened her eyes to see him gazing at her in wonder and deep appreciation.

"Ah, lass," he whispered, "yer more lovely than I'd dreamed."

With a feather touch he trailed his fingertips down her throat, over the curve of her breast, and down her stomach. She had seen that look on his face before. Laughing softly she said, "You're looking at me the way you look at horses, Daniel O'Brien."

"What?" He seemed to come out of a daze. "What do ye mean?"

"When you're carving a horse and you're sizing up the animal, you look at him that way. As though you were memorizing his every curve."

Daniel chuckled and looked a little embarrassed. "I must admit, I was just thinking how fine it would be to carve you in wood. A bonny figurehead for a ship you'd make." He leaned back and surveyed her with an artist's eye. "I can see you now there on the front of one of those fine clipper ships, yer hair blowin', yer lovely breasts bared to the wind, salt water on yer face and lips."

She watched his amber eyes and saw the moment that the artist disappeared and her lover took his place.

"Are ye really going to be mine, darlin'?" he asked. She heard the vulnerability in his voice and the fear that matched her own. The fear that someone or something would, once again, come between them.

"All yours, Danny . . . tonight."

An hour later they lay side by side on his bed, snuggled beneath the thick, red and blue star-patterned quilt. Running her fingertips over his chest, Eirinn was allowing herself the luxury of getting to know his body, just as he had explored hers when he had first brought her to his bed.

She had seen him with his shirt off many times before, but until this time she had never noticed the tiny white scar that ran through the thick hair just above his navel.

173

"When did you get this?" she asked, tracing the line with her fingernail.

"In a pub tussle, I'm afraid," he said. " 'Twas only skin deep, lucky for me."

"And this?" She pointed to a dark red pucker on his right hip.

"Nicked by a Rebel bullet." His voice was strangely flat, and it occurred to her that a wound of that kind could hardly be called a nick.

"And these?" She pointed to the long jagged scars that ran down his left thigh and calf, deep scars that represented a terrible injury. "Did you get those in the war too?"

Daniel sighed and closed his eyes, but not before she saw the pain registered there. "No. Those were from a long time back."

He was silent for so long that she thought he was finished. Apparently the memory was too much for him.

But finally he opened his eyes and said, "Have ye heard of the Night of the Big Wind?"

She thought carefully. "I think so. Wasn't that the awful hurricane that destroyed so much of Ireland back in 1840?"

He nodded. "The very one."

"But you were just a baby then."

"A wee lad, I was. Still in the cradle."

She didn't know if she should push him, but she wanted so much to know. "What happened, Danny?"

"Me father's house was ruined that night," he said. "A big oak tree fell on it. Destroyed it entirely. And when the wall came crashin' down, I was there to meet it."

"Oh, Danny, how dreadful. Was it very painful?"

He laughed grimly. "Can't say as I remember the wound itself. But I do remember livin' with it afterwards. 'Twas a terrible trial. I limped badly back then, couldn't run and play with the other garsoons. But Michael encouraged me to walk until, as the years went on, I got stronger. And when I was tired he carried me around on his shoulders, he did. We went on long hikes across the fields and the Kerry mountains. 'Twas like sittin' on top of the world to be sittin' on Michael McKevett's shoulders."

Eirinn thought of all the times she had ridden on her father's broad shoulders. She thought of how much it must have meant to a little lame boy to have such a big, strong friend to show him affection and attention. "No wonder you love him so much," she said.

"Aye, Michael gave me a sense of what it was to be a man. He gave me the woodcarvin' and a father's love." Daniel reached down and stroked her cheek with his fingertips. "And tonight he gave me what he loves most in the world. I only hope I can take care of you, Eirinn, and love ye as ye deserve to be loved."

Her hands moved over his body, stirring the feelings and desires that had only begun to be satisfied. "Oh, I think you could love me as I deserve to be loved, Danny," she said playfully.

"Again?" he asked with a mock groan.

She shrugged. "If you want to, that is."

He reached down, and pulled her up beside him, and began to nuzzle her breasts. "Ah . . . 'twill be a hardship, for sure," he murmured. "But I'll bear up."

Chapter Fourteen

She rode across the horizon of his dreams, a woman on a white horse, her golden hair streaming out behind her in the night wind. On her shoulder sat an owl. Behind her ran a wild boar and a wolf. The Night Mare.

Galloping across the moon-silvered fields of County Kerry, she brought Death with her. Death, starvation, pestilence.

Famine.

In the ditches on either side of the road crouched the living skeletons with their outstretched hands. Men, women, and babies, begging the woman for a scrap of bread to relieve their misery.

She brought relief. But her relief was that of eternal sleep. As she rode those country lanes, village streets, and city alleys, they fell. Hundreds. Thousands. Hundreds of thousands falling beneath her mare's hooves.

At the edge of one of those roads Daniel watched in silent horror as he had night after night, year after year. These were his people who were dying. His friends, neighbors, and family. And there was no way to stop the slaughter.

He was only a little boy, and a lame boy at that. What could he do in the face of one of the world's greatest tragedies?

"Come, lad," said a deep voice behind him.

The lad turned and saw his friend, Michael McKevett, walking across the dark field toward him. Daniel rushed into the man's strong arms for protection.

"There's a ship leaving for America," Michael said, "and we must be on it."

"Leave Ireland?" the boy asked, his heart pounding in his throat.

"Aye. If we don't, she'll get us, too."

Daniel watched the Night Mare as she turned east toward County Cork. "But can't she follow us to America?" he asked.

"Aye. She can. And she surely will. No one truly outruns the Night Mare. When it's your time, she'll find you, no matter where ye hide. But there's no sense in staying here, in her very path, so to speak."

Michael lifted the boy onto his shoulders and they walked down the road in the opposite direction from the death rider.

But Danny had to look back at her, just once. He knew he shouldn't. But he had to.

She was following them . . .

"No!"

Eirinn woke to find Daniel sitting up in bed, shivering so violently that the iron bed frame shook. She reached for him; his body was covered with cold sweat.

"Danny, what is it?" she asked. "What's wrong?"

He passed a trembling hand across his brow and mumbled something about a mare. She realized that he was still half asleep.

Shaking him gently, she said, "Danny, are you having one of your bad dreams?"

He blinked his eyes as though seeing her for the first time. "Aye . . . a bad one it was."

"Do you want to tell me about it?"

He shook his head, and she felt an invisible wall

slide up between them.

"No," he said. "But I think ye should be goin' back to yer room now."

"Danny, I don't want to leave you now." She laid her hand on his bare shoulder. "You need me."

" 'Tis best, lass. Truly it is," he said, and she had never heard him sound so sad, so defeated. "I thought that with you at my side, she'd stay away. But it seems she's with me forever."

"Who, Danny?"

"The Night Mare." He shuddered. "I swear, she'll haunt me 'till the day that she and I meet, face to face."

"Where's Da and Ryan?" Eirinn asked when she walked into the kitchen and took her place beside Daniel at the breakfast table.

"Yer father's in the shop, admiring his new carousel, and the good God only knows where Ryan is," Caitlin replied as she placed a plate full of food on the table in front of Eirinn.

Eirinn reached beneath the table and squeezed Daniel's knee. He gave her a sad, tender smile and she was reassured. It had really happened after all. They had been lovers. And, other than his nightmare and the fact that he had sent her back to her room in the middle of the night, it had been wonderful.

It was spring. She was in love. All was right with Eirinn's world.

She wondered for a moment if it showed on her face. Casting a sideways glance at her mother, Eirinn wondered if her mother's quick eyes would detect the difference. Would she guess that they had been together last night?

But Caitlin seemed preoccupied and weary this morning. Her usually ruddy complexion was pale with a tinge of gray, and dark circles made her large eyes seem enormous.

"What's wrong, Caitlin," Danny asked as he shoveled the food into his mouth. "Ye look a bit peaked about the gills this mornin'."

She avoided his eyes as she poured herself a cup of coffee and sat down with them. "I don't know," she said. "Didn't sleep well at all last night."

"You weren't worrying about us, were you?" Eirinn asked as she reached across the table and patted her mother's hand. "I thought you were happy for us."

Caitlin smiled tiredly. "Ah, I am happy for ye both. Happy, indeed. I can hardly wait to see ye wed." She looked down into the depths of her coffee and her eyes were distant, as though seeing the future in that amber liquid. "I had dreams last night . . . bad dreams."

"What did you dream?" Eirinn asked.

Caitlin shook her head as though trying to rid her mind and heart of the night's darkness. "I mustn't speak of it before breakfast," she said, quoting a bit of Irish pishogue. "If a bad dream's put to words before breakfast it'll come true, sure."

Eirinn's eyes met Daniel's in an uneasy understanding.

"The Night Mare," Danny muttered, but only Eirinn heard him.

"Ye've been workin' too hard, Caitlin," Danny told her. "But we'll all have a short rest as soon as this machine is delivered and set up. Though it won't be a very long holiday, what with Eirinn selling machines faster than we can build them."

Eirinn looked across the table at her mother's drawn face and a quiver of fear went through her. Life was never this perfect. Just when you thought it was, something always went wrong.

As Michael stood looking at the machine that he, his family, and employees had built, a wash of pride swept over him. He reveled in the moment, savoring the joy that came too seldom but that was glorious enough to keep him going through the long, backbreaking hours of constructing the next one.

He walked around the machine and admired Daniel's intricate carving and the horses that he himself had brought into the world from chunks of glued-together wood. He noted with satisfaction Josef's and Ignacio's delicate painting that brought the figures to life. The mechanism was strong and precise. Every piece had been crafted in the forge located at the back of the old livery. Michael's only regret was that Sean Sullivan hadn't worked on this machine.

"Ye would be proud of this one, friend," he whispered, "if only the Night Mare hadn't snatched ye away from us so early."

Michael walked up to the wheel and braced his massive shoulder against one of the support rods.

This was the magic moment, when the carousel was turned for its first rotation. A horse from the stables would be used to move the heavy wheel, as very few men could budge this much weight. But Michael would allow no animal this honor. He had turned his own wheels since he had built his first one twenty years before in Ireland. And he would turn this one, too, even if it were the largest yet.

With over two hundred pounds of muscle, honed by a lifetime of smithing and carving, Michael pushed. At first he felt nothing, then it moved with him. His wheel, his muscle, his dream, moving together as one.

The machine turned faster and faster, the precision gears meshing, like the finest clock. Only this device didn't measure time, only happiness — the joy of the generations of children who would ride it in the years to come.

Happiness exploded inside Michael's chest and burst forth in an incoherent cry of joy. This was what Michael McKevett lived for, the ecstasy of creativity. Princess Niav's flying horses. They came through him, from his mind, his imagination, and through his hands into the world, where they could be enjoyed by all who saw them and rode them to the Land of the Ever Young.

Michael stopped pushing and allowed the wheel to turn on its own. Tears clouded his eyes and he didn't bother to wipe them away.

He didn't see the untightened cable as it strained and slipped in its housing on the center pole. He heard the small click of metal against metal, and his brain registered the sound, a sound that was wrong.

When the cable snapped, whipped around and struck his temple, Michael felt nothing, saw nothing except the blackness that swept over him in a wave that obliterated all senses. He dropped to the floor where his giant body lay motionless.

The wheel continued to spin . . . one . . . two . . . three revolutions before it finally stopped. Michael McKevett's machines were precise.

Behind closed lids Michael saw nothing but darkness. Then, gradually, he realized that he was no longer in the carousel shop in New York City. He stood on the banks of Killarney Lough, its black water lapping gently at his feet.

Overhead, a full moon glistened, and as his eyes adjusted to the silver light he could discern in the distance the snow-tipped, crooked peak of Carantuohill, the tallest mountain of the Macgillicuddy's

Reeks. He took a deep breath and filled his lungs with the sweet smell of Ireland. He felt her feminine presence, embracing him, cradling him in her maternal arms.

"Ah, sweet land, how I've missed you," he said as tears streamed down his face. " 'Tis so good to be home."

Then, before his eyes, the waters parted and a figure rose up from the lake. It was a woman with long, streaming hair seated on a white horse. She rode toward him, a smile on her pretty face, her hand stretched out to him. The horse's mane was gold, its bridle silver, studded with precious jewels. Around its graceful neck hung garlands of lilies and roses.

Michael recognized the horse. He had carved this pony many times in the past twenty years, and he was surprised and pleased, seeing it now with his eyes instead of his imagination, how accurate he had been.

"Princess Niav," he whispered as he walked into the cool water. "You've come for me, to take me to the Land of the Ever Young."

She nodded as she reined her horse in beside him. He marveled at her unearthly beauty. Her hair was golden, like the horse's mane, and it flowed in glorious profusion down to the saddle. Her eyes were warm and kind. Like Caitlin's, he thought as he walked toward her. Her lovely face was so very like Caitlin's that he felt as though he knew her, had always known her.

With a wave of one graceful hand she invited him to join her on the horse, and without hesitation he did.

The horse turned and headed back toward the center of the lake. Michael knew where they were going. She was taking him beneath the waters to the enchanted land that he had heard of all those years ago in Ireland. The Land of the Ever Young, where there were no disappointments, no sadness, and everyone remained a child forever.

It wasn't until they had neared the center of the lake that Michael noticed the owl on her shoulder. An icy chill washed over him as he turned in the saddle and looked behind. Following them was a bristly wild boar and a large gray wolf.

"Ye've tricked me," he said to the woman who sat in front of him and held the silver reins in her delicate hands. "Ye aren't Princess Niav at all."

She said nothing, but the horse suddenly rose above the water and soared like an eagle over the peak of Carantuohill. Looking down onto that snowy peak, Michael felt his heart soar with the horse. A flying horse. Like the ones he had carved.

Somehow, it no longer mattered that she wasn't Princess Niav. Michael knew that she would take him to that enchanted land. So, he closed his eyes and turned his face into the cold night wind that swept through his hair. He put his arms around the woman's waist and embraced the Night Mare.

Daniel decided that he had given Michael enough time to spin his new wheel and enjoy the fruits of his labor. Danny understood Michael's ritual and how much it meant to him. Some things were better enjoyed alone, and Daniel didn't want to intrude.

When he opened the door and stepped inside the shop, Daniel's first thought was that Michael wasn't inside. Often, even if Michael were silent, Daniel could sense his presence. There was a bond between the two that few people would have understood. Only those who had faced life and death together could have understood that tie.

Daniel walked around the carousel and when he

reached the other side, he saw the limp cable. And he saw Michael's body.

Michael lay facedown on the wooden floor in a relaxed position, as though he were sleeping. For a moment Daniel allowed himself to think that he was asleep. But he knew better. Daniel had seen too many dead men on the battlefield and in the ditches of Ireland to believe that Michael McKevett was still alive.

Danny stood still for a long moment. He didn't speak. He didn't breathe. Then his body shook as though buffeted by a strong wind and he fell to his knees beside the body.

"Michael. Dear God . . . no."

His mouth spoke the words of denial, but he knew the truth. His friend was dead. As dead as those corpses in the ditches.

A thousand memories raced through his mind. Michael carrying him on his back for long rides across the moonlit fields in Ireland. Those were the good times, before the Great Hunger.

Danny saw Michael placing a box of carving tools in his hand and showing him how to coax a living, vibrant horse from a hunk of wood. He remembered that day in Ireland when he had shown Michael his first carved horse, and Michael had hugged him and told him that it was the loveliest thing he had ever seen.

Daniel had thought, after the war and Stephen's death, that nothing could truly ever hurt him again. But he had been wrong.

He reached out and smoothed the hair away from his friend's forehead, where a small trickle of blood dripped. It had been a quick death. Painless. Not slow and obscene like so many Daniel had witnessed. Not like Stephen, thank God.

But it didn't hurt any less. Michael was still dead. And Daniel knew that the pain that was

184

knifing through his heart was going to get worse, much worse, long before it got better.

He looked at the loose cable and in the back of his stunned mind it occurred to him that Michael had been killed by the very thing he loved. It was a bitter irony. But life was bitter. Daniel knew that.

Feeling the grief rising in him, he fought it down. This was too great a sorrow to feel all at once. If he allowed it all to come at one time it would destroy him. So he pushed it down as far as possible, and it lay there, boiling and seething. More rage, more pain. More ghosts.

He reached down and closed those sightless green eyes. It wasn't much, and he wished he could do more for his friend. Never in his life had Daniel O'Brien felt so helpless.

A scream shattered the silence. Daniel jumped to his feet and whirled around. Eirinn stood only ten feet away, her hand clasped over her mouth, her face as white as her father's. Daniel hadn't even heard her walk in.

"Da! Danny, what's wrong with him?" Her voice was already shaking with sobs. She knew. Just as he had known.

She ran toward her father's body, but Daniel caught her halfway.

"Don't darlin'," he said. "Ye don't want to see him now."

"Is he . . . ? He's not—?"

"Aye, love, he's dead."

"No!" She tried to push away from him, beating his chest with her fists, but he held her tightly. "Let me go. I want to see him. Oh, God, he can't be dead!"

As quickly as he had grabbed her, Daniel let her go. It was a terrible thing—to hold the dead body of a loved one in your arms. But Danny knew that she had to do it, just as he had.

He watched as she fell down beside Michael, gathered him to her, and rocked him, just as Daniel had seen Michael rock her so many times over the years.

Daniel had thought that he had felt the sharpest stab of pain when he had first seen Michael's body sprawled there on the floor. But as he watched the woman he loved hold her dead father, kiss his face, and beg him not to be dead, Daniel felt the tip of that knife stab deeper than he had ever thought possible.

And, dear God, there was still Caitlin.

Chapter Fifteen

Caitlin dipped the washcloth into the porcelain bowl and wrung the water from it. Walking over to her bed, she moved like one asleep, her motions slow and methodical.

Lovingly she washed Michael's face, taking care to remove every trace of blood. Her touch was as gentle as though she were bathing a newborn babe when she moved the cloth over the rough stubble of his heavy beard.

This is the last time I'll touch him, she thought. She recalled the first time she had touched Michael McKevett. They had been young and carefree that summer before the famine. Beneath a tree beside the River Laune they had whiled away a Sunday afternoon, talking of everything and nothing, kissing, touching, exploring. Little did they know that afternoon what lay before them. The deepest sorrows and the greatest joys.

It had been a good life, rich in experiences. Caitlin couldn't help feeling bitter that Michael's life had been cut short so early. Yet he had lived more in his forty-two years than most people did in eighty.

So many people came into the world and left it without anyone knowing they had been there. But Michael had left the legacy of his carving, of his beautiful flying horses, and of the love he had given to those closest to him.

Caitlin embraced all these comforting thoughts

as she bathed his body, preparing it for the under-taker. She thought that perhaps she should sum-mon a priest to administer last rites, but she decided against it. Michael had rebelled against the Catholic church long before he had left Ireland. If he had chosen not to live as a Catholic, why should he die as one?

Maybe the ancient ones, the druids, had been right about a soul coming back to earth again and again. Caitlin hoped they were right. Perhaps in another lifetime she and Michael would be together again.

Finished with the bath, she sat on the side of the bed, took his huge, calloused hand and lifted it to her lips. Suddenly the comforting thoughts weren't enough to keep the grief at bay. Michael was dead, and the quality of his life and the hopes of a hereafter didn't matter. The man she loved more than life itself was gone forever.

Choking on her sobs, she lay down beside him, put her head on his chest as she had done every night for twenty years and wrapped her arm tightly around his waist.

Michael was gone. This body that she was em-bracing was empty, and Caitlin knew it. But it was all she had left of him. She wasn't ready to let go just yet.

She lay there and wept until she had no more tears. It was when she was finally spent, her emo-tions totally expended, that the thought came to her. A thought that gave her comfort and purpose. There was something she could do for Michael after all. She would do it.

She sat up on the bed and pulled a sheet over his body. Laying her hand along his cheek, she smiled.

"I'm going to take you home, love," she whispered. "Ye'll be able to rest forever in ol' Erin's soil. 'Tis the only place yer soul will be truly at rest . . . in the shadow of Carantuohill."

"I hope ye'll understand why I must do this," Caitlin told Eirinn and Daniel as the three of them sat at the table, glasses of whiskey in their hands to drink a final toast to Michael.

"Of course we do, Mama," Eirinn said, and Caitlin was relieved to see that, although there was sorrow in her daughter's eyes, there was strength. She was going to survive this tragedy. She was a daughter of Ireland, and Erin's daughters thrived on adversity.

"I would be glad to go with ye or even in yer place, Cait," Daniel offered, his deep voice soft with sympathy. "I can take him back if it's back ye want him."

"No. 'Tis something I must do meself. But I thank ye for the kind offer. I've booked passage on a ship that sails tomorrow morning. The undertaker is preparin' him now for transport."

Caitlin reached out her hands and they each took one. Closing her eyes, she drew strength from the two people she loved most in the world. "I'll leave the shop in yer hands, Danny," she said. "And yers equally, Eirinn. It will never stay alive without the two of you workin' night and day the way Michael and I worked. But I know ye'll not let Michael down."

"We'll not let you down either, Caitlin," Daniel assured her. "The shop will never be the same without Michael. He was its heart and soul. But it will survive. We'll see to it."

"I've no doubt," she said. "Me only concern is Ryan and what he might try to do now that his father's gone."

At the mention of Ryan's name, all three of them caught their breaths.

"Dear Jesus," Caitlin gasped. "No one's told Ryan that Michael's dead."

Daniel stood and tossed the last few drops of whiskey down his throat. "I'll tell him," he said. "If I can find him."

It was two o'clock in the morning before Daniel found Ryan. He was in a hotel room over one of the seedier casinos in Coney Island. When Ryan answered Daniel's knock, he was dressed, but he had obviously been sleeping in his clothes.

Daniel held his breath as the odors of stale alcohol and an unwashed body assaulted his nostrils.

"May I come in?" he asked.

Ryan glared at him with red eyes. "I've nothing to say to you."

"Don't be an arse, Ryan. Let me in," he said as he forced his way into the room. "I have to talk to ye. Sit down and keep a shut mouth for a minute, if ye can."

Ryan sat, or rather collapsed, onto the bed, his arm wrapped around one of the four posts. He leaned his forehead on his arm. "I suppose you've come to gloat about your engagement to Eirinn."

"No."

Perhaps it was something in Daniel's tone that made Ryan sit up and suddenly become alert. "What is it? What's happened?"

"You and Michael. . . ," Daniel began, "you two were adjusting the support cables yesterday."

Ryan glanced away uneasily. "Yes. So?"

"Did ye get them all tightened up proper?"

"Ah, no. When we quit for the night they weren't all tightened yet. Michael said he'd do it first thing in the morning."

Daniel said nothing as he mulled over this information, which somehow didn't ring true. Michael had turned the wheel, and he would never have done that if he had known that the cables weren't tightened down and carefully adjusted. But Daniel reminded himself that he had no proof that it was Ryan's fault. Besides, he had come to give this man some tragic news. There was no reason to make it harder with unfounded accusations.

"Why are you asking about the cables?" Ryan inquired warily.

"Because there was an accident at the shop this mornin'."

"What kind of accident?"

Daniel swallowed and cleared his throat. "The worst kind. One of the cables slipped out of the housing when the wheel was turned . . . and Michael was kilt by it."

Danny thought at first that Ryan hadn't heard him because he simply sat there, staring at him as though not comprehending. Then he whispered, "Dear God," and covered his face with his hands. His body began to tremble violently.

For a moment Daniel considered walking over to him and putting a comforting hand on his shoulder. If it had been anyone in the world other than Ryan McKevett, Daniel would have done so without hesitation. But he couldn't bring himself to touch the man, even now. Besides, he didn't think Ryan would welcome his touch.

"Are ye all right, lad?" he asked softly. When Ryan didn't answer, he added, "Is there anything I can do for ye?"

Daniel stood there, shifting his weight from one

foot to the other, until Ryan dropped his hands from his face and looked up at him with haunted, but dry, eyes.

"Yes," Ryan said, "there's something you can do for me. You can get the hell out of my sight."

Daniel shrugged and left the room, grateful for the fresh air in the hall.

I'll tell ye one thing, McKevett, he thought as he walked away. *I'd better never find out that you had anything to do with Michael's death. Or surely ye'll be as dead as himself.*

Caitlin stood in the ancient graveyard of the tiny Irish village of Lios na Capaill and wondered if she had made the right decision. She had buried Michael, not beside his former wife, Annie, but next to the grave of Michael and Annie's baby. Caitlin knew, probably better than anyone, how Michael felt about Annie. Their relationship had been a stormy one and had ended tragically when she had died giving birth to Ryan. Caitlin didn't believe that Michael would want to lie beside Annie for all eternity.

Kneeling down on the freshly laid patch of sod, Caitlin placed a bouquet of bluebells on the grave. She was so glad that she had brought him back to Ireland. Her heart was still broken, but at peace because Michael was at peace, and that was all that mattered.

"Rest well, my love," she whispered. Then she left the cemetery and walked down the narrow dirt road that she hadn't walked for twenty years.

The last time Caitlin had been in this town it had been nearly empty; the villagers had died of starvation or fevers, or had emigrated. Now the town was thriving again. Children played in the streets and dogs chased flocks of flapping chickens, ducks, and geese through the fields.

She recognized a few of the faces, but most were strangers. They stared at her curiously as she passed. Some nodded and smiled. Caitlin's heart swelled in her chest.

Dear God, it was good to be home.

She passed the forge with its horseshoe-shaped door, the forge where Michael had learned his trade. To her left was the police barracks and behind it the old oak tree where she had seen her friends and neighbors hanged for such villainous crimes as stealing a loaf of bread from an English landlord.

Across the fields to her right was the ancient ringed fairy fort, where the Good People lived. Michael had slept there one night—an act that had proved to the villagers that he was daft, indeed—and the spirits of the fort had given him the dream of the carousel.

But straight ahead was the small stone building that Caitlin had longed to see for the past twenty years. It was her pub. The tavern that had been left to her by her father so long ago that it seemed like another lifetime.

The place hadn't changed. It looked exactly as she remembered. Even the sign that Michael had carved for her still hung over the door. She reached up and touched it lovingly before opening the pub.

When Caitlin stepped across the threshold into the dark, dusty interior, she felt as though her heart would surely burst with joy. She was home. Not just her body, but her soul itself had come home.

Throwing the curtains open she allowed the sunlight to stream in, revealing the rough-hewn tables and chairs, the rush lights, and the bar that had once sparkled but was now covered with twenty years worth of dust.

Against the far wall was the fireplace that had warmed many a cold, weary traveler. When she saw the small stool pulled close to the hearth, tears flooded her eyes. Michael had sat there, night after night, carving the tiny horses that had, years later, become his enchanted flying horses. *Ah, Michael,* she thought. *How can I ever live without you?*

Suddenly, Caitlin knew how. The answer was as clear as though he had just whispered it in her ear. She could feel Michael close by, his love, his strength and concern for her.

She walked over to the bar and picked up the towel that she had folded and laid there twenty years before. With a sense of purpose she hadn't felt in a long, long time, Caitlin began polishing the bar, her grandfather's and her father's bar. Her bar.

Eirinn walked into the office and sat down at her desk. She was exhausted. All day long she and Daniel had combed the shipyards, searching for carvers. The ship building trade had always proved a good source of talented craftsmen, experienced in carving the figureheads for the bows of the magnificent clipper ships. But today their search had yielded nothing, and with the orders that were steadily coming in, they needed all the help they could get.

When she and Daniel had returned to the shop, they had found Ryan going through the company books. Daniel had threatened to flatten him then and there, and if Eirinn hadn't intervened on Ryan's behalf, she was sure that he would have been sporting a black eye and a leg plaster.

If only the two of them could get along, she told herself, it would make her life much simpler, but that was probably asking too much considering how different they were. She only wished that she didn't love them both so much and that she didn't feel so pulled between them.

On the one hand was her love and passion for Daniel, her lover. But Ryan was her only brother, all that was left of her family except for Caitlin.

Eirinn picked up the pile of mail on her desk and quickly shuffled through it, separating bills from payments. Then she stopped short. The blue envelope in her hand carried an Irish postmark, and the address was neatly penned in Caitlin's careful hand.

Her fingers trembled as she tore open the letter. This was the first word they had received from Caitlin since she had left. Eirinn had been trying, with little success, to banish thoughts of shipwrecks and a thousand other fears.

She sat down in her mother's chair and read the carefully printed words.

Dearest children,

I have reached Ireland's blessed green land safely and your father has been laid to rest beneath the sod in his own village of Lios na Capaill. I can't tell you how happy I am to be home again. Any soul born in Ireland is never at peace anywhere in the world except in this lovely land. I never knew until I stepped off that ship how dead I felt inside when I was away from here.

That is why I must tell you of a difficult decision I have made. As much as I love you all, I simply can not return to America. My heart breaks at the thought of being away from the ones I love, but I could never find the strength again to leave Ireland.

Michael is here with me. I'm not speaking of his body which is buried in the graveyard, but of his spirit which walks this green land with me. I feel him beside me every moment. He is in the air I breathe, the waters of the River Laune, and in the clouds that pass over Carantuohill. I can't leave Ireland. I can't leave Michael.

One of my deepest sorrows is that I won't be there to see the two of you wed. Think of me on that day and be sure that I am there with you in spirit. I've no greater joy than to know that you will share the kind of love that Michael and I enjoyed all those years. Dear God, how I miss him.

Please find it in your hearts to forgive me for not returning to America. Know that my door and my arms will always be open to you, as I hope you will come to visit me often. I leave the shop in your care, knowing that you will honor Michael's memory in all your dealings.

May God keep you in the hollow of His hand, and may He never close his fist too tightly on you.

With love,
Caitlin

Eirinn crumpled the letter in her hand. Her mother wasn't coming back. She couldn't believe it. Caitlin wouldn't be there to see her and Daniel take their marriage vows. It was more disappointment than Eirinn's mind could take in at once. Everyone she loved was disappearing. How could a mother simply run away to Ireland and never return?

In the back of her mind a voice whispered that she wasn't being fair. She was no longer a child who needed her mother's nurturing. She was a woman, perfectly capable of running the carousel shop, especially with Daniel O'Brien to help her. But Eirinn didn't feel like a woman. She felt like a little girl in need of her mother's warm embrace. She needed Caitlin to hold her and tell her that her world wasn't really crumbling around her.

But Caitlin wasn't there. And she wasn't going to be. She was in Ireland where she belonged. And most important, Caitlin was happy.

Eirinn smoothed the crumpled letter lovingly with her palm, then held it to her chest. It wasn't as good as a mother's embrace, but it would have to do.

When Eirinn reached the hotel room with a lop-sided "68" nailed to the door, she thought for a moment that she had the wrong room. The door was standing half open, and Ryan would never have left his door unlocked, let alone open. He was always afraid of being robbed and was overly careful about such things.

She had come to the hotel to find Ryan, to inform him of Caitlin's decision. He hadn't come to the shop for the past week, not since his argument with Daniel. But because he was forever complaining about not being informed about what was going on in the family, she had decided to come to his room over the casino and show him Caitlin's letter.

"Ryan?" She knocked on the door, and at her touch it swung open the rest of the way. Apprehensively she stepped into the semidarkness. What if she had the wrong room? She had heard that all types of lowlifes inhabited this hotel. It would be just her luck to stumble into some den of thieves . . . or worse yet, murderers.

Her eyes quickly adjusted to the darkness and she saw Ryan lying sprawled across his bed. He was naked. And something told her that he wasn't merely asleep but unconscious.

She grabbed his robe, which was hanging on the bedpost, and tossed it over him. "Damn it, Ryan. Wake up," she said, shaking him roughly by the shoulder.

He moaned and opened his eyes.

"You're drunk," she said. Then she saw the pipe and the velvet pouch on the table beside the bed, and she knew that his stupor wasn't caused by alcohol. She had never seen opium, but somehow she knew what it was.

"Eirinn, what the . . ." He struggled to sit, but she pushed him back onto the bed.

"Don't bother to get up," she said, hurt and disgust apparent in her voice. "I came by to talk to you about an important matter, but I see you're in no condition for a serious conversation. When you get yourself together, come by the shop and we'll talk."

She had turned to go when she heard another low moan. It was coming from the pile of blankets and pillows on the other side of the bed.

The stack parted and a dark head appeared. The woman's black hair was dirty and unkempt, and her large eyes were as bloodshot and darkly circled as Ryan's. Obviously she had been partaking of the same vices as her bedpartner.

Eirinn fought the bitter taste that rose from her stomach. She had always imagined Ryan's casino lifestyle to be glamorous and worldly. It had never occurred to Eirinn that her dapper brother lived in squalor such as this.

She looked over at Ryan and saw that he was fully alert now. It was apparent that he was deeply embarrassed for her to see him this way.

Eirinn turned and fled the room. She ran, knowing that she would never perceive Ryan McKevett the same way again. The image of her brother as she had always thought him to be had collapsed. It was one more loss that her heart must grieve.

Chapter Sixteen

"Get out of here, you two-bit whore! Get out of my bed before I kill you."

Ryan kicked Bernadette in the ribs. Tumbling out of the bed, she landed in a tangled heap of sheets on the floor, lodged between the bed frame and the wall.

"She saw you!" he shouted down at her as he leaned over the side of the bed. "I'll never be able to look her in the eye again now that she's seen me with a worthless slut like you."

Gathering the sheets and the remnants of her pride around her, Bernadette struggled to her feet. "You're a fine one, calling me a whore. Who was she anyway? Your wife? I should have known you were married, you bastard."

"That was my sister, you fool."

"Your sister?" She stared at him incredulously. "You're this upset because your sister caught you in bed with another woman?"

"Not just another woman. With *you*. Anyone can tell by looking at you that you're a slut."

Bernadette winced, but lifted her chin in a pose of pathetic haughtiness. "I'm a *singer*," she said. "And if you don't apologize to me this instant, I'm going to walk out that door and you'll never see me again."

He rolled off the bed, scooped up her clothes from the floor, and threw them at her. "The sooner the better."

She dressed frantically, tears streaming down her gaunt, rouged cheeks. As she buttoned her bodice she turned to him and said, "I still don't understand what you're so upset about . . . unless you've got something funny going on with your sister."

In an instant Ryan had crossed the floor and slapped her so hard that she was sent sprawling on the floor. Just as quickly he opened the door, yanked her up from the floor and threw her out into the hall.

He slammed the door, but he could still hear her shouting, "If she's really your sister, you're crazy, Ryan McKevett! Do you hear me? You're sick. You're in love with your own sister!"

Bernadette hated herself when, two hours later, she knocked on Ryan's door. It was moments like this when Bernadette knew that she wasn't a singer; she was a whore. What else would you call a woman who went crawling back to a man who beat her, a man she didn't love or even particularly like? She went back because he fed her and provided her with a bed every night. And, of course, there was the opium. Bernadette could no longer afford to support her habit. And the best thing about men like Ryan McKevett or Padraic Brady was that they always had a supply and didn't usually mind sharing in exchange for sex.

Bernadette couldn't fool anyone into thinking that she was a singer on her way to fame and stardom. She couldn't even fool herself anymore.

With shaky legs she pushed the door open and walked inside. Ryan was stretched out on the bed again, where he had spent most of his time since Michael's death. At first she was afraid that he would rise up from the bed and throw her out as he had before. But as she walked closer to him, she saw that he was in no condition to quarrel with anyone.

Bernadette had spent enough time in opium dens to recognize the signs of overdose: his clammy, blue skin, his livid eartips, his shallow, erratic breathing.

If he didn't get medical help immediately, Ryan would die.

Remembering his cruelty only hours before, she considered letting him die. It would serve him right. If she hadn't come back he would have died, and his body probably wouldn't have been discovered for days.

Bernadette turned and walked out of the room. But by the time she reached the hall, she was running—racing for the doctor to save the life of a man who had beaten her. Because Bernadette decided that even if she was a whore she was a good person. She couldn't just let him die.

"Do you really think we can do it, Danny?" Eirinn asked as she stared at the beginnings of a carousel: piles of wood everywhere, templates, and rough-hewn block figures.

He left the steaming pot of pungent glue and walked over to her. Wrapping one arm around her shoulder, he said, "Of course we can, love. It won't be the same without yer dear father and mother, but we'll do it just the same. We've no choice. We owe it to them."

As he looked down into her green eyes, he saw her fear and her pain that never seemed to heal completely before the next wound was inflicted. He wanted to kill Ryan for causing her this latest grief.

"We'll do it," he repeated. "Never you worry. Come along to me room and I'll make ye a cup o' tea."

With one arm around her waist he led her to his room upstairs over the shop. It was small but cozy, with a Franklin stove in one corner that blazed cheerfully. His only furniture was a small table, two chairs, and a bed, spread with a colorful quilt. Against the far wall was a work bench. Daniel carved long hours in the shop, then came up here to carve objects that pleased him, works of art that weren't for sale.

"What's this?" she asked, walking over to the bench and holding up a small wooden head and arm.

He set a kettle of water on the stove, took two cups from a small cupboard, and put them on the table. " 'Tis a puppet," he said, "a marionette for one of the wee ones who comes to the shop sometimes. He's a good lad, but he has no toys to play with. A child without a toy is a sad sight indeed."

Carefully she laid the tiny head on the bench and joined him at the table. "Did you have toys when you were a child, Danny?" she asked as she sat down.

He smiled and nodded. "I did, indeed. Had a whole menagerie of animals that yer father carved for me." He was quiet for a long moment, then drew a deep breath. "Would ye like to see them, lass?" he said, and she could hear the emotion in his voice.

"I would."

He walked to the bed and knelt beside it. From beneath the bed he pulled a small chest. Eirinn had never seen this chest before. It was very old and scarred with leather straps that were brittle and broken, but Daniel handled it as though it contained the queen's coronation jewels.

She left her chair and knelt beside him on the floor. "You brought this from Ireland, didn't you?"

He nodded. "Held it on me lap almost every

minute on the voyage to prevent anyone from stealin' it." He opened the lid; its rusty hinges complained. A musty, pungent scent wafted from the dark interior. "That's the smell of peat," he said. "That's the blessed smell of Ireland herself."

He lifted out a dark brick that was charred on one end. Breaking off a corner, he pressed it into her hand. "That's turf, darlin'," he said. "We kept ourselves warm day and night by diggin', dryin' and burnin' those bricks of turf. And a fine scent it was floatin' on the night air."

He laid the rest of the brick aside as Eirinn turned her piece over and over in her hand.

" 'Tis no wonder yer mother couldn't leave Ireland," he said wistfully. "If I were ever to see that green land again, a jarvey with ten mules couldn't pull me away from her."

Lifting up a small black bag, he said, "Hold out your apron there, lass."

She did as she was told and he poured the contents of the bag into her lap. Eirinn gasped with delight as two dozen or more tiny figures tumbled out: a dog, cat, hare, bird, chicken, duck, and a herd of delicate horses.

"Oh, Daniel, they're lovely. Did Da really carve them all?"

"All except this one." He picked out a comical, misshapen hare with legs that were too short and ears too long. " 'Twas the first thing I ever carved, a gift for Michael. I was after throwin' it away, but he wouldn't allow it."

Eirinn took the hare from him and pressed it to her lips, thinking of the beautiful pony he had carved for her birthday. "I'm glad you kept it. I'm glad you kept all of these."

One by one she examined the figures, touching them, holding them tightly in her palm, feeling a link with her father that she hadn't felt since his death. Unbidden, tears came to her eyes and rolled down her cheeks.

Just as Michael had always done, Daniel reached up and wiped them away with his calloused fingertips. "Don't cry, darlin'," he said gently. "Yer father will always be with us. We have our memories of him and the lovely things he made. 'Tis a fine legacy he left behind."

She sniffed and nodded.

"We'll give these to our children someday," he said. "And I wouldn't be surprised if some of the wee ones have yer father's green eyes and his love for carvin'."

Eirinn couldn't contain her grief any longer. "Danny, I miss him so . . ." The rest of her words dissolved in sobs.

"I know." He drew her into his arms. "I know, love."

They held each other for a long time, the toys in her lap a poignant reminder of all their loss. Finally, Eirinn wiped her eyes with the corner of her apron.

"I know it isn't proper for us to be married now, with Da just recently deceased," she said. She reached up and laced her fingers through his thick waves. "But I need to be married to you, Danny." Hugging him close, she pressed her full breasts against his chest. "I need to sleep beside you at night, every night." She pulled back and looked into his eyes. "Do you need me too?"

A surge of desire so acute that it was pain, shot through him. He closed his eyes and nodded. "Ah, yes, love. I need you."

"Then say we'll be married soon. I know that Da would understand."

"Soon, darlin', very soon."

He stood and drew her to her feet. "But for tonight we can hold each other . . . and pretend."

With one hand he pulled back the quilt on the bed and then lowered her gently onto the linen sheets.

He reached down and pulled off his boots. The rest of his clothes soon followed. Slipping beneath the quilt, he aligned his body with hers.

"Danny," she said, cuddling close to his warmth, "there's something I want to say."

"And what's that, love?"

She raised up onto one elbow, looked down at him, and laced her fingers through his hair. "If the Night Mare pays you a visit tonight . . . I'm not leaving. So don't even ask me to. Understand?"

He said nothing, just looked at her for a long time. Then he nodded. And pulled her into his arms.

Bernadette stood in the middle of Ryan's room, staring into the empty wardrobe. She couldn't believe her eyes. She should have known. She should have anticipated this. But, trusting, naive soul that she was, it had never occurred to her that he would simply leave town without even saying goodbye.

She had saved Ryan's life, the bastard. If she hadn't summoned the doctor that night he would have been dead and buried, where he deserved to be. Where he *would* be if she found out where he was.

She ran to the dresser and searched the drawers for her small cache of jewelry. Even that was gone. Damn him! If she could only get her hands on him she'd—

"Well, well, what have we here?"

Turning around, Bernadette saw that she was no longer alone. Two men stood in the doorway, wearing leers on their battered faces, which were nearly as ugly as the grease-stained suits they wore. One sported a ginger-colored mustache with drooping ends. The other one was less attractive, his face bisected diagonally with a jagged purple scar.

She recognized them instantly as O'Mahoney and Ferris. They worked for a neighboring casino, the Blue Moon; their specialty was collecting unpaid gambling debts.

"So, where's your boyfriend, sugar?" O'Mahoney asked, toying with the limp end of his mustache.

"I don't know," Bernadette said, feeling the twist of fear in her belly. These two were bad. Very bad. There wasn't anything they wouldn't do or hadn't done. "Ryan left without a word—and took my jewelry too. I'll kill him if I find him."

Ferris smiled, showing a row of jagged front teeth. "You'll have to wait your turn, lady. By the time we're finished with him, there won't be much left."

O'Mahoney closed the door behind him and slowly, deliberately turned the lock. Her heart hit her shoes. Should she start screaming now? Would it help if she did? The clientele in this hotel heard shouts, cries, and gunshots at all hours and paid no attention.

Both men walked toward her. She backed up against the wall until she could go no further.

"Why don't you just tell us where McKevett is, lassie, and save us all a lot of pain and trouble?" O'Mahoney said.

"Yeah, I'd hate to skin up my knuckles on that pretty face of yours." Ferris seemed genuinely concerned.

In the circles that Bernadette traveled, she had faced this sort of situation many times before. She knew that the answer was to start talking. Fast.

"Really, Ferris. I'd tell you fellows if I knew. If nothing else, to get even with him for running out on me, the dirty bastard. But he took off without

207

telling me where he was going. I'd give you the money he owes you myself, but I'm broke. He even stole my mother's jewelry and—"

"Don't give us that, girl," O'Mahoney interjected. "We know where you get your jewelry, and it ain't from your sainted mother."

"All right, that's true," she said, bursting into sobs. "But I don't know where Ryan is. I swear I don't!"

"Well, I guess we'll have to mess her up." O'Mahoney raised one meaty fist.

"Wait!" She held up her hands, cringing. "I don't know where Ryan is, but I know how you can get your money back."

The fist hovered menacingly in front of her face. "How?"

"Ryan has a sister. Her name is Eirinn. Eirinn McKevett. She has money. They live in Brooklyn and they have a carousel shop where they make those things . . . those merry-go-round things like the one down on the boardwalk. She might even know where Ryan is, because they're very close. The other night . . ."

But apparently O'Mahoney and Ferris had no interest in Ryan's relationship with his sister, because they were already leaving, slamming the door behind them.

Bernadette's knees gave way, and she sank to the floor in a limp heap. Thank God she could think on her feet.

For a moment she felt guilty that she had turned those animals on an innocent woman. But Bernadette had learned long ago how to dispel guilt as quickly as possible. She was a survivor, and survivors had to travel light. They couldn't be burdened by the weight of an overly sensitive conscience.

Besides, she couldn't help feeling jealous of a woman who had obviously supplanted her in

Ryan's affections. Bernadette still remembered the look of disgust on Eirinn's pretty face when she had looked down on her that night as she lay next to Ryan in a drugged stupor.

If Ferris were going to skin his knuckles on someone's face, better Eirinn McKevett's than hers.

Eirinn breathed a small sigh of relief when she rounded the corner and saw the carousel shop ahead. Daniel had warned her about going out tonight. In fact, he had forbidden her to go, but Eirinn had decided that no man was going to give her orders before he became her husband. She wasn't so sure that she was going to obey him afterwards, either. Caitlin had taught her that a woman should use her own mind rather than rely on others to do her thinking.

And tonight Eirinn had decided to go see Ryan. The trip had turned out to be fruitless. Ryan had disappeared and no one seemed to know where he was.

She hadn't heard from him in several weeks, not since she had visited him in his hotel room that miserable night. How she wished that she could erase that evening from her memory. Her fantasy of Ryan's life had been so colorful, so glamorous. So far removed from reality. It seemed she had no heros anymore, except Daniel.

She thought of the way Danny had made love to her last night, and she felt safe and loved. It was a wonderful feeling. And now, as she walked toward the shop, she felt a warm glow just to be coming home to him.

But as she approached the shop door she saw two men step out of the alley that separated the carousel shop from the bakery next door. Every nerve ending in her body tingled with premonition.

There was nothing particularly threatening in the way they were strolling toward her. In the dark she couldn't see their faces, so she had no reason to think they were watching her. But they were. She could feel their eyes on her.

Quickening her pace, she hurried toward the shop door. They matched her stride. She was in trouble, and she knew it.

With one hand on the big, brass door handle she yanked as hard as she could. It was locked. One glance over her shoulder told her that they were rapidly closing the distance between them and her.

"Daniel, open up!" She pounded on the door, knowing that he was probably upstairs asleep. It was late. He had been right after all. She shouldn't have been out this late. "Danny! For God's sake open the—"

Her cry was shoved down her throat by a big hand that clamped over her face. An enormous arm circled her waist like a steel cooper's band and lifted her off the ground.

She fought, kicked, tried to scream, but she couldn't even breathe.

"A hellcat, this one," she heard one of them say.

"Fine with me," replied the other. "That makes it more fun. Come on, Ferris. Take her in the alley."

He dragged her along as though she weighed nothing at all. Once her foot landed squarely on his instep. He cursed, but didn't stop until they were well into the dark alley.

"Where's your brother?" the other one asked.

The man who held her loosened his hand just enough for her to answer. Instead she screamed, a loud, hysterical shriek of fear, like a frightened hare.

A hand came crashing across her face, and she felt the pain of her own teeth biting into her jaw and tongue. The salty, bitter taste of blood filled her mouth.

"If you try that again, I swear we'll kill you right now." He twisted her arms behind her and she thought surely her shoulders were dislodged.

"Now we'll give you one more chance to tell us where Ryan McKevett is, and then we're gonna hurt you bad. Understand?"

She nodded and the hand over her mouth moved away again. "I don't know where he is. I just went to see him myself at the hotel, but he was gone. I don't know where."

"She's protecting him," the big one announced. "We'll have to show her we mean business."

Eirinn closed her eyes and steeled herself for another blow to her face. But, to her horror, she felt something worse.

The big, hairy hand grabbed at her lace collar, and she heard the sound of her dress ripping. All the way down the front.

For some reason she thought of Tomas, and hate welled up inside her to give her strength.

"No!" she screamed, but this time it was a cry of rage.

Chapter Seventeen

The cold, hairy hand closed over Eirinn's breast and squeezed hard. She screamed again. The sound was shattered by an explosion that lit the alley's darkness. A gun shot. At close range.

Suddenly the hand dropped away from her chest and a heavy weight collapsed across her, the body of one of her attackers.

"Take that ye bloody devil," she heard Daniel say. "Hurt my woman, will ye?"

As though through a haze of shock she heard him say, "After the other one, lads, and be certain that he doesn't get away."

The enormous body was rolled off her. It fell to the ground with a muffled thud.

"Are ye all right, darlin'?" Danny asked. She felt his arms, strong and gentle, lifting her.

She nodded and fought to control the violent shudders that rippled through her body.

Holding her tightly against his chest, he said, " 'Tis all over now. They'll not hurt ye again."

She looked down at the body on the ground. "Is he dead?"

"Aye. I'd say that Death has knocked upon his door and found him at home. But yer not to worry about the likes of himself. Surely the world won't miss him."

As he carried her out of the alleys he felt the hard press of steel against her side. "Is that a gun?" she asked. "Are you the one who shot him?"

"Aye. And it's proud I am to have done the deed." At the front of the shop he carefully set her on her feet and unlocked the door. With a comforting arm around her waist he led her inside. His eyes scanned the ragged tears in her bodice and the dark red scratches that were rising into angry welts across her white breasts. "I only wish I'd arrived a few minutes sooner. Are ye sure yer all right, love?"

Because her shaking legs would no longer hold her, she sat down on a paint drum and buried her face in her hands. In an instant Daniel had knelt in front of her, his hands on her shoulders. "Tell me what happened, if ye can," he gently coaxed.

"I went to Coney Island to see Ryan," she said, then waited for him to scold her, but he didn't. "And he wasn't there. Apparently he left town, because nobody knows where he is. I was almost home when these two men stepped out of the alley and they followed me. I knocked on the shop door, but there was no one to let me in."

Daniel's amber eyes reflected his regret as he stroked the back of her hand. "The lads and I were out lookin' for ye, lass. When we discovered ye gone, we were worried that ye'd gotten yerself into trouble."

"Seems you were right," she admitted. Silently she blessed him for not chastising her like a naughty child.

"Go on," he said.

"Then they grabbed me from behind and dragged me into the alley. They asked me where Ryan was and—"

"Ryan? What the bloody hell does that bastard have to do with this?"

Eirinn felt her temper rise, as always, at hearing Ryan attacked. "Nothing. I mean, it couldn't be his fault that those bums attacked me."

"I'm not so sure, but let's have the rest of yer

213

story."

"And when I told them that I didn't know where he was, they didn't believe me. And they hit me, and the big one tore my dress."

"The one I shot?"

She nodded.

"If I'd known that, I'd have beaten him first, cut his throat, and *then* shot him."

She looked into Daniel's eyes and knew that he meant exactly what he said. She had never seen this side of her gentle Danny, and it frightened her. But at the same time, it made her feel safe to have such a man for her protector. Wrapping her arms around his neck, she drew him close.

"Thank you, Danny."

"Ah, darlin' girl, 'twas no bother at all."

The shop door opened and they both jumped. She saw Daniel's hand go to the gun that was jammed into the waistband of his trousers. But it was only Iggie and Josef.

They both bore the swollen lumps and purpling bruises of a fight on their faces, along with expressions of grim satisfaction.

"Did ye take care of the other one?" Danny asked.

"We took care of things," Ignacio said, his thin chest expanding with pride. "We taught him a lesson his children will remember. No man harms a lady who is friend to Ignacio. You are all right, signorina? Did those bestia hurt you very bad?"

"I'll be fine, Iggie, thanks to the three of you," she said and was rewarded with his bright smile.

"We . . . ah . . . disposed of the one in the alley," Josef told Daniel in a conspiratorial tone. "There won't be any need for this to be reported, or for Miss Eirinn to have to answer any embarrassing questions."

Eirinn looked up into the faces of the three men

who had saved her life. These men had just killed for her, but in their eyes she saw only their concern for her well-being. "Thank you," she said. "I owe you one."

"Ye owe us two, darlin'," Danny reminded her. "There was a pair of those ugly devils and big ones they were at that. It's two ye owe us, and we'll surely collect someday."

"I'm glad you're here, Ryan." Eirinn laced her arm through his and led him into the carousel shop, which had been transformed into a ballroom for the evening. Eirinn, along with the neighborhood children and their mothers, had hung garlands of flowers and ribbons from the rafters.

Daniel and his ever-growing team of carvers had graciously donated the use of over fifty horses for the evening. Every animal bore a child, from eight to eighty, on its back as the party gained momentum.

Eirinn and Ryan walked over to the band, which played atop a makeshift stage: two pipers, a fiddle, and an elderly man who played the traditional Celtic drum, the bohran.

"I'm relieved that you would welcome me back, Eirinn," Ryan said, and the sadness in his blue eyes went straight to Eirinn's heart.

She held out her arms to him and in an instant he was holding her tightly. "You're all the family I have left," she said. "How could I ever turn my back on you?"

"But after what those men did to you . . . how can I ever forgive myself?"

She pulled back and looked up into his eyes, trying to convey her love to him. Ryan needed to be loved. That was all he had ever needed. No one but her had ever seemed to understand that.

"You didn't know they would come after me. I don't hold you responsible."

"Daniel believes it's my fault. He told me so in no uncertain terms. In fact, he let me know that as far as he was concerned I wasn't welcome to show my face around here."

Ryan cast a surreptitious glance toward the other side of the room, where Daniel chatted with his friends and employees. Daniel stopped talking long enough to glare back.

Eirinn saw the looks exchanged between the two men and it twisted her heart. Why, on this night when she and Daniel were celebrating their coming marriage, couldn't the men she loved get along?

"This party isn't Danny's alone," she said. "It's mine as well, and I'm very glad you came. I just wish you would spend more time here in the shop. We could use your expertise, you know."

Ryan laughed grimly. "Daniel despises me. He would never allow me to work with you in father's business."

"But it's your business too. If you want to work with us, all you have to do is say so. I'll see to it that Danny cooperates."

"Do you really think you have that much influence with him?"

Eirinn's eyes met Daniel's across the room. His gaze skimmed briefly over her tightly fitted new party dress, conveying a message that made her ache for the wedding that was to take place in one week.

"Oh, yes," she said answering Daniel by the twinkle in her eyes. "Danny would do anything I asked. Just as I'd do anything for him."

Ryan had stepped outside to catch a breath of fresh air and to escape Daniel's watchful, critical eye. He was glad that he had. If he hadn't come out onto the street he would never have intercepted Bernadette as she stepped out of a carriage and walked toward the door.

"What the hell are you doing here?" he asked as he grabbed her forearms.

"I came to see you," she said, pursing her lips in what Ryan supposed she intended to be a playful pout. To him it merely looked simpering. "You've been avoiding me since you came back to town. I guess it's because of my jewelry that you took, and I just wanted to tell you that it's all right as long as you—"

He pulled her into the dark shadows at the corner of the building, and his grip on her arm tightened until she whimpered.

"I know what you did, you little bitch," he hissed in her ear. "You turned my sister over to O'Mahoney and Ferris. Because of you, she was nearly killed. You're lucky that I don't just break your neck here and now."

"I don't know what you're talking about, Ryan." She tried to pull her arm out of his grip, but he twisted it behind her back. She gasped from the pain. "I'd never do anything to hurt you or anyone in your family."

"Do yourself a favor, Bernadette. Get back into that carriage, and in the future make sure to stay out of my sight. If I ever see you again, I swear, I'll hurt you badly. Do you understand?"

"But, Ryan . . ." She sniffed loudly. "I love you. I've been good to you. We had some good times together, don't you remember? One time you said you loved me too. Don't you love me anymore?"

He gave her a shove toward the street and she nearly stumbled off the curb and into the gutter.

"But Ryan, I don't have anywhere to go," she wailed.

"Go to hell, Bernadette." He turned to walk back to the door.

"All right. That's where I'll go, Ryan McKevett," she called after him. "And I'll wait for you there. It won't be long until you join me."

Ryan chose the lad carefully. He was a boy of about ten with an intelligent, greedy look about him. Summoning the child to a quiet corner of the room, Ryan gave him a set of meticulous instructions, four coins, and a pat on the head.

As Ryan strolled around the room, keeping a close eye on his pocket watch, he saw Eirinn and Daniel dancing together. Jealousy, bile-bitter, welled up in his mouth, obliterating the taste of the fine Irish whiskey that was flowing like Torc Waterfall through the crowd. He watched as Daniel bent his head to hear Eirinn's words, words that brought a smile to his face and caused him to hold her even more tightly against him.

I'll be damned if I'll let him marry her, he thought. *I'll kill him before I let him touch her.*

Then Ryan smiled, a smile that didn't touch his eyes. If his plan went as he intended, they would never stand before the priest, and most important, they would never sleep in the same bed.

Ryan stood in the middle of Daniel's bedroom, hating the man. He looked at the bed with its colorful quilt and hated the thought that Daniel might have already taken Eirinn there.

I should just murder him, he thought. But Ryan was afraid to kill Daniel O'Brien.

In the first place, his crime might be found out, and Ryan didn't, couldn't bear the idea of ending his life on the end of a rope. Too many Irish peasants had died that way. He didn't want to follow in his ancestors' footsteps.

Besides, Daniel O'Brien had been a soldier. A damned good one. And he might not die that easily.

No, the plan he had was much better. It had its risks, certainly, and it wouldn't be accomplished without the shedding of some blood. But it would be worth it.

As Ryan lifted the whiskey bottle in his hand and took a deep draught, he thought of Eirinn, of her shining black hair and green eyes. Yes, she was worth the price. He tilted the bottle again — and poured what remained down the front of his coat.

"Mr. O'Brien." The boy tugged at Daniel's coat sleeve. "There's a man upstairs in your room. I saw him go in there just a minute ago. I think it was Mr. McKevett."

For a moment Daniel thought the lad meant Michael. *The* Mr. McKevett. Then his heart reminded him with a jolt.

"Who is it yer talkin' about, boy?" he asked, ruffling the child's curls. "Ye surely don't mean Ryan McKevett."

"Yes, he's the one. I saw him go into your bedroom upstairs, and I just thought you should know."

"Thank ye much." Daniel handed the boy a coin. "Yer a good lad."

As Daniel walked away, the child slipped the coin into his pocket, where it joined the others. Tomorrow morning on the way to school, he would buy out the candy store.

"What are you doing in my room?"

219

The smell of whiskey hit Daniel in a wave the moment he opened the bedroom door. There, sitting at his table, was Ryan McKevett, an empty bottle clutched between his hands, his eyes red and staring into space.

Daniel walked over to him and shook him roughly by the shoulder. "Who the bloody hell do ye think ye are, comin' into me room and makin' yerself at home like this?"

"I had to get away for a while." Ryan's voice was heavy and slurred. Daniel couldn't remember seeing him this drunk before. Drugged yes, but not drunk. "Needed some . . . quiet."

"Well, this room isn't the place for you to be seekin' yer solitude. I'll ask ye to be on yer way now, or I'll be seein' ye to the door with a gentle tap of me hobnails."

To Daniel's surprise, Ryan burst into tears and hid his face with his hands. "I can't stand it anymore, Danny," he said. It clicked in the back of Daniel's mind that this was the first time Ryan had ever called him "Danny", a name used only by his closest friends.

"What is it ye can't bear?" he asked, not even pretending to care.

"Livin' with the guilt."

Ryan had Daniel's full attention. "And what is it yer feelin' guilty about?"

"The fire."

Daniel felt his heart stop beating, then leap against his ribs. "The fire that destroyed the shop?"

Ryan sniffed and nodded his head. "I started it. To get even with Michael. He told me that I wasn't his son and I hated him for it. So I set that fire."

Daniel took one step toward him, his fists clenched.

"And Michael's accident," Ryan continued, his hands still hiding his face. "It was my fault. Michael told me that night to tighten up the support cables, but I didn't do it. I was tired and I was angry. So I just went to bed and forgot about it." He dropped his hands and looked up at Daniel with dripping eyes. "I killed him. It's my fault he died."

Daniel felt as he had on the battlefield. Rage flashed through him, red and searing, followed by a coldness that went all the way through him to the marrow of his bones.

This worthless, selfish bastard had killed Michael. He had burned the shop and Michael's carousel to the ground. Then he had caused Michael's death with his laziness and irresponsibility.

Daniel thought for a moment of the gun beneath his pillow, but he decided against it. He was going to kill Ryan McKevett with his bare hands. And he was going to enjoy doing it.

Chapter Eighteen

"Miss Eirinn, I thought you should know that there's two men fighting upstairs. It sounds pretty bad. I just thought I should tell you."

Eirinn looked down into the boy's big blue eyes, which were wide with concern. A bolt of fear shot home. Instinctively she knew who the two men were. And if they had actually come to blows after all these years, it would be no ordinary bar brawl. "Thank you for telling me, Edward."

Seconds later she was flying up the stairs, holding her new skirt and multiple petticoats high in front of her. If she didn't stop them, they would kill each other. Maybe it was already too late. "Please, God, don't let it be too late," she whispered as she ran.

Even from the top of the stairs she could hear the blows. She winced, feeling the pain herself, because no matter who was giving and who was receiving, they were both men she loved.

Flinging the door wide, she rushed into the room. "Oh, God!" she cried when she saw Ryan, stretched backward across Daniel's table, his face covered with blood, his arms up before him trying to ward off Daniel's fists. "Danny, what are you doing?" she screamed as she launched herself at him and attempted to pull him off her brother.

"Eirinn . . ." Ryan whimpered her name and held out one hand to her in pathetic supplication. ". . . help me."

"Danny, please don't!" she sobbed. "You'll kill him!"

Daniel stopped, his fist in midair, and looked over at her. He seemed shocked to see her. He looked down at Ryan's battered face and his own blood-splattered fist.

Quickly Eirinn wedged her body between them. Tears streamed down her face as she said, "Danny, why? Just before our wedding you try to murder my own brother?"

"This bastard isn't yer—" Daniel choked on his words. He stood for a long moment, looking down at Ryan. Eirinn could feel the tension radiating between the two men. "He isn't worth yer love, darlin'," Daniel said at last. "He's caused ye more grief than ye'll ever know."

"Don't say that. I won't listen to you saying such bad things about someone I love."

She reached down and wrapped her arms around Ryan's neck, supporting his head. Blood poured from several lacerations on his skull and his eyes were nearly closed from swelling. She couldn't believe that Daniel had done this with his bare hands. But he had. His knuckles were cracked and bleeding, and his face wore the same look as the night he had shot that man in the alley . . . the look of a killer.

"I don't understand, Danny. You've always been so gentle and kind with me. How could you do such a thing to my flesh and blood? Ryan is the only family I have left."

Daniel said nothing. The anger that glittered like frost crystals in his eyes frightened her. Who was this stranger who could murder another human being?

"If he's all ye have left in the world, lass,"

Danny said, "I pity ye. Because surely this heap of dung isn't much."

He reached over and pulled Ryan up by the front of his shirt, and Ryan's head lolled to one side. Eirinn steeled herself to see Daniel strike him one more time.

But he didn't. He said to Ryan, "Ye can thank the good God that I love her as much as I do. 'Tis the only thing that saved yer hide tonight."

Daniel turned and walked over to the bed. As he pulled out the small chest, tucked it under his arm and headed for the door, he said, "I know it's a hard decision, darlin', to choose between yer brother and me. But 'tis a choice ye must make. I can't live under the same roof with the man, or be in the same business with him. I'll surely kill him if I try. Ye'll let me know what ye decide."

He walked out the door.

Eirinn had that familiar, aching feeling that Daniel had just left her . . . again.

Eirinn lay in her bed and stared at the stars through her window. Tears rolled from the corners of her eyes down her neck. She was hurt, but pain was something she had learned to deal with. Mostly, she was confused.

When she had asked Ryan what had started the fight, he had told her that they had quarreled about the carousel business. Ryan had said that Daniel insisted he stay out of it completely, and Ryan told him that he wanted to follow in his father's footsteps, preserving and enhancing Michael's dream.

Eirinn supposed it could have happened that way. Daniel was certainly passionate about anything having to do with Michael or the carousels. Those were two things that Daniel cared enough about to kill someone. And, of course, he cared that much for her. He had proved it in that dark alley.

So, if he loved her so much, why had he walked out on her? What did he expect her to do? Come groveling after him? Was she supposed to turn her back on her only brother and rob him of his inheritance?

She supposed that she should have asked to hear Daniel's side of the story. But, then, he had made no attempt to defend himself. If Daniel had been justified in his attack, he would surely have told her himself. Besides, Ryan's side of the story made perfect sense. Daniel could be violent when something he loved was threatened, and he had made no secret of the fact that he considered Ryan a threat to Michael's business.

She was surprised to hear that Ryan was suddenly interested in the carousels after all these years, but it was a change that would have pleased Michael. As long as Ryan chose to be a part of the business, how could she deny him that opportunity?

It wasn't fair of Daniel to make her choose. So she wouldn't. She simply wouldn't speak to Daniel until he came to his senses and apologized to Ryan for the beating and to her for walking out on her.

Having made her decision, she felt better. She only hoped that Daniel would come around soon. After all, their wedding was only a week away, and she wanted all of these hard feelings to be dead and buried by then. She didn't want anything to ruin that perfect day.

I should never have made her choose, Daniel told himself. *She'll choose him. God knows why, but she'll choose him.*

He tossed and turned on the hotel bed, tangling himself in the blanket. If only he had been able to tell her, to explain why he had attacked Ryan. If he hadn't been so damned self-sacrificing he could have told her that Ryan wasn't really her brother at all, that he had burned the shop and caused Michael's death.

But he had watched Eirinn slowly recover from her latest shock, regaining her strength day by day. He couldn't take that away from her again. Even if it meant losing her to that bastard, Ryan, he couldn't hurt her that much.

So, what do you think it will do to her if you don't show up at your wedding? he asked himself. *Don't you think that will hurt her, too?*

Of course it would. Daniel knew that Eirinn loved him dearly and that she wanted to be his wife. But how much did she want him? Enough to tell Ryan to go to hell? It was a lot to ask, but if she really loved him, she would do it.

God knows, he loved her enough to do anything for her. Anything except work and live with Ryan McKevett. Some people simply couldn't be in the same place at the same time without courting disaster.

If she loves me, she'll throw Ryan out and send word to me before the wedding, he thought. *But if she loves him more than me . . .*

Daniel couldn't even consider the possibility. So he allowed himself to drift off to sleep.

That night, for the first time in months, the

Night Mare rode through his dreams. And with her she brought the dead, scores of them. Daniel searched their gaunt, pale faces to see if Ryan McKevett was among them. Then he remembered that he hadn't killed him after all. How he wished he had . . .

"I'll never have the chance to wear it, Ryan," Eirinn said as she held her wedding dress before her and considered her reflection in the mirror that hung over the fireplace in the parlor.

"That's a shame," he replied, his voice dripping with sympathy, as he sat and watched her from his seat on the sofa. "You'd look so beautiful in it."

Sadly, she folded the gown and returned it to its box that lay on the floor. "You say such nice things to me, Ryan. All brothers should be as kind as you."

He stood, walked over to her and slipped his arms around her waist. "All sisters should be as lovely as you." He pressed a kiss to her cheek.

No longer able to hold the tears back, she buried her face against his chest and cried. "There won't be any wedding tomorrow," she said. "If he still intended to marry me, he would have come back before now."

Ryan fought down the joy that bubbled inside him and tried to sound as disappointed as she expected him to be. "I'm sorry, sweetheart. I'll go have a talk with him if you like. I'd be glad to give him a piece of my mind about how cruelly he's treating my little sister."

"No. Don't even consider it. After what he did to you the last time he saw you, I don't want you

227

near him."

Ryan breathed a sigh of relief that he wouldn't have to carry through with the offer. "As you wish, dear. But I'd like to give him a good thrashing to show him the error of his ways."

"I forgave him once before when he ran away and left me alone," she said, "and I took him back into my heart. I won't do that again, Ryan."

He held her tighter, aware of the swell of her full breasts against his chest, the softness of her hair, the warmth of her body. When he pressed his lips to her cheek, he had to fight the impulse to kiss that red mouth. She wasn't his sister, after all. Eirinn was a woman, a beautiful woman. And God, how he wanted her.

"I don't blame you, love," he said. "I'd never speak to him again if I were you."

"Do you think he'll come to the church tomorrow?"

The very thought filled Ryan with dread. He wished he had the courage to kill Daniel. Anything to make sure that he didn't appear for the wedding. "I doubt it. I think he's forgotten all about you. It pains me to say so, but I do."

Her sobs redoubled. "If he doesn't come to the church tomorrow," she said, "I swear, I'll never forgive him."

"For your sake, I hope he comes." Ryan held her even tighter. "I'll pray that he does."

As Daniel neared the small brick house between the bakery and the carousel shop, his fists clenched and unclenched inside his jacket pockets. The wedding was tomorrow. Damn! Why hadn't she sent word to him? He had made sure that

Ignacio had dropped the hint that he was staying at the Island Plaza, the newest hotel on Coney Island. So, why hadn't she come to see him?

The answer was obvious enough, or so at least Daniel thought. Eirinn was a proud woman, like her father and mother, and she was waiting for him to come to her.

When he had walked out the other night he had fully intended to stay away until she came to him and assured him that Ryan wouldn't be a part of their lives. But every time he thought of her, crying, hurting, wondering whether or not he still wanted to marry her, his heart melted.

He would be the one to take the first step. Not that his demands had changed. He still wanted Ryan out of their lives and out of the family business, but he was willing to go to her and ask if they could talk. If they could only hold each other and share what was in their hearts, Daniel knew that they could work things out. Their love was strong. Surely it could surmount an obstacle like Ryan McKevett.

With resolve he mounted the front porch steps and walked up to the door. He stopped, his hand raised to knock.

Through the beveled glass oval in the center of the door he saw them. Eirinn and Ryan stood in the parlor, their arms wrapped tightly around each other, Eirinn's head resting on Ryan's chest.

Eirinn's back was to him, but Ryan was facing his way. Ryan glanced toward the door and saw him. A grin, the one that Daniel hated, slid across his face.

Once again, Daniel regretted having spared the man's life. He had only done it for Eirinn, and he had lost her anyway.

He watched through the glass for another moment, torturing himself. He saw her arms tighten around Ryan, pulling him closer. Deliberately, Ryan kissed the top of her hair, then her cheek, his eyes never leaving Daniel's.

Daniel turned on his heel and left the house without looking back.

He should never have asked Eirinn to make a choice between him and Ryan. Now he knew without a doubt who she loved most. Daniel only wished that it was anyone in the world other than Ryan McKevett, the one man Daniel wanted most to see dead and buried.

Eirinn stood at the front of the church in her wedding dress. Every person she knew and loved had gathered to watch her be married to that fine and upstanding lad, Daniel O'Brien. Everyone that is except Danny O'Brien himself. Her groom had left her standing at the altar, and Eirinn hated him for it.

This time her hatred wasn't hot, youthful and passionate. It was cold and hard, like a slab of uncarved gravestone. Not a girl's hatred, but a grown woman's.

She listened stoically as the priest dismissed the congregation, and she watched as one by one they filed out, giving her a nod or smile of sympathy.

"Are you ready to go home, sweetheart?" Ryan asked, his hand on her arm.

She shook him away. "Yes," she said. "I should never have come in the first place. I knew he wasn't coming."

"I'm so sorry. You must be terribly embarrassed, having all your friends and neighbors here

230

to witness this—"

"I'm not embarrassed," she said. And she meant it. "I'm angry. And I'm going to make him pay."

She looked up at Ryan, her green eyes blazing with the same fury that had driven her father to murder back in Ireland, years before her birth. "No man is going to leave me standing alone in a church on my wedding day and not pay the price," she said. She lifted her chin and squared her shoulders, and she had never looked more like Caitlin O'Leary McKevett. "I'm going to hurt him, Ryan. I'm going to find a way to make Daniel O'Brien pay for this. One way or the other."

Chapter Nineteen

"I still have to look at the McKevetts' carousels before I make my final decision," said Herman Altman, a potential customer, as he stood in the middle of Daniel O'Brien's shop and surveyed the current carousel in progress. "But I have to tell you, I'm very impressed with your workmanship. Beautiful. Absolutely beautiful."

Daniel flushed with pride. He had always taken great personal satisfaction in the carousels he and Michael had built. But this shop was his own, the carousel being produced here was his own. And it felt wonderful.

At first he had struggled with an overwhelming burden of guilt for leaving Eirinn and deserting Michael's business. But he knew that Eirinn would survive and keep the shop afloat. After all, she was Caitlin's daughter.

Besides, he believed that if Michael were alive, he would understand why he couldn't stay. The last thing Daniel wanted was to make life difficult for Eirinn by competing with her. But it didn't exactly depress him to think that he was giving Ryan McKevett a run for his money.

"Aye, well, I'm sure ye'll find the McKevetts building a fine wheel," he said. "It just all depends on what yer after, whether ye'll prefer mine or theirs."

Mr. Altman pulled the felt hat from his head and scratched his balding pate. "I looked at Padraic Brady's wares last evening. Now that was something to behold. He has jewels all over those horses of his, and a thousand twinkling lights on his carousels. Though he does ask an enormous price for all that."

Daniel shrugged. "I suppose that's fine if it's what yer after." He walked over and lovingly stroked the velvet flank of an Indian pony. "But as for meself, I fancy the horse itself. 'Tis the most lovely creature on God's green earth." *Except Eirinn,* he thought. "And I believe it does the animal an injustice to put all those spangles on him."

"Yes, I think I agree with you." Mr. Altman replaced his hat, carefully tilting it to one side. "So, give me your best price on a wheel like we just discussed, and after I look at the McKevetts I'll get back to you."

Daniel wrote the detailed estimate out for him. As he handed Altman the paper, he said, "When you see the McKevetts . . . ah, Eirinn McKevett Sullivan, that is, please tell her that I . . ."

"Yes?"

Tell her I love her, he thought. *Tell her I miss her and I can't sleep at night because I'm lying there aching for her.* "Never mind," he said. "Just give her my regards."

"Daniel O'Brien sends his regards," Herman Altman told the pretty black-haired woman who stood before him, a ledger in hand, the end of a pencil sticking out of her mouth as she scowled

233

at the numbers she had just written.

At his words her eyes flashed green fire. "You can tell Mr. O'Brien to go to hell in a tinker's kettle," she replied as she continued to figure the estimate.

"Ah, yes, quite," Herman stammered, embarrassed to hear a woman curse. It was almost as bad as having to discuss business with a member of the fairer sex. "I'll convey your sentiments to Daniel the next time I see him."

"There'll be no reason for you to see Daniel," she said, shoving the finished paper under his nose. "He'll never be able to beat this price."

Altman raised his eyebrows and whistled softly. The price was almost half what he had been quoted by Brady or O'Brien. "Can you really deliver a quality carousel for that price?"

"In three months," she said without batting an eyelash.

"And would you be willing to put that in writing?"

She snatched the ledger away from him, scribbled across it, tore the page out, and handed it to him. "There you are, sir. Just sign at the bottom and we'll begin your carousel today."

Altman shook his head in amazement. Perhaps dealing with a woman wasn't so bad after all, especially one as pretty as this one. And as eager to make a deal.

He held out his hand and she grasped it in a handshake that made him wince.

"Thank you, Mr. Altman. You'll be pleased with your decision to buy a McKevett carousel, I promise you."

He chuckled. "If you keep those prices down

234

there, you're going to put your competition out of business."

She smiled, her green eyes glittering. But this time Altman didn't consider her smile pretty. In fact, something about it frightened him. Women were supposed to be soft, feminine, sweet creatures. They weren't supposed to smile as though they wanted to eat someone for breakfast.

In that moment Herman Altman was glad that he was a simple concessions owner. He was glad that he wasn't Padraic Brady. And he was especially thankful that he wasn't Daniel O'Brien.

Eirinn sat at the head of the table in the chair where her father had sat for so many years. No one seemed to mind or to question her authority. Not even Ryan, who sat to her left. To her right were Ignacio and Josef. Further down the table were Nicholas, David, and the McKevetts' newest employees.

"I sold a carousel today," she announced.

The room exploded with applause and shouts. The gang had waited a long time for this news. It meant they all had a job for a while longer.

"Mr. Herman Altman ordered it." She took a deep breath and spoke the words that she knew would spoil the cheerful mood. "There were others bidding on it, and to get the job I had to sell it to him at half the price we are accustomed to getting."

There was a heavy silence around the table. The men's joyous expressions melted into confusion and then quickly turned to anger.

235

"So that means you'll each be paid only half of what you received before. I'm sorry. But thanks to Daniel going into business against us, the prices will have to stay down for a while."

"But we were only barely able to feed our families as it was," Josef said, his voice trembling with indignation. "You're not just cutting our wages in half, but the food on our tables, too."

"For me, I don't eat much," Ignacio said, squaring his already thin shoulders. "But what can I tell my mama? For her I am the man."

Eirinn squirmed miserably. Josef's criticism had simply made her angry, but Iggie's gentle reproach tugged at her heart. These men had given her their best over the years. They were master craftsmen. They deserved better.

The new employees agreed, but quietly, not secure enough in their positions to complain too bitterly.

Eirinn cast a sideways look at Ryan. It was too much to expect him to come to her aid.

She decided to let them have all the bad news at once and be done with it. "And I had to promise to deliver the machine in three months."

"Three months! How the hell can we produce a quality carousel in that amount of time?" Josef demanded. "Even Padraic Brady takes six months, and look at his shabby workmanship. Michael would turn over in his grave if he knew about this."

Eirinn's temper soared. She looked again at Ryan, but he sat passively as though he found the entire proceeding immensely boring.

"This isn't open for discussion," she said. "Setting prices and delivery dates is my responsibility.

I did what I had to do to get the order. If I hadn't made this sale we would have been closing our doors in two weeks, and we would have all been without a job. So if you can't be grateful, at least stop your complaining." She stood, clearly signaling the end of the meeting.

When the last sullen face had filed out of the room and the door was closed, she turned on Ryan. "Thank you so much for the great show of support, brother. For one who wanted so badly to be in the carousel business, I don't see you taking a very active role."

He shrugged. "Why should I? You were doing fine by yourself. Besides, I don't agree with what you did."

"What are you talking about?"

"We can't afford to produce a carousel at that price and you know it. But you were willing to put us all on the line just to hurt Daniel O'Brien."

He stood, walked around the table and placed his hands on her shoulders. "Though I can't blame you, considering that he abandoned you at the altar, so to speak."

"I did this *for* us, not *against* Daniel."

He patted her long black hair. "Of course you did, sweetheart. Don't worry about it. I think that destroying Daniel is a worthwhile occupation, and I intend to help you in any way I can."

"You told me to go to hell, Ryan. This place was the closest I could come." Bernadette wrapped the black lace robe with its ludicrous ruffles more tightly around her thin body. She

237

walked over to the broken-down bed, dropped the robe to the floor, and crawled between the dingy sheets.

Ryan glanced around the shabby room in disgust. "A whorehouse. I should have known that's where I'd find you."

A light of hope flared in her big blue eyes. "You came looking for me?"

"Yeah," he lied without hesitation. Better she think he had been combing the city for her than that she know he had simply walked into the nearest whorehouse in search of some female company. Of all the rotten luck. As usual he had requested a black-haired beauty. But the madame had informed him that it was a busy night and he would take what he could get. He had opened the door and found Bernadette, even thinner and paler than he remembered.

But thin or not, she was female. As his eyes caressed the flesh that she had bared for him, he remembered that holding her had not been without its pleasures.

She didn't have black hair or green eyes, but he would turn out the lights when he took her, and maybe in the dark, he could pretend that she did.

The woman with the black hair was down the hall, in bed with Daniel O'Brien.

Daniel had arrived early in the evening and had been given his pick of the lot. Without hesitation he had chosen Cecilia. He didn't want to think about why. He wanted to think it was because she had a nice, warm smile and a softly rounded body. It couldn't be because of her thick black curls or green eyes.

"I'm sorry," she said as she buttoned his shirt and helped him slip into his jacket. "I feel really bad that you didn't—"

"Don't worry about it," he said brusquely. Then his expression softened and he reached out to stroke her cheek gently. " 'Twasn't yer fault. Yer a bonny lass, indeed, and ye do know how to please a man. Me heart was somewhere else, I suppose, and me body followed it."

She shrugged. "It happens sometimes." She led him to the door and stood on tiptoe to kiss his cheek. "I hope you come back soon. Maybe we could try again."

He looked at her for a long time before he answered. "I thank ye kindly for the offer, but I don't think so, lass."

The girl smiled knowingly. "She's a lucky woman."

"Who's that yer speakin' of?"

"The lady who your heart was visiting this evening."

Daniel pressed some money into her palm. He had already paid the madame downstairs, but this girl looked as though she needed it more than he. Then he turned and walked out the door into the hallway.

It was at the first bend of the corridor that he ran into Ryan. Literally. The two men stood, head to head, eye to eye, each of them loathing the sight of the other. It was their first encounter since the night Daniel had beaten Ryan.

"You just never know who you'll meet on the streets of hell," Ryan said, looking terribly pleased with himself for catching Daniel at a disadvantage.

Daniel would have loved to remove that look from Ryan's face with a few taps of his knuckles, but he curled his fingers into tight fists, reining in his temper.

"What would Eirinn say if she saw you in a place such as this?" Ryan said.

Daniel pulled those reins tighter. "I don't give a tinker's damn what Eirinn thinks," he lied. The last thing he wanted was for her to find out that he had visited this place. He hadn't realized just what a seedy house this was until he rounded that hallway and ran into Ryan McKevett. If Ryan was an example of this establishment's clientele he would find another place to frequent.

"I don't suppose yer here to distribute alms to the poor," Daniel said, his voice dripping with sarcasm.

"As a matter of fact, I was visiting an old friend of mine, a poor girl who's gone to ruin."

"If she's a friend of yers, 'tis no wonder she's ruint."

Ryan stepped toward him, his fists raised.

Daniel met him halfway. "Do it, man," he said. "Nothin' would please me more than to finish what yer sister interrupted, and her not here to save ye this time."

Ryan flushed with anger, but he lowered his fists.

"You're going to pay for what you did to me that night," he said. "I'll not rest until you've paid."

As Ryan turned and walked away, Daniel thought of what he had lost that night. He had lost Eirinn to Ryan McKevett. What greater price could he have paid?

Though it was nearly midnight, the night air was still sultry and oppressive. Sweat trickled down Eirinn's face to her throat and on down to the bodice of her light cotton dress. But her perspiration was as much from nervousness as from the heat of the summer night.

If she could only get into the arcade, see Daniel's new carousel, and get out without being recognized. Pushing her way through the crowd, she entered the octagonal building that housed the new carousel that was the toast of Coney Island. Eirinn's eyes swept the throng but there was no one there she knew.

When she saw it she caught her breath, and unexpectedly a wave of joy swept through her. It was glorious, the most beautiful creation she had ever seen.

In that instant her hate was put aside and she felt only pride and happiness that something this lovely had come into the world through the talents of people she loved.

Mirrored panels in gilded frames caught the golden light of a hundred lanterns, causing the machine to glitter like a giant twirling gem. The scenery panels were exquisite oil paintings, pastoral scenes painted in the most delicate of pastels. Highly polished brass sparkled like burnished gold, and jewels twinkled as the carousel whirled, spinning its riders into the Land of the Ever Young.

But the horses . . . they were the most beautiful creatures Eirinn had ever seen. She had known that Daniel was a master, but now she knew that he was a magician, creating beauty out of nothing.

"Do you like it, Eirinn?"

The voice came from behind her; it was deep and husky with emotion.

"Danny." She turned around and stood, quietly drinking in the sight of him. The crowd around them faded from her senses, and they were alone. Just the two of them. And the carousel. "It's wonderful."

He shrugged. "Aye, 'tis a fine one if I do say so meself."

He smiled and she felt it all through her body, warm and tingling. For the moment the past year was forgotten. The pain of rejection put aside. She felt like a little girl again, admiring her big, wonderful Danny and his latest creation.

"Would you like to ride it?" he asked, his heart shining in his amber eyes.

She nodded.

Turning to a young man who hovered nearby, Daniel said, "Armand, please get these people out of here. We're closing early tonight."

Five minutes later, Eirinn and Daniel were truly alone and the carousel was empty.

"Which horse are ye after ridin'?" he asked as he led her around the wheel.

"I want to ride the lead horse, of course," she replied.

Every carousel had a lead horse, the one animal that was always carved by the shop's master carver, the most beautiful and ornate horse on the wheel.

This lead was obviously Daniel's masterpiece. He was an armored horse with intricate chain mail drapings and a jeweled faceplate and chestplate.

She stepped up onto the platform and grasped the horse's brass pole. With a thrill of awareness she felt Daniel's hands close around her waist and lift her onto the horse that was the largest she had ever sat upon.

"He's as large as a real stallion," she said.

"Aye, that's what I intended. I wanted the children to know what it was like to ride a real horse."

He walked over to the control panel and flipped the switch. The wheel began to turn, faster and faster. So fast that it took her breath away and she had to hang on to the pole to keep from falling off.

So enthralled was she that she didn't notice Daniel until he swung into the saddle behind her and wrapped his arms around her.

"Daniel, what are you — ?"

"Hush," he whispered in her ear. "Just close yer eyes and feel yerself flyin'."

She reached down deep inside her heart, trying to grasp her anger and hate. This man had hurt her, deserted her. Twice. How could she let him hold her like this?

But his body was warm and solid against her back. And his arms around her waist were heavily muscled, the hard, rounded biceps pressing into the sides of her breasts. His fingers were splayed across her ribs.

She gave into the lassitude that robbed her of strength and leaned back into him. Her anger

243

and hate were too far out of reach.

"I've missed ye, darlin'," he said, his breath moist and hot against her neck. "Dear Jesus, how I've missed holdin' you like this."

No. Her heart rejected his words the instant he uttered them. He had no right to say things that stirred those old emotions, feelings that she had thought she had carefully buried.

"Don't say that."

His arms tightened around her and his lips pressed against the side of her neck. The motion of the horse brought their bodies closer and closer together.

"But 'tis true. Not a day's gone by I haven't thought of you. To be honest, not even an hour."

"Don't say that, damn you."

She wriggled and tried to pull away from him, but he held her fast. Her head was spinning faster than the carousel they were riding.

"I love you, Eirinn." His lips moved up her neck to her ear. "I've never stopped lovin' you. And you love me too. That's why you came here tonight."

"No! That's not true."

Twisting out of his arms, she slid off the horse and tumbled down onto the platform. In an instant he had dismounted and was pulling her onto her feet.

"Don't be a fool," he said. "Ye could have hurt yerself."

Ignoring him, she stumbled to the edge of the platform and jumped off. She landed on the ground in a crumpled heap.

In an instant Daniel was beside her. "Eirinn! Are ye after killing yerself entirely?" he demanded. Once again he pulled her to her feet, but this time his touch was anything but gentle. His fingers dug into her shoulders as he pulled her roughly against him. "Don't ye ever do a stupid thing like that again, girl. 'Tis a wonder ye didn't break both yer legs and yer neck besides."

"Don't you tell me what I may and may not do, Daniel O'Brien," she said, fighting back the sobs that threatened to choke her. "And don't you dare tell me that you love me and that you miss me. You're the one who left me. You're the one who didn't show his face on our wedding day."

"Ye didn't need me!" he shouted back, his nose nearly touching hers. "Ye had that worthless heap of dung, Ryan, to keep ye company. I gave ye a choice and ye made it."

"He's my brother, my flesh and blood. If you really loved me you never would have asked me to choose. You don't love me. You never did, or you wouldn't have left me. Ryan or no Ryan."

His eyes blazed and she felt scorched by the heat. His breath was hot on her face when he said, "Ye can say I left ye, because 'tis true, I did. And ye can say I wasn't fair to ye, if ye think I treated ye badly. But don't you tell me that I never loved ye, girl, because I know better than you what I felt. What I still feel."

His hands moved from her shoulders to her hair and became tangled in her silky black curls. Holding her tightly, he bent his head and kissed her. His lips were hot and wet against hers, his tongue bold as he invaded those soft recesses.

She resisted, but only for a moment. Then she

was returning the kiss, welcoming his tongue's thrusts and answering him with flicks of her own, hating herself all the while.

How could her mind curse him while her heart and body responded to him?

He was the one to finally break the kiss. They both stood there fighting for breath, holding on to each other as though their legs alone couldn't support them.

"Tell me ye hate me, if it pleases ye," he said. "But don't ever tell me I don't love ye."

"You left me," she said, all of her pain expressed in those three words.

"Ye chose Ryan over me."

It couldn't be that simple. She wouldn't let it be that simple.

"I hate you, Danny O'Brien." And then, because even she couldn't really believe her words, she drew back her hand and slapped him as hard as she could.

He didn't flinch. He didn't even put his hand to his cheek. If her palm hadn't been stinging she wouldn't have been sure that she'd struck him. It wasn't enough. She had to know that she had hurt him.

"And I didn't come down here to see you," she added. "I came to see your carousel. I heard that you had a marvelous new engine that turned it and I had to see it."

She looked at the carousel that was still whirling at breathless speed. "We have to stay informed about what our competition is doing."

Turning back to Daniel, she saw the disappointment and deep pain registered in his amber eyes.

She had hurt him . . . badly. And it was enough.

Perhaps it was too much. . .

Chapter Twenty

"I see that you McKevetts are installing your own carousel here in Coney Island." Padraic Brady tilted back his head and puffed a white cloud into the already smoke-choked atmosphere of the private poker room of his casino. The other three players had moved on to the less costly vices of drink and women. Only Brady and Ryan remained, and since Ryan had long ago depleted his supply of chips, they had settled into a comfortable conversation about the amusement business.

"Yes, and a nice one, too," Ryan replied proudly. "We got it set up last week and it hasn't stopped spinning yet."

"I saw your sister there, supervising the operations when your boys were setting it up. She's a pretty little thing, and full of vinegar too. She was obviously the one in charge. I see now who my competition is." He smiled, deepening the creases in his jowls. "And to think that all this time I thought it was you."

Ryan saw the contempt in Brady's eyes and it stung him deeply. He hated this man. So why did he spend so much time with him? Ryan knew that answer to his own question the instant it crossed his mind. Brady was successful; he had money, lots of it. And Ryan hoped that if he hung around Brady long enough an opportunity would present itself. Someday Brady's money would be his. Part of it, at least.

"Yeah, she's a beauty all right," Brady expounded. "All that pretty black hair, those wicked green eyes, and a body that would make a man—"

"That's my sister you're talking about," Ryan interjected with a fury that surprised them both. "You'd better be careful what you say."

A flicker of respect lit Brady's eyes as he said, "No insult intended, old boy. I was just saying that she's obviously a very special lady. Does she have any romantic interests at the moment?"

Ryan thought carefully before answering. He had an inkling where this conversation was heading, but he wasn't sure how to head it off. "None at the moment. But then, Eirinn doesn't take time for courting and such things. She always has her head buried in the business."

"Sounds like a good woman. Maybe I'll come knocking on her door one day soon with a bouquet of flowers. Any woman has time for courting if the right man comes along."

"Stay away from Eirinn." The words escaped Ryan's mouth before he had the chance to censor them.

"What are you talking about? She's a grown woman and a widow. She can certainly decide for herself if she's interested in a suitor. Besides, you're a shrewd businessman, Ryan. I'd think that you'd be able to foresee how beneficial this arrangement might be for both of us. Brady-McKevett Carousels. Rolls off the tongue nicely, don't you agree?"

"Stay away from her. She isn't interested in

marrying again."

Brady laughed and the ugly cackle raised the hair on Ryan's neck. He looked down at those beefy, chafed hands and thought of them caressing Eirinn's soft, white body, and for some reason he thought of the pistol buried in his coat pocket. He would kill this weasel before he would let him touch her.

"What's the matter, McKevett?" Brady asked, and his grin widened. "Do you have something going on with her yourself?"

The pistol suddenly appeared in Ryan's hand. Later he wouldn't even remember reaching for it. "Don't you ever say that again," he hissed through gritted teeth.

Ryan's eyes glittered with insanity. Brady recognized the symptoms and dropped his boisterous bravado. Holding up his hands in surrender, he said, "Now, I was only joking with you, Ryan. I never meant to cast aspersions on the lady's integrity. Or yours either, for that matter. Put that away before you hurt someone."

Slowly, Ryan slipped the pistol back into his pocket. Then he folded his trembling hands on the table in front of him and closed his eyes, trying to gain control of his emotions. When he finally opened his eyes, Brady was gone.

"I know why you don't want Brady to marry your sister," Bernadette said as she unhooked her corset and dropped it to the floor beside her rumpled petticoats.

Ryan watched her from the bed, his arms folded behind his head. Scowling, he reached down and pulled the sheet up to his waist. "How

250

do you know about that?"

With a shrug and a smile she climbed into bed beside him. "We girls hear all kinds of things. I heard that he practically asked for her hand last week and you turned him down. Pulled a gun on him and everything. Of course, I know why. But don't worry, I won't tell anyone."

He reached over and lightly wrapped his long fingers around her throat in a gesture that would have frightened most women, but Bernadette chatted on happily. "Can't say that I blame you. Old Brady isn't a very appealing sort. I don't suppose you'd welcome him into your home . . . let alone your sister's bed."

The fingers tightened ever so slightly, but she didn't notice. "But if they did get married, your sister and Brady, that is, you wouldn't have to be jealous. Believe me, I've spent the night with Brady and I know."

His hands slid down to her small breasts. "What are you talking about?"

"Well, I really shouldn't talk about him, he's been nice to me. But since it's you." She drew a deep breath and lowered her voice to a whisper. They were alone, but the hotel walls were thin. "Brady talks a lot about liking women, and from the things he says you'd think he was a great lover, but—"

"He isn't that wonderful?" Ryan remembered that once before she had mentioned that Padraic Brady was lacking on the cot. Thinking of the passionate session they had just shared, Ryan thrilled to a feeling of superiority over this man whom he had envied for so long.

"Not at all." She moved her lips closer to his ear. "He can't even . . . you know . . ."

251

"Really?" This was better than he could have ever hoped.

"It's true. And not just with me either. The girls love it when he asks for them because they know they can spend the night sleeping and still be paid. He just gets drunk, touches them a little here and there, and then passes out. Sound asleep. Every time. I used to think it was only because he didn't like me. But the other girls say it's the same with them."

Ryan's hands moved on down her body with a boldness born of confidence. So, as he had suspected, Brady was impotent. He saw the man in a whole new light now—the man, and the prospect of him marrying Eirinn.

It would be nice to have Padraic Brady for a brother-in-law and business partner. This was the opportunity he had been waiting for to get his hands on the man's money.

And if he was impotent, that made him the perfect husband for Eirinn.

The wind battered the house, shaking the windows in their sills and causing the walls to creak and complain with ever increasing urgency. Eirinn set two bowls of soup on the table, one for herself and the other for Ryan.

"Jesus, Mary and Joseph," he muttered as he sat in his chair and spread the napkin on his lap. "This is no ordinary storm. It's a full-blown hurricane if I ever saw one. It's a wonder I even got home."

"Where were you all evening?" she asked, tasting the soup and deciding that if it wasn't as good as Caitlin's it would still do on a chilly autumn night.

"With Padraic Brady."

"Gambling again? Ryan, you know we can't afford for you to throw your money away like that."

"We were discussing business. Personal business."

"What kind of personal business would you have with someone like Brady?"

"Brady's a good man, Eirinn. Don't sell him short. He's a brilliant businessman and a pretty nice chap when you get to know him."

She stared at him in amazement across the table. "Are we talking about the same man? I thought you considered him a lying cheat."

"Maybe I did at one time, but that was before I got to know him. Now I count him among my friends."

"And just what has Brady done to warrant this abrupt change in your opinion of him? Has he raised the dead or walked on water?"

Ryan's blond eyebrows knit together in a frown as he shook his head sadly. "Really, Eirinn. Sarcasm doesn't become you. Nor does blasphemy. I swear, you're getting more outspoken every day. Whatever happened to your sweet disposition?"

"It was trampled with muddy boots once too many times."

"And because Daniel O'Brien broke your heart, you're going to take it out on every man you meet for the rest of your life?"

"No, Ryan," she said, lifting the spoon to her lips. "Only you."

They stopped arguing long enough to listen to the wind, which was getting worse by the moment.

"If you don't work on getting back a bit of your sweetness, Eirinn," he said, "you'll never catch a husband."

She laughed, but there was no humor in the sound. "Why would I want a husband when I already have one man to take care of? I should think that you would be burden enough for any one woman to bear."

Hours later, Eirinn lay in her bed listening to the storm rage outside her window. The mournful sound of the wind answered a sadness in her heart as she thought of Sean, the baby, Michael, and Daniel. It was too much to lose, too fast. Even though she worked hard all day to keep the memories at bay, in the night hours they came rushing in, bringing a melancholy that she couldn't rise above.

And then there was her mother. Caitlin's letters came regularly every month, but a letter wasn't enough. Eirinn missed her terribly. That was another wound that she was afraid would never heal.

Only one thought gave her relief, only one area of her life was fulfilled. Her father's dream was alive. With the revenue from the new carousel, the business was finally secure. Michael had foreseen a day when the McKevetts would permanently install a carousel of their own on Coney Island, and it had been a good idea. It had been a hard battle, squeezing the funds out of a floundering company to build an extra carousel on the side and still meet their customers' orders.

But they had done it. Eirinn had done it.

She smiled and allowed herself to wallow in the

satisfaction the realization brought. The business was going to survive, and it was because she had been resourceful and had worked so hard. Eirinn drifted off to sleep, her doubts and fears temporarily relieved.

It was just before dawn, when the worst of the storm hit, that Eirinn woke with a terrible thought. Coney Island was undoubtedly being battered even worse than Brooklyn. What was the wind and water doing to the new carousel?

Eirinn lifted her skirts as she picked her way through the sodden debris of splintered boards, scattered timbers, and broken glass. Coney Island was devastated.

All around her was the aftermath of the hurricane, and with every step she took, her anxiety rose. The carousel couldn't have survived, not when structures that had stood here for fifty years had been battered to the ground. Even the sturdiest buildings had their shutters, doors, and signs torn loose and their windows shattered. In the streets, which were nothing more than rivers of mud, the shop owners stood, their mouths agape at the results of Nature's fury.

Eirinn ran the last few blocks to the boardwalk where the carousel tent had stood. If the wheel had been inside a building it might have survived, but with only canvas to shield it . . .

She rounded that final corner and stood, shocked by the expected. Nothing in that pile of rubble even vaguely resembled what had been there only yesterday. It looked as though a giant hand had picked the wheel up by its center pole and then dropped it from a hundred feet in the air.

Stunned, Eirinn walked among the wreckage of gaily painted rounding boards and shredded canvas. Saddest of all were the ponies that lay on their sides as though slaughtered.

Eirinn thought of all the long hours that the men in the shop had spent building this carousel. She thought of how she had juggled the funds to buy the materials and pay for the labor on this machine. An investment for the future it was to have been. For the next century this carousel should have spun, garnering profits for the Mc-Kevetts and their children's children. And now it was a heap of ruin . . . like her father's dream.

"I'm sorry, darlin'." She turned and saw Daniel standing behind her, his head down, his hands thrust deep into his pockets. " 'Tis a terrible loss," he said.

Her first inclination was to run into his arms, and in her heart she knew that he would welcome her. But she was angry. Deeply furious with him, with Fate, with the world.

"Why should you care, Daniel?" she asked, her voice crackling with sarcasm. "It's just that much less competition for you. I suppose your carousel fared just fine in that nice building of yours."

She saw the anger flare in his eyes, but not enough to extinguish his sympathy. "It'll need a few repairs, water damage and all, but yes, it fared well enough, considerin'."

Eirinn thought of Daniel's beautiful carousel, so much more graceful and elegant than this one that her poor factory with its unskilled labor had put together. "I'm glad it survived," she said, surprising herself that she meant it.

He walked up to her and put his hands on her shoulders. Through the fabric of her jacket she could feel the heat from his palms, and her pride was the only thing that stopped her from wrapping her arms around his waist and melting into him.

"And what about you, love?" he said. "Will you survive this loss?"

She shrugged. "I've survived all the others."

"So ye have. And it's made ye stronger."

"Strong, angry, and bitter," she added.

He nodded. "I've seen the change in ye. Yer a woman now, surely. A girl no longer."

"She seems another person . . . the girl I used to be," Eirinn said as dark sadness swept over her. She felt like her carousel—windblown, ragged, twisted and disjointed to the point of being unrecognizable.

"What's the worst, love?" he asked. "Tell me what's the worst thing happenin' to ye right now."

Eirinn could see the concern in his eyes. She could feel herself responding to that concern, and she hated herself for it. Her anger rose to give her the strength to resist the more tender emotions.

"I'm losing my father's company," she said. "We were sinking before. That's why we built this carousel. For the first time since you left I thought we were going to make it. And now this . . ." She waved an arm toward the wreckage.

"I'm sorry," he said simply.

"You should be." She shook his hands off her shoulders. "If you hadn't left us, none of this would be happening."

257

Abruptly he stepped back from her, and the look on his face was the same as when she had slapped him that night. But he quickly looked down at the ground, shuttering his eyes and whatever he was feeling.

"Anytime ye want me to work alongside ye instead of against ye, all you must do is get rid of that worthless baggage ye call yer brother and I'll be there."

"I can't deny my brother his birthright. You know that."

"I know that it's a fool ye are, Eirinn Mc-Kevett-Sullivan," he said. "To be throwin' away everything yer father worked for, to be denyin' yer own happiness for a man who isn't worthy to—"

"I don't want to hear this. You have no right to say it. You're the one who hurt me, who left me. He's always been there for me."

"Is that so? Then where is he now, Eirinn? Only a moment ago ye needed someone to hold ye and tell ye what a strong woman ye are. Does he ever tell ye that? No. He just uses yer strength for his own purposes. And when he's used ye all up he'll find another woman to use. That's the way of a man like that."

His words reached deep inside her and rang true. Ryan did drain her. She was the one who always took care of him. Where was he when she needed a little comfort? Daniel was the one who was there when she needed to feel someone else's strength. Danny was there when . . .

She cast the thoughts out of her brain before they could find their way to her heart. Lifting her skirt out of the mud, she turned and walked away. He didn't follow her, and she was surprised that she felt more than a little disappointed.

"If some money would help ye out a bit," he called after her, "maybe I could—"

"To hell with you and your money! I'll find a way, Danny O'Brien, and it'll be without your charity."

Chapter Twenty-one

"That was a lovely dinner, Eirinn," Ryan said as he handed Padraic Brady a glass of brandy and his customary cigar. "I hope the two of you will forgive me for having to leave so abruptly this way. But there's a matter down in the shop that requires my attention."

Eirinn sighed inwardly as she sat down on the parlor sofa, as far away from Brady as possible. Ryan was so transparent. Since when had he been needed in the shop?

She already felt imposed upon. This was the fifth time in two weeks that Ryan had brought Brady home for dinner unannounced, and she knew very well why he hadn't asked her permission beforehand. She would have said no. Part of Ryan's genius was knowing when not to ask.

"I can't tell you how much I've enjoyed the time I've spent with you and your brother here in your lovely home," Brady said as Ryan left the room. "And your cooking is superb."

"Just Irish peasant fare," she replied coolly. "The kind my mother taught me to cook."

"Ah, yes, your lovely mother. And how is Caitlin these days?"

"She's doing very well. I receive a letter from her regularly every month. She has reopened her pub there in Lios na Capaill and business is brisk."

"I've no doubt. Your mother was a fine businesswoman. It runs in the family, I suppose." He lifted his brandy glass to her in an exaggerated salute.

As she returned the toast, she thought, not for the first time, that perhaps she had been too hard on Padraic Brady all these years. During his recent visits Eirinn had seen a side of the man that she had never dreamed existed. He could be quite charming, an excellent conversationalist, and rather pleasant all the way around.

Eirinn had learned quite a lot from him about the carousel business, as he had generously shared with her his knowledge and strategies. To little avail, she thought, her business was too far gone to benefit from his advice.

As though reading her mind, Brady said, "I heard that you had to let go of some of your best workers. I was sorry to hear that."

"That's true, Mr. Brady. The skies aren't very bright over McKevetts' Carousel Manufactory today."

"Please, call me Padraic," he said as he reached down the sofa and placed his hand on hers.

Her first inclination was to pull it away, but she resisted the urge. After all, he was only being sympathetic. At moments like this she could almost think of him as a friend.

"Is there anything I can do, Eirinn? Your father made such a contribution to the carousel industry. Some even say that he invented the flying horses. I'd hate to see his shop go under."

"There's nothing you can do, but I thank you for your concern."

He sighed and squeezed her hand. "Actually, I

have an offer for you. I've been waiting for the right moment to discuss it with you."

"What kind of offer?"

"I was thinking that if you and I pooled our assets, it might be a winning combination. I think we would make a good team."

Carefully, Eirinn removed her hand from his. "Have you discussed this with Ryan?"

"Of course. He thinks it's a wonderful idea."

So, that was why Ryan had invited Padraic over so many times lately, why he had conveniently left them alone. Ryan wanted Brady for a partner.

"Well, if Ryan thinks it's a good plan, I don't suppose I have any objection," she said doubtfully.

His face fell. "I was hoping for a slightly more enthusiastic reaction than that," he admitted.

"I'm sorry, Mr. . . . I mean, Padraic. It's just that I hadn't really considered taking on a business partner. I'll have to grow accustomed to the idea."

"A business partner?" He threw back his head and laughed. "Who said anything about you being my business partner? I want you to be my wife."

As his words filtered into Eirinn's brain her thoughts skidded to a stop. *Wife?* Padraic Brady's *wife!*

"I . . . I don't understand."

He shrugged. "It's really very simple. I admire you. I enjoy talking to you and looking at you. You're a very lovely woman, Eirinn, and I'm fond of you. Surely you guessed."

"Ah, no. I'm sorry, I didn't know. You were talking business and I just assumed that . . ."

"I broached the subject from a financial point

of view because I thought that would appeal to you most. I didn't think you would sit here while I recited love sonnets in your ear."

He was right. She would never have allowed him to court her, this man with the rounded belly, receding hair, and drooping jowls. But when viewed from a financial standpoint, the idea of marriage to him was less appalling than the alternative—bankruptcy.

"You don't have to give me your answer to-night, Eirinn. Think about it for as long as you like. I've been a bachelor all these years and I can wait a bit longer."

"I'm sorry, Padraic, but I can't see you as my husband. I can't see us . . . together."

He smiled and patted her shoulder. His touch was awkward, forced, as though he weren't accustomed to physical affection.

"Don't worry about that. We'll sleep in separate rooms. I wouldn't have it any other way. And I promise I'll never visit your bed."

Her eyes searched his face. Surely he didn't mean . . .

"Never?"

"Well . . ." His gaze swept over her. "Not unless you insisted."

She looked him squarely in the eyes. "I *wouldn't* insist."

He stood, picked his bowler up from the table and set it on his head. "Fair enough. You think about it and give me your answer as soon as you decide."

He walked toward the door, but before he reached it Eirinn had weighed her choices and chosen the least of her two devils.

"I accept," she said. "But you must promise me two things."

Smiling broadly he said, "Anything."

"First, that you'll do everything in your power to see to it that my parents' shop continues to manufacture carousels."

"I swear. And what's the second thing?"

"That you'll help me put Daniel O'Brien out of business."

As Eirinn stood before the priest and repeated the sacred vows of matrimony, she wondered what it would have been like to make these promises out of love and not necessity.

Twice now she had pledged her life to a man, not because she wanted to spend the rest of her days with him but because she felt it was the only option left to her.

The ceremony was a blur, and for that she was thankful. This day wasn't a memory that she would cherish forever. And the sooner it was over, the better.

After the Mass she and Padraic stood on the church steps greeting friend after friend and a host of Padraic's relatives. His family seemed to consist solely of elderly women who were delighted that "dear Paddy" had decided to "settle down at last." And with such a lovely bride, too.

Among his friends there were several young women who eyed Eirinn jealously and made her uncomfortable. She suspected that it was Padraic's money they begrudged her, rather than the man himself.

"How do you suppose she got him to marry her?" one of them asked within her hearing.

"Well, we both know he didn't get her pregnant." They both collapsed in fits of giggles and Eirinn blushed scarlet. She and Padraic had been married less than an hour and already it seemed the entire world knew the details of their private life.

She looked around for Padraic, but he was deeply engrossed in conversation with Ryan and another friend of his, who was eyeing Eirinn with a lecherous eye.

"Congratulations, darlin'," said a familiar voice. She turned around to see Daniel standing beside her with a strangely sad look on his handsome face. Her heart thudded against her ribs, but she quickly convinced herself that it was from anger, not joy at seeing him. "Yer lookin' lovely today," he said. "I always knew ye'd make a pretty bride."

Before she had the chance to say a word, he had taken her into his arms and was kissing her. His mouth was hot and moist as it moved over hers in a kiss that was hungry and possessive. She wanted to pull away but she couldn't. He wouldn't let her, and neither would her own desires.

Finally, long after etiquette was breached, he ended the kiss, but he didn't release her right away. He stood there with his arms around her waist, and the fire in his eyes made her knees weak. How different his kiss was from the quick little peck that Padraic had given her at the end of the ceremony.

Out of the side of her eye she saw the elderly matrons watching them with lifted eyebrows. And she saw someone else. Padraic. He was coming down the steps toward them with Ryan at his heels, both of them walking with determined strides.

"No one invited you to this wedding," Ryan told Daniel when they reached the bottom of the stairs. "I'll ask you to please leave immediately."

Padraic nodded his agreement.

Daniel looked down at Eirinn. "I'll be on me way when the bride herself asks me to go," he said quietly, "and not before."

Eirinn looked from her brother to her new husband and back to Daniel, the man she loved, the man she hated. "Leave, Danny, please," she said.

"As ye wish." He bent his head once again and his lips brushed her cheek in a socially acceptable kiss. "I had to kiss ye once more," he whispered in her ear. "And I had to make it a good one." Then for all to hear, he said, louder, "I'm sorry. I'll be off now. And all me best to the bride and groom. May ye grow old together in peace and harmony."

"I thought you said you hated Daniel O'Brien." With every shot of whiskey Padraic's disposition was deteriorating. So was his conversational skill. He had questioned her on the subject of Danny O'Brien four times already in the past hour, and Eirinn was growing weary of the interrogation, *and* of her new husband.

"I'm tired, Padraic," she said as she folded her lace veil and carefully placed it in the cedar chest that sat in the corner of the parlor. She was remembering the last time she had tucked it away, the night she had married Sean.

She looked over at Padraic, drunk and sullen. Recalling Sean's gentleness on their wedding night, Eirinn wondered how she could have married such a man as this. In vain she tried to convince herself that she had done it for Michael and Caitlin, for their dream that, thanks to Padraic's money, would survive. But in her heart she

266

knew that neither of her parents would have condoned this marriage. Caitlin, being as pragmatic as she, might have understood it, but she would never have approved.

"Did O'Brien ever touch you? Did you go to bed with him?" Padraic's mind kept returning to his jealousy like a tongue to the space vacated by a newly pulled tooth. "Tell me right now, before I have to beat it out of you."

She looked over at him, sprawled across the parlor sofa, and felt more distaste than fear. "I told you before, Padraic, I don't love Daniel O'Brien. I despise the man. You have nothing to worry about."

"That's good," he said, his speech beginning to slur. He leaned his head back and closed his eyes. "You'd just better stay away from him. I may not choose to sleep in your bed, but that doesn't mean I'll allow you to have another man in it. Do you understand me, woman?"

"I understand."

But that night, as she slept, another man came to Eirinn's bed . . . in her dreams. A man with soft chestnut curls, amber eyes, and gentle hands. His clothes smelled of freshly cut wood and he spoke with a lilting brogue.

"Ye didn't have to sell yerself to Padraic Brady," he said as he pulled her close to his warm, hard body. "I would have helped if ye'd only let me."

"But you didn't want me. You left me."

" 'Twasn't yerself I walked away from. 'Twas Ryan. I wanted ye, lass. I'll always want ye. But I can't live and work with Ryan. If I'd tried, one of us would have ended up dead, surely."

267

"You loved me? You only left because of Ryan?"

He nodded.

"Oh, Danny, why didn't you tell me before I married Padraic?"

"I tried, darlin'. God knows I tried. But you were too angry to listen."

Tears filled her eyes and spilled down onto her pillow. "And now it's too late," she said.

"Aye." He sighed and buried his face in her hair. " 'Tis too late."

Chapter Twenty-two

Eirinn strolled through the Brady-McKevett Carousel Factory. The shop was bustling as it had been for the past eight months now. Every amusement operator in Coney Island wanted a carousel, and they wanted to buy it from this shop.

Only yesterday she had heard that Daniel O'Brien's business was suffering, due to Brady-McKevett's low prices and fast delivery schedules.

A few people were willing to pay more and wait longer for the exquisite workmanship that Daniel and his staff produced, but not many. The crowds didn't seem to mind if the ponies were true-to-life works of art or quickly chiseled out, awkwardly shaped creatures. Young and old, they lined up to ride the flying horses, nickels in hand.

Eirinn should have been happy. She had secured her parents' dream. She had beaten Daniel O'Brien, or at least made life unpleasant for him.

But as she walked through the shop and saw the slapdash workmanship, the shoddy carving, doubts pricked at her. Was this really what Michael and Caitlin would have wanted? Prosperity at the price of quality and reputation?

And what about her own life? She had shown Daniel that she could sell more carousels than he, but every night, when she slept alone in her empty bed, she thought of him, longed for him. And the worst part was that she suspected he knew how much she wanted him. So who had really won after all?

As she passed the painters she saw one of their newest employees, a fellow named Nick Muglia, applying jewels to a roaring lion. The McKevetts had used these round, faceted bits of glass for years to enhance the saddles and bridles of their animals. The glittering jewels accented the drapings of the more dramatic horses nicely when used sparingly.

But Muglia was gluing the jewels all over the poor beast. Across its forehead, down its legs, over its chest, obliterating the carver's work.

"What in heaven's name are you doing there?" she demanded.

"He'sa nice. Bello. The king of all the beasts."

"He looks ghastly," she said. "You can't see the animal. Whatever possessed you to do such a thing?"

Muglia looked at her, a confused expression on his face; his English vocabulary apparently did not include the word "possessed."

"Why are you doing that?" she asked. "Why?"

He grinned broadly, comprehending now. "Ah. Mr. Brady. He tell me to put on jewels. More is good, he say."

Her heart sank. "Oh, he did, huh?"

Walking toward the office, she tried to control her temper. This time Padraic had gone too far.

The last time a carousel had gone out of the shop with the horse's manes painted red, green, and orange, she had blushed with shame, but she hadn't said anything. She had bit her tongue when she had seen the purple frog and the pink giraffe. But this was too much.

"Well, hello, Eirinn," Ryan said as he looked up from the ledgers spread across the desk.

At his side sat Padraic, the cigar that Eirinn

had grown to loathe hanging from the corner of his mouth. Padraic reached over and closed the ledgers one by one, in a manner that Eirinn guessed was meant to appear offhand, but seemed more deliberate.

"Good afternoon, dear," Padraic said. "How nice of you to grace us with your lovely presence."

"Please, Padraic, I'm not in the mood for your sarcasm. I want to know why you gave orders for that lovely lion to be covered with jewels. The damned thing looks like it has the measles."

"Don't say 'damned', dear. Cursing doesn't become a lady," Padraic expounded as ash flaked from the end of his cigar and spilled down his jacket lapel.

"I'll curse if I *damn* well please, and you didn't answer my question."

Ryan, always one to desert the scene of a battle, stood and walked toward the door. "I'll leave the two of you alone to discuss this. Good luck to you both, and may the best man win," he added with a sneer.

Eirinn cast him a disparaging look as he left, quietly closing the door behind him.

"So, you don't approve of my new idea, dear?" Padraic's words and tone irritated her. He never used endearments except when he was condescending to her, which he seemed to be frequently these past few months.

"No, I don't. It looks like hell. Carousels are supposed to be elegant, beautiful works of art. You're producing gaudy monstrosities that look as though they came out of a brothel. And what's worse, they bear my family's name."

Padraic's face flushed dark red and she knew that she had pushed him too far.

He stood and walked over to her. Even from

271

three feet away she could smell the whiskey on his breath. It was only two o'clock in the afternoon and he was nearly drunk already.

"I'm not really interested in what you think," he said. "When and if I do want your opinion, I'll ask for it. Do you understand?"

She nodded. "Oh, yes. I understand. You're slowly closing me out of every aspect of my own business. Between you and Ryan, I haven't been allowed to look at the books for almost four months now. I'm no longer allowed to speak to prospective customers, and now you're telling me that I can't speak my mind about design." She stepped closer to him, her face set in grim lines. "This business was mine long before I married you, Padraic. I won't be shut out."

Before she even saw it coming, he slapped her hard across the face. The blow knocked her backward against the drawing table. Putting her hand to her cheek, Eirinn fought back the tears of fury.

"Don't tell me what you will or won't have, woman," he said, his breath hot on her face. "I'm your husband, and I'll say and do whatever I please to you."

Eirinn's temper flared, her fear turning to rage. "How dare you hit me!" she said. "My own father never raised his hand to me, and I'll be damned if I'll take stand here and let you—"

His fist slammed into her jaw. She reeled from the blow and felt herself falling. The floor rose up and hit her. Then everything went black.

"My husband doesn't know I'm here, Father," Eirinn told the elderly priest who sat behind his desk in his rectory office. His hands were folded before him, the forefingers lifted to form a steeple as lofty as the one on his cathedral. "I want an annullment, but I'm afraid to tell him. I'm not sure what he's capable of . . ." She pointed to the dark swelling on the left side of her face, "considering what he did to me yesterday."

"Are you trying to tell me that Padraic Brady inflicted those bruises on you?" the priest asked, obviously doubtful.

"Of course he did. I just told you that."

"I find your story difficult to believe."

"Why?"

Tapping his forefingers together thoughtfully, he said, "Padraic is such a devout man, comes to confession twice a week, pays his tithes as regularly as clockwork, attends Mass every Sunday."

"And drinks to excess, is unscrupulous in his business dealings, and strikes his wife when she displeases him," Eirinn added.

The priest shook his head in disbelief. "That doesn't sound like the Padraic Brady I've known all these years."

Eirinn felt her heart sinking and her anger rising. "Father, why would I lie?"

He shrugged. "There are many reasons why a woman might want to break her marriage vows, but none that God would condone. Just because you have an occasional quarrel and—"

"Quarrel? The man knocked me unconscious. It wasn't a simple difference of opinion."

"Still, my child, you married Padraic for better or for worse. Marriage can't be discarded as easily as yesterday's newspaper."

This wasn't going as she had hoped at all. She should have known that Father McMurtry would take Padraic's side and not hers. Padraic was a faithful follower of the Church. And perhaps more important, he was a generous contributor.

On the other hand, like her parents, Eirinn seldom attended Mass. Unlike most of the Irish she knew, she had not been taught to revere the Church. For some reason, which they had never shared with her, Michael and Caitlin seemed to have a grudge against the Catholic church. Eirinn suspected it had something to do with their experiences in Ireland.

Following the dictates of the Church had not been considered as important in the McKevett household as following the dictates of one's own conscience. Eirinn had consulted her own heart when making her decisions. And now that she needed the Church's help, it seemed she had waited too late to seek that assistance.

"I'm sorry, child," the priest was saying, "but there's nothing I can do. You don't have grounds for an annulment."

"Isn't cruelty and violence grounds enough?"

"It's his word against yours. And I'm sure he would deny that he struck you if called to account for the deed."

She nodded tiredly. "That's true. He would." Reaching deep into her deck of resources, she pulled out her last card and dealt it. "Father, Padraic hasn't made love to me yet. We've been married eight months and the marriage hasn't yet been consummated. Isn't that grounds for an annulment?"

The priest squirmed in his chair. "I suppose it would be if it were true. But really, Eirinn, you can't expect me to believe that in all this time you and Padraic have never come together as man and wife."

"It's true."

"Once again, it would be his word against yours and—"

"Never mind, Father," she said, suddenly weary. She stood, picked up her coat and headed for the door. "Thank you for your time." Pausing in the doorway, she said, "Just out of curiosity, Father . . . if it had been Padraic here, asking you for the annulment, and he had told you that I had refused to bed him all this time, would you have believed him?"

"I'd rather not say. It isn't important."

"It's important to me. I want to know."

The priest thought carefully before answering. "I would have believed Padraic."

"Why, when you didn't believe me?"

"Because Padraic is a devout Christian."

"And I'm not?"

He lifted one bushy white eyebrow. "You tell me."

Eirinn looked around the office at the crucifix and the pictures of the saints. She didn't love this place. She didn't even like it. And she didn't feel as close to God here as when she walked in the park and felt the summer sun warm on her face or when she woke on a spring morning and heard the birds singing.

"No," she said, "I suppose I'm not as devout a Christian as dear Padraic."

Bernadette looked up at the sign over the shop door and read: "Brady-McKevett Carousel Manufactory." Shoving her hands into her skirt pockets, she clenched her fists and tried to stop trembling. She swallowed hard, but nothing could rid her mouth of the bitter taste of nausea.

Ryan had told her never to come here, to his work or to his home, but she had to see him. Since his sister and Padraic had gotten married she had seen little of Ryan. In all the time she had known him, she had never seen Ryan McKevett more interested in work than pleasure. Until now. It had been three months since he had last visited her in the humble room he had rented for her over Brady's casino. He hadn't paid the rent in two months, and Brady's manager, Tim O'Day, was daily threatening her with eviction.

But that was the least of Bernadette's worries today.

She opened the door and peeked into the shop. Having waited until late in the day, she found the place deserted and dark. At first she thought she had missed him altogether. Then, on the opposite side of the shop, she saw an open door with lamplight streaming out.

With her heart in her throat she walked to the office and stepped inside. He sat at the desk with three open ledgers before him. His handsome brow was furrowed in a scowl of concentration.

Bernadette felt a tug deep inside her, like that of a silver cord attached to her heart, binding her to this man. She didn't know why. True, he was the handsomest man she had ever been with. And at times he was kind to her, giving her an unexpected bauble, an unsolicited compliment, and, once in a great while some word of affection that bordered on love.

But usually he was cold, distant, aloof. When she was with Ryan, Bernadette often felt alone, as though she had been left standing in the sleet and snow on the porch of a great house, and he had slammed the door in her face.

Bernadette knew as she stood there in his office that she would probably have that door shut on her again. But she had to run that risk and put her heart on the line. She had no where else to turn.

"Ryan," she whispered softly.

He turned around, and the instant he saw her anger flared in his pale blue eyes. "What the hell are you doing here?" he demanded, rising from his chair. "I told you to stay away from here."

"I know, but it's been so long since I've seen you, Ryan." Bernadette could hear the desperation in her voice, and she hated herself for it. It must be nice to be strong, like Ryan, and not need anyone. She wished to God that she didn't need him, but she did, especially now.

"I've been busy," he said. "I have other things to do, you know, than roll around between the sheets with you."

She swallowed the insult and braced herself for more. "The rent is two months behind on the room," she said. "I'm going to be evicted."

"So pay it."

"Ryan, I don't have any money. I stopped . . . working . . . at Miss Rafferty's months ago. You know that. You're the one who told me to stop. Tim says he's going to throw me out tomorrow if I don't pay up."

He shrugged. "Tim's a friendly sort, and he's had his eye on you for a long time. I'm sure you could work out some kind of arrangement with him."

The ugly smirk on Ryan's face left no doubt about his meaning. For a moment Bernadette wondered how she had ever thought him handsome. Tears flooded her eyes. This wasn't how she had intended this conversation to go. Not at all.

"Is that what you really want me to do, Ryan?" she asked, her voice trembling.

"I don't care what you do."

Bernadette felt her world crumbling beneath her

feet. If he wouldn't even help her pay her rent, how could she ever expect him to help her with—

"I'm pregnant, Ryan," she blurted. Drawing a deep breath, she plunged ahead. "I'm three months along. You're going to be a father. Congratulations."

She watched his face as he took an emotional tumble off his pedestal. In that instant Ryan McKevett wasn't aloof, he was frightened. Bernadette would have preferred that he had been happy, but it reassured her to know that he could be afraid too, if only for a moment.

Then she felt his door slam shut again and she could read nothing on his face or in his eyes. Once again she was standing on the porch in the freezing rain.

"Bernadette," he said, his voice heavy with feigned sympathy. "I'm sorry that you've gotten yourself in this predicament. But surely you can understand that I can't take responsibility for a child I don't even know is mine."

"It's yours and you know it. I stopped working months ago and you're the only man I've been with since then."

He walked over to her and lifted his hand. Thinking that he was going to strike her, she cringed, but he simply laid his palm on her shoulder.

"As I said before, I'm truly sorry, but I can't marry you or even go on paying for a room that I'm no longer living in. You have to understand, Bernadette. You're a whore. You always have been. You always will be. And whores get pregnant every day. It's one of the hazards of your trade."

He reached into his pocket, pulled out a handful of coins, and pressed them into her palm.

"There. That's for old times' sake. We did have a few good times, didn't we?"

Bernadette needed the money, even a paltry amount such as this. With this change she could eat a nice dinner and pay for another night or two at the hotel.

But as she stood staring down at the coins she wondered. Was this all she was worth to him? Was this the price of her companionship? Of the child inside her?

"Yes, I've bedded men for money," she said. "And I suppose that makes me a whore. But I never took money from you, only food and shelter. And I thought you were offering that as my friend." She threw the money at his feet. "I was never a whore with you, Ryan. Only a fool."

Chapter Twenty-three

"Ryan will kill me if he finds out I've been here to see you," Bernadette said as she set her tea cup on its saucer and tried to keep her hand from trembling.

From the opposite end of the sofa Eirinn watched and listened, her mind unable and unwilling to comprehend the story she was hearing. Ryan couldn't be this cruel. Surely the girl was lying.

"Ryan wouldn't hurt a woman," she argued. "Especially one with child. He's . . . a gentleman."

The young woman with the old face laughed grimly. "You think so? Well, I know better. Remember that night when you came into our room and caught us—"

"Yes, I remember." Eirinn stared down into her tea cup. How could she ever forget? That had been the beginning of the end. The moment when her image of Ryan had been shattered. The events since that night had only served to further disillusion her.

"Well, after you left, he threw me out. And I mean *threw* me out. Cracked two of my ribs."

"I don't believe you."

"Then maybe you'll believe this." She rolled up both sleeves of her dress, a garment that had once been elegant, but was now worn to the point of being shabby. Holding up both arms, she displayed a series of dark bruises just above her elbows. "That's what Ryan did to me yesterday when I came to the shop and told him that I was pregnant. We had an argument and he ended up pushing me out the door."

Eirinn winced when she saw the bruises, and her heart went out to this young woman. She knew what it was to be hurt by a man, to be treated as less than human, and she knew the fear and pain of being an unmarried woman carrying a child.

"He called me a whore and tossed me out," Bernadette lamented.

"Are you?" Eirinn asked softly as her eyes roamed over the other woman's rouged cheeks and low-cut bodice. She had the look of a woman who had been mistreated by more than one man.

"What do you mean?" Bernadette's blue eyes filled with tears.

"Forgive me," Eirinn said. "I don't mean to insult you. But you've come·here asking me for money. I don't know you. How can I be sure that you're even pregnant, let alone that my brother is responsible for your condition?"

Bernadette nodded and bit her lower lip. "I understand. There's no reason why you should help me. But I had no where else to turn and I need the money to get myself taken care of."

"Taken care of? What are you talking about? I thought you wanted me to help you raise your child."

Shaking her head, Bernadette said, "It's too late for that. If Ryan won't marry me I can't have the baby. I'd never be able to take care of it myself. There's an old woman, a fortune-teller, there in Coney Island who'll take care of it for me. But she charges a lot of money, and I just don't have it."

Eirinn's mind refused to entertain the idea of Michael and Caitlin McKevett's grandchild meeting its end that way.

Besides, she had heard about those back alley

281

surgeries that often left the woman dead or damaged for life.

"Please, you mustn't do such a thing. I'll help you any way I can. If necessary, I'll even raise your baby as my own. But promise me you won't go to that woman."

Bernadette set her cup on the tea table and stood. Her face was gaunt and pale, her limbs thin and brittle-looking. "I can't promise you anything," she said wearily. "I don't know what I'm going to do."

"Go home and rest. I'll do what I can, I promise."

The young woman's blue eyes searched Eirinn's. For what, Eirinn didn't know. But she could see by the hopelessness in those eyes that Bernadette hadn't found what she was looking for. She couldn't think of any way to reassure her.

"Really. I'll help you, and everything will be fine. You'll see."

Eirinn showed her to the door and down the front steps. As she watched the woman walk away, Eirinn had a terrible premonition that everything wasn't going to be fine. Not at all.

Eirinn stood beside the poker table, its green felt top dimly lit by the tasseled lampshade that hung low over its center. Padraic and Ryan sat on opposite sides of the table, their heads bent over their cards, which they were playing close to their vests. A stack of chips lay on Padraic's side of the table. Only three remained on Ryan's. Apparently his luck was running true to form tonight.

For a while she said nothing, waiting for them to acknowledge her presence. It soon became apparent that neither of them intended to greet her. But tonight she didn't care. She was too hurt and angry

surprises than other men the woman than other
mere

"Ryan, I need to speak to you," she said.

"In a minute." He tossed one of his remaining chips into the center of the table.

"Now."

Both men looked up from their cards, astonishment in their eyes. It had been a long time since Eirinn had spoken with an authoritative tone. It had been months since she had felt so strong. Perhaps some of her strength came from having someone weaker to defend.

"I want to speak to you about Bernadette," she said. "You remember her—the one I found you in bed with several months ago."

Ryan cast an uneasy glance across the table at Padraic, who folded his cards and scooped his chips into his bowler.

"Since I have nearly all of your money anyway," Padraic told Ryan, "I might as well leave the two of you alone to have your little chat. Don't let her get the best of you, man."

Eirinn fought down her loathing as she watched him leave the room. How had she ever been so foolish as to marry a man like that? She looked down at Ryan, who sat fondling his one remaining chip. What had she done to deserve having two such men in her life? The answer, which troubled her deeply, was that she herself had chosen to be with both of them.

With a sigh of fatigue she sank onto the chair beside him and picked up the stack of cards. Tossing them, one by one, onto the table, she said, "Bernadette came by to see me today."

She could feel him tense as he fumbled with the chip. "Did she now? And what did she want?"

"What does everyone want, Ryan? Money. She needs money to abort your child."

"Did she tell you that she's a prostitute?"

283

"She admitted that she once was. But she told me that you're the only man she's been with for months."

"And you believed a whore?"

"I believed that woman. Whatever she may have done in the past, I don't think she was lying to me."

"You're gullible, Eirinn." He shook his head in disgust.

She nodded. "Obviously so. I thought all these years that you were a good person. I loved you and insisted that everyone else try to love you. But they could see through you, Ryan. They all knew what you were, what you were capable of. Everyone except sweet, trusting, gullible little Eirinn." She leaned across the table toward him. "How could you have turned that girl away? She's carrying your baby in her belly. How could you abandon her like that?"

"Dammit, there's nothing I can do for her. You don't really expect me to marry someone like her, do you?"

Eirinn looked him up and down as though seeing him clearly for the first time. "No, I don't. She's much too good for you. But unfortunately she doesn't know that. She wants you. God only knows why."

"I'm not going to marry her, Eirinn, not even for you. So don't ask me to do that. If she wants to get rid of the baby, I think that's a wonderful solution to a difficult dilemma." He looked across the table at her, his eyes colorless in the dim light. He picked up the one chip, flipped it into the air, and caught it with a practiced flick of his wrist.

"There's just one little problem," he said. "Thanks to your husband's uncanny skill at poker, I'm flat broke. Could you lend me the money for a few weeks?"

She stared at him a long time before answering. She wanted to seal this moment in her mind forever. The day might come when she would ask herself why she had turned her back on her own brother. Recalling this moment would dispel all guilt.

"You're despicable, Ryan McKevett," she said as she stood to leave. "I look at you now and I wonder why I ever loved you, why I ever thought you were so big, brave, and strong. You're weak and cruel and the most selfish person I've ever known. I want you out of my life, out of my home and my business. And I'll do everything I can to see to it that you are out."

No longer able to bear being near him, she turned and headed for the door.

"Wait!" He stood and hurried toward her, hands outstretched. "I love you, Eirinn. I always have. I don't think I could live without your love and your respect."

His heart was in his eyes. He meant it, but she didn't care. "Of course you can, Ryan," she said. "Just give it a try."

He was either going to marry her or kill her, and he had to decide which before he reached her hotel room.

How dare she go behind his back to Eirinn, Ryan thought as he stormed down the hallway of the casino hotel toward the room at the end of the hall. That ungrateful wench. After all he had done for her—fed her, clothed her, bought her jewelry, even if he had been forced to pawn it to pay his gambling debts, and he had paid for this room for over a year.

Then, just because he skipped a few months rent and refused to marry her, she had tattled to his sister. He wanted to break her neck or maybe just strangle her slowly and enjoy every minute of it.

There was only one thing to stop him. If he killed her, Eirinn was sure to find out, and then there would be absolutely no way to win her back.

On the other hand, if he married Bernadette and did the honorable thing, at least in Eirinn's eyes, it would go a long way toward winning back her love and respect.

He couldn't live knowing that she hated him, that she felt only contempt for him. Ryan had always defined himself in terms of how Eirinn saw him. He had endured the ridicule of his family and peers because she had thought him wonderful, intelligent, and sophisticated.

Whatever he had to do to restore her faith in him, he would do. Even if it meant marrying a worthless little strumpet like Bernadette.

He could do worse, he supposed. With a bit of grooming and some refinement, she could probably be introduced to some of his society friends. And she certainly did know how to please a man in bed. Yes, he could do worse than Bernadette.

By the time he reached the door at the end of the hall he had made his decision. He wouldn't murder her after all. He would marry her.

Slipping his key into the lock, he found that the door was already unlatched. The moment he opened it and stepped inside, he smelled it. That sweet, sick smell of blood. A lot of it.

The room was dark, so he quickly lit a lamp. It didn't take long for him to find her. She lay face down in the middle of the floor. The dark stain of blood covered the threadbare carpet beneath her.

"Bernadette," he whispered, knowing that she would never answer him. "Dear Jesus, what happened to you, girl?"

Even before he had taken the three steps to her

body and knelt down beside her, he was shaking violently. He had never seen so much blood in his life. Her petticoat was drenched in it. She wore no bloomers or stockings, but her legs were covered with the thick, dark stuff. A chill of horror went through him when he saw the long knitting needle that was still clenched in her right hand.

"No. You didn't. . . ."

He stood and backed away from her, trying to distance himself from the body and from the realization that was flooding over him. She had done this to herself, trying to abort the baby—his baby.

He had known she was desperate, but, dear God in heaven, he had never thought she would try something like this.

His knees buckled and he sat down abruptly on the side of the bed. Bile, bitter and thick, rose in his throat, and he choked it down. His brain churned out a thousand thoughts and just as many memories.

What could he do? He couldn't just leave her here like this. How long had she been dead? If he reported her death would the police question him? And what about the scandal? Would everyone find out that she had been pregnant . . . with his child?

He recalled how she had devoured her food that first night he had brought her to this room. She had been so young and innocent then, with roses in her cheeks and adoration in her wide blue eyes. He had never really loved her, but there had been a time when he had liked her. He hated to see her die in this obscene way.

And then Ryan remembered another time. A time that he had conveniently shoved into a far corner of his mind. Only now it came rushing forward, demanding to be remembered and considered.

Bernadette had saved his life that night when he

had tried to end it all with opium. She had found him, summoned a doctor, and rescued him.

Guilt, hot and searing, scalded his conscience. It was a new feeling for Ryan, an unbearable one.

He lost the battle with his stomach and ran to the washbowl on the dresser. This was his fault. He had killed this girl as surely as if he had held that damned knitting needle in his own hand.

She should have allowed him to die that night. If she had, she would be alive now. He stood there, gagging over the washbowl, wishing he were dead.

He didn't want to live any longer. He was tired of the way he had spent his life, tired of himself.

But most of all, he didn't want to live because after this there was no way in the world that he could ever regain Eirinn's love. She would never, *never* forgive him for this.

Chapter Twenty-four

Eirinn sat staring down at the ledgers spread before her on the desk. She couldn't believe her eyes. No wonder Ryan and Padraic had kept her from seeing the books all these months. Neither of them would have wanted her to know that little by little Ryan had been losing the McKevetts' half of the company to Padraic. The pay off for gambling debts, no doubt.

How could Ryan have done it? How could he have gambled away Michael's and Caitlin's business? An enterprise that had taken them a lifetime to build had been lost in less than one year.

Perhaps worst of all, Eirinn had a gnawing, sick feeling that Padraic had planned this all along. Like a fool she had married him, thinking that she was saving her family's business. In fact, she had sold out to the devil.

Eirinn slammed the ledger closed and sat there trembling with rage. She wanted to kill them both. How had she been so naive as to think them honorable men?

Many times she had heard Michael say, "If a man fools you once, shame on him. If he fools you twice, shame on you." Ryan and Padraic had made a fool of her once, but never again. She would find a way to bring her company back under her own control, at least her half of it.

Hearing the door open behind her, she turned in her chair and saw Padraic walk into the office. As always when she saw him these days, her heart began to pound against her ribs. Her body still remembered the beating he had given her and it reacted with fear. Her mind and heart reacted with fury.

His eyes scanned the ledgers on the desk, then locked with hers. She stared back at him unflinching. Instinctively she knew that this was no time to show weakness.

"What the bloody hell do you think you're doing there, girl?" he roared, pointing an accusing finger at the books.

"Finding out what you and my worthless brother have been hiding from me all these months. This business is hardly a partnership anymore, is it?"

"Your brother has an appetite for gambling and no income to support his habit." He shrugged. "I've only taken what was rightfully mine."

She stood and walked over to him, pulling herself up to her full five feet, four inches. She was still at least five inches shorter than him, but in her anger she didn't care. "Ryan's half was my half as well. He had no right to pay you off with my property, and you had no right to take it without my knowledge."

"Your property?" He laughed sardonically. "You're a woman. And a woman can't own property."

"I'm an *Irish* woman, like my mother," she said. "And she taught me that under the old Irish law, a woman is equal to a man in every way."

"But this is America, not old Ireland, and you can't own anything. So get used to the idea." He moved closer to her, and she could smell the rancid scent of whiskey on his breath. "I own this company, Eirinn, and I own you. I'll do whatever I damned well choose with both of you, and don't you forget it."

Her temper flared and common sense evaporated. "What do you think I am? A horse or a deed to a piece of property? I'm a human being, God damn it, and you'll treat me like one or—"

His hand cracked across her face and the air rang with the sound of it. Eirinn stepped back, her hand to her cheek. She was trembling violently, but from anger, not fear.

"If you ever do that again, Padraic, I swear I'll kill you," she said in a voice that was so deep and menacing she didn't recognize it as her own.

He took one step toward her, his fists raised. But he hesitated. Perhaps it was something in her eyes that stopped him. He stood there staring at her for a long moment then he turned and walked away.

Eirinn was surprised. She had fully expected to be hit again and again. She had also expected to follow through with her threat. She had had enough of being beaten and used by men. Tomas had raped her, Ryan had cheated her, and Padraic had abused her. Never again.

A covey of pigeons fluttered and cooed at Eirinn's feet as she tossed the last bits of bread onto the grass. All afternoon she had sat on this park bench, looking out over the lake, thinking, remembering.

It had been a spring evening like this when Daniel had taken her out in the boat to the middle of the lake and asked her to marry him, when he had made love to her that night in his room. For the first time in her life, Eirinn knew what it was to truly regret. If she could only go back to that afternoon and erase all that had happened since. If she had only had the wisdom to see Ryan for what he was, to understand why Daniel had refused to work and live with him. Now she knew that Daniel had rejected Ryan, not her. She had been the one who had given him the ultimatum: accept me, accept my brother.

She had felt deserted by Daniel, but Daniel must have felt that she had chosen Ryan over him. Danny had realized then what Ryan was, as she was only now comprehending. No wonder he was unable to be around him.

She was grateful that Daniel didn't know what had happened to Michael's business. He would have died rather than lose it to Padraic Brady.

With a sick, aching emptiness inside, Eirinn watched a pair of lovers step into one of the boats and row their way to the center of the lake. Their laughter carried across the waters on the still evening air, and the sound made her all the more melancholy.

She missed Danny. She wanted him. But it had been so long and so much had happened. Did he miss her? Did he still want her?

Tossing the last of the bread to the pigeons, she stood and dusted the crumbs from her lap. There was only one way to find out.

Seated on his parlor sofa Daniel watched as his housekeeper, Mrs. Clancy, served the dainty cakes frosted with pink and lavender icing along with cups of steaming tea. He was grateful that Mrs. Clancy knew how to entertain a young lady of good breeding such as the one sitting on the opposite end of the sofa. At times like these Daniel was acutely aware of just how little he knew about such things.

Miss Elizabeth Hampton was definitely upper crust. The daughter of a Manhattan banker, she could have picked any number of eligible gentlemen from the social registers. And Daniel was flattered that she had chosen to spend this afternoon in his humble home, sipping tea.

These days Daniel found himself surrounded by more and more people of this woman's social standing—wealthy, prominent people who admired his art and seemed to place great importance on the many awards that were being lavished upon him by civic art groups.

The attention and adoration was nice, but Daniel wasn't comfortable enough to wallow in it. He was convinced that someday soon they would all realize that he was only an Irish immigrant who carved horses out of wood, not the great artist they proclaimed him to be.

But for now he was enjoying the company of the lovely Elizabeth Hampton. Or at least, he was trying to. She was beautiful, refined, educated, and intelligent, and Daniel was bored to tears.

"Daniel O'Brien, where is your mind today?" she asked, a pretty pout on her heart-shaped face.

He shook his head as though coming out of a trance. "I beg yer pardon, ma'am?"

"That is the third time you've yawned in the past five minutes. Obviously you're not interested in hearing about the ambassador's ball or what everyone was wearing."

"But I am, darlin'. Ye must tell me all about it."

His interest in her conversation—and in the lady herself, for that matter—was feigned, and the fact was painfully obvious.

Daniel could see the light of infatuation in her hazel eyes, and the hurt of knowing that her feelings weren't returned. He felt terrible. The last thing he had intended was to hurt this gentle lady.

He had forced himself to see her, half-heartedly to pursue her. Anything to get his mind off Eirinn. It wasn't fair, to himself or to the ladies he had used for momentary distraction.

"I think I'll be going home now, Daniel," she said as she rose from the sofa and slipped on her white gloves. "Thank you for a lovely afternoon."

" 'Twasn't a lovely afternoon at all, I'm afraid," he replied with regret in his voice. "And I must be apologizin' to you for me behavior. I've a lot on me mind at the moment and—"

"I know what you have on your mind, Daniel," she replied. Tears brimmed in her luminous eyes. "You're still in love with Eirinn McKevett. Everyone knows that . . . except maybe you."

" 'Tisn't true at all, at all," he protested. "That woman's the bane of me existence, she is. 'Tis a wonder I haven't murdered her already and put her out of me misery."

The lady lifted her chin and walked toward the door. "Keep saying that Daniel," she said, "and maybe someday you can make yourself believe it. But you'll never convince me. You love her and you always will. And as long as she's in your heart, there's no room in there for me or anyone else."

He opened his mouth to argue, but nothing came out. So he closed it and stood there, staring down at the floor. He had misused this good lady as surely as he had misused those whores. She was right of course. He did love Eirinn. And what made it worse—he knew that she loved him too. Then he thought of Ryan. Yes, Eirinn loved him, but obviously not enough. Not as much as she loved Ryan.

"I'll take ye home now," he said as they walked out the door and down the front porch. "Just give me a moment to hail us a hack."

A moment later he handed her into a hansom cab, but when he tried to climb in beside her, she stopped him with an upheld palm.

"No, Daniel. I'd rather go home alone. Thank you anyway.

"Ye'll do no such thing," he said. "I'll be seein' ye home, sure as the world."

"I said no. I'll be fine, and I truly prefer it this way. Good afternoon, Daniel."

With a wave of shame Daniel realized that Miss Elizabeth Hampton was about to cry, and that she didn't want him to see her tears. Out of respect for her wishes, he leaned into the cab and kissed her, sweetly and tenderly on the lips.

"Good afternoon, Miss Hampton. Ye'll understand if I don't call again, ma'am. Yer right. There is

294

another in me heart and mind. But yer a lovely lady and I'll long remember you with fondness."

Daniel waved the driver on and watched until the hack was out of sight. He had run the social gambit now — from prostitutes to socialites. But in all that searching he hadn't found one woman who could help him forget that black-haired beauty with Ireland in her green eyes.

For the first time in years, Eirinn was happy. Her step was light, her eyes glittering as she hurried along the sidewalk through Daniel's brownstone neighborhood. She had made a mistake, a terrible mistake, by choosing Ryan over the man she loved.

Michael and Caitlin had always taught her that family came first. But Danny was family too. You didn't have to be joined by blood to be a member of a family. There were more important things that bound people together — love, loyalty, dedication.

Daniel had proven himself in every way. Even these past months, when she had been doing everything she could to undermine his business, he had done nothing to retaliate. He had been a perfect gentleman in all his dealings and she had hated him for it. She hated him because his honesty showed up her bitterness for what it was — petty and shallow.

And to think that all this time she had thought that she no longer loved Daniel. Of course she still loved him. She had simply redirected her passion into anger. But all the feelings were still there, boiling beneath the surface, threatening to erupt at any time.

She would tell him how she felt, she decided. As soon as she got to his house, she would tell him that she still loved him, that she had been a fool, and she would beg his forgiveness.

He would welcome her back with open arms. Of that she was certain. He still loved her. He had to. All

295

she had to do was convince him that she wanted him back and was willing to put her pride aside to gain his love and trust again.

By the time she rounded that final corner she was nearly running. She couldn't wait to speak those words of love, to see the joy in his eyes, to feel those strong arms around her.

Then she saw him. She froze in mid step and stood there watching, her breath and her heart caught in her throat.

He was walking a beautiful young woman out to the curb and putting her into a hack. Then he was kissing her. Eirinn was too far away to see the expressions on their faces, but she could clearly see that this was no ordinary woman. She was a lady, and Daniel was treating her like one. He was handling her with a gentleness and respect that went straight to Eirinn's heart and caused a deep, searing pain to shoot through her.

When he kissed the woman it wasn't a quick, fraternal peck. It was a kiss with feeling and affection, the kind he had given her so many times. The kind of kiss that she had been looking forward to receiving when she told him that she was still in love with him.

Tears flooded her eyes, and she whirled around, afraid that he might see her. The last thing she wanted was for him to know that she had witnessed this tender moment between him and his new lover.

As she walked away, Eirinn tried to hate him for loving another woman, but she couldn't. It was all her own fault.

She had taken him for granted, assuming that when she was ready to come back to him he would be ready and eager to take her back.

But she had waited too long. It was too late.

Chapter Twenty-five

As Eirinn looked around the manufactory a flood of memories swept over her, washing her in melancholy. Everywhere she looked there were reminders of the people she had loved and lost.

Even with the changes that Padraic had brought, there were still ghosts in this shop. In her mind's eye Eirinn saw her father moving around the room, changing a line on one of the life-sized sketches, stopping beside an apprentice carver, gently advising and directing, pausing at Daniel's table to watch a master craftsman's hands work their magic. She saw Michael putting his giant shoulder to the finished wheel and turning it for the first time. She remembered how he had died, killed by the thing he loved most, that which he himself had created.

With a pang of longing she thought of Caitlin, working beside Michael all those long years, quietly supporting him, supplying solid business advice to her less than practical, artistic husband. If Michael had been the heart of the business, Caitlin had been its mind, a queen with sword in hand, protecting the ground they had gained, striving to conquer new horizons.

Eirinn walked over to the master carver's bench and looked at the tools carefully spread there and covered with a soft cloth. Those should have been Daniel's tools, not those of the Italian whom Brady had just hired. Daniel was the true master, always had been. When the McKevetts' shop had lost him it had lost its hands and the magic they created. Daniel had carved anything that Michael's imagination had spun. But since both of them had left, nothing truly wonderful had been brought to life here in this shop.

All around her Eirinn saw the sad, misshapen ponies with their too-long noses and too-short legs. They were the product of unskilled hands who were pushed to work too fast. They bore no resemblance to the magnificent stallions or the dainty mares that had once pranced in this shop.

She had lost it all. The realization came to Eirinn along with an aching pain that coursed through her body, leaving her weak and shaken. Everything that her father and mother had built she had lost.

It wasn't only Ryan's fault. He had gambled it away on paper. But she was the one who had killed the dream, killed it with hatred, her determination to ruin Daniel. So what if they produced four carousels a year compared to his one? His were works of art that would endure and provide pleasure for generation after generation. She knew, better than anyone, that the machines the McKevetts had produced this past year would do well to survive the decade.

"I'm sorry, Da," she whispered into the dark silence. "I'm so sorry."

To her surprise she heard a response—not with her ears, but with her heart. Michael understood and, as always, forgave. But it didn't make her feel any better.

Without thinking where she was going, she walked to the back of the shop, to a door that opened into a small storeroom. She hadn't stepped into that room for years, since they had first moved to New York. But tonight she was drawn there, to the object that was in the corner covered by a heavy dropcloth.

Pulling the canvas away, she unveiled the dainty mare that Danny had carved for her sixteenth birthday. The pony's green eyes glowed in the dim light that shown through the half-open door, and Eirinn could feel those eyes on her, watching with gentle sadness, feeling her pain.

She reached out and laid her hand on the horse's smooth neck. She could almost feel a life force surging through the wood. The horse had a soul, and Eirinn knew whose it was. It was the essence of Daniel O'Brien, captured there in the wood. His power, his gentleness, his love for her.

"Oh, Danny," she whispered as tears ran down her cheeks and sobs choked her throat. "I've lost you too. I've lost everything."

She hugged the horse, burying her face against its neck. So absorbed was she in her grief that she didn't hear the footsteps in the shop or the creak of the door as it opened wider. She didn't know he was there—until he reached out and grabbed her shoulder.

"I don't have to ask why you're crying over that horse," Padraic said as he whirled her around, his thick, sausagelike fingers digging into her shoulder. "And I don't have to ask where you went today either. I know. You went to see that damned Daniel O'Brien."

She tried to pull away from him, but he held her too tightly. "If you really followed me," she said, "you'd know that I didn't say a word to him."

"Only because he was busy with another lady. Not because you didn't want to."

The humiliation of the afternoon washed over her again, adding to her anger. "You followed me?"

"Don't flatter yourself. I have better things to do than chase your skirt all over town. I had Tim

O'Day follow you."

Tim O'Day? When Eirinn thought of that burly oaf trailing after her, watching her every movement, her temper soared. "You've got a lot of damned nerve, having your bloodhound sniff around after me."

He released his grip on her arm, but her relief was short-lived. A second later he backhanded her across the face. The pain blinded her. She fell back against the horse, her hand to her stinging cheek. "Don't you ever do that to me again, Padraic," she said. "I mean it!"

In answer he struck her again, only this time with his fist. The punch landed on her ribs and knocked the breath from her body. She collapsed onto the floor.

"I told you before," he said as he hauled her to her feet, "I'll do whatever I please with you. You're my wife and I own you." He grabbed a handful of her hair and yanked her head backward. "I could kill you right now and no jury would convict me of murder. Not when I tell them that you've been sleeping with another man."

"I haven't been with Daniel," she said. The cold voice of logic in the back of her mind was clammering to be heard above her rage and fear. It was telling her to pacify him, to say anything at all, to get out of this room. Get out and run. To safety. To Daniel.

"You lying bitch. I saw the way he kissed you that day. Our wedding day. You almost married him once. Daniel's still in love with you. Everybody knows that."

Even in her fear and pain, Eirinn's mind clutched at his words. Was Daniel really still in love with her? *Did* everyone know except her? The very thought caused a surge of happiness that brought a momentary half-smile to her face. Quickly she wiped it away, but not soon enough. Padraic had seen it.

"You *are* still in love with him, damn you." He grabbed for her again, but this time she got away from him. Far more agile than he, she ducked under his arm and raced out the storeroom door and into the shop.

He ran after her and caught her beside Daniel's workbench. "Have you been with him?" he shouted into her face. "I know you have. But I want to hear you admit it."

With one hand he shoved her backwards across the bench, his fingers clasped menacingly around her neck. Not squeezing, but threatening.

"I've been faithful to you," she gasped, trying not to cry out as the sharp edge of the bench bit into her spine. "I swear I have."

"You're lying. You're a lying whore and I'm going to kill you."

He meant it. She could see it in his eyes. She heard more than felt the blow that snapped her head backward and caused her vision to blur. But even through the haze of pain she saw it, the red smear on the fist held in front of her face. It was blood. *Her* blood.

Fear, and its paralysis, disappeared. Fury took its place. An animal fury born of the need for self-preservation.

Suddenly she was back in that dark alley again, fighting for her life. Only this time her attacker wasn't a stranger. He was her own husband.

Slowly, as though drifting in a dream, she watched that blood-smeared hand rise and fall. She heard the horrible liquid thuds as his fist landed on her face and body.

Danny! her mind and heart screamed. But Daniel

301

couldn't help her this time.

She flailed at him with her fists, but he didn't even wince. The only sign that she had even struck him was his increased rage as the blows came harder and faster.

She could hear him screaming at her, but her mind couldn't take in the words. It didn't have to. His message was clear. He wasn't going to stop until she was dead.

Something told her that if he ever got her down on the floor, he would quickly finish her off. But her legs were giving way beneath her, too weak to support her any longer. As her knees buckled she slid to the floor, clutching at the edge of the bench. But she grabbed only a handful of the sheet that covered the carver's tools.

No sooner had she hit the floor than he was on her, his hands around her throat in a grip that cut off her air. She thrashed and tried to scream, but it was only a gargled gasp. Insanely she struck at his chest with her clenched fists. He gasped and she saw a look of surprise and pain on his face. So she hit him again and again, shocked that her blows were actually affecting him.

Grabbing at his chest, he rolled off her and onto the floor beside her, where he lay groaning.

There was blood everywhere. Somehow Eirinn knew that this time it wasn't her own blood. It was his.

She watched in fascinated horror as his body quivered and his eyes rolled back in his head.

He was dying.

She had hit him in the chest with her fist, and he was dying.

Staring down at her hand, she didn't recognize it as her own. This was a stranger's hand that had just murdered someone. And it was holding a bloody chisel.

From the shadows he watched. He had walked into the shop just in time to hear her scream and to see her throw the chisel away. She scrambled away from the body on the floor and ran, her hand over her mouth, out the back door.

Ryan knew what had happened. Somehow he had known all along that it would come to this. Soon after Padraic and Eirinn had been married, Ryan had realized the depth of violence that Brady had been capable of. He had known each time that Brady had beaten Eirinn and Ryan knew Eirinn well enough to know that she wouldn't submit forever.

This showdown had been inevitable. Ryan was deeply relieved that it was Brady who was dead and not Eirinn. The weight of Bernadette's death was already more than his conscience could bear.

Ryan walked over to the corpse and stared down at it. He thought how similar Brady's body looked to Bernadette's. Both had been covered with blood, both stared up at him, seeing past him into their own private hells.

But Ryan didn't get sick this time. He was glad that Padraic Brady was dead. Eirinn was free now. Free of the trap that he, himself, had laid for her.

Padraic Brady deserved to be killed, Ryan decided as he walked over and picked up the blood-slick chisel. And by getting himself murdered, Brady had supplied Ryan with a way to show his love and devotion to Eirinn.

He shoved the chisel into his coat pocket, grabbed Brady's limp arms and, using all his strength, pulled the heavy body across the floor to the door.

He smiled as he left the shop and headed toward the livery to get his buggy.

Yes, after this, Eirinn would always know how very, very much he loved her.

Eirinn's mind raced as she threw her clothes into two carpet bags. Ireland. She would catch the next ship bound for Ireland. If she was lucky she would find one leaving tonight. Waiting until morning would be risky. Someone might find the body and . . .

She should have hidden it. Buried it. But even though her life depended on it she couldn't bring herself to set foot inside that shop again, let alone touch him.

Her hands were shaking so much she could hardly unbutton her dress, the dress that was still stained with her blood and Padraic's.

She should probably burn it, she thought. Then she remembered that it didn't matter. With an overwhelming surge of grief and regret she looked around her bedroom and realized that by tomorrow she would be sailing far away from here.

Away from her home and the shop.

Away from Daniel.

The corpse lay sprawled in the middle of the floor of the shabby room that had been Ryan's home for the past three weeks. It was a tiny hovel, no more than a shack, behind the restaurant of the Blue Moon Casino. Deluxe suites in classy hotels had long become a thing of the past for Ryan.

He scurried over to the room's one window and carefully pulled the threadbare curtains. The last thing he needed right now was a midnight customer to come knocking at his door, trying to buy some opium. Ryan wasn't open for business tonight. He needed every bit of the precious black powder for himself.

But first things first.

Pulling the chisel from his coat pocket, he laid it on the floor beside the corpse which he had dragged there only moments before. Then, after reconsidering, he picked the chisel up, closed his eyes, and plunged it into the body's chest.

There. That ought to be convincing enough.

Taking a wide path around the body, he walked over to the small table in the corner of the room, took out a pen and some paper, and sat down on the table's one chair.

Slowly he began to write a letter to Eirinn, choosing each word and phrase with the utmost care, knowing that others besides her would read it.

Dearest Eirinn,

Please forgive me, darling, for the terrible murder that I have committed this night. But I couldn't bear to see the way he was abusing you, day after day with no end in sight. I was responsible for getting you into this destructive marriage. I had to be the one to release you.

When I look back over my useless life, I realize that I alone am to blame for the great sorrows that have afflicted you. And I must confess it all to you now.

First I must tell you that had it not been for me, Sean Sullivan would be alive today. I set the fire that destroyed the factory. Sean died of heart failure witnessing that tragedy, so I am to blame. Though Sean wasn't the love of your heart, he was a good husband to you and I am to blame for you losing him. From the shock of his death, you miscarried your child. So that death is also to my discredit.

Secondly, I must confess that I was also responsible for your father's death. My mistake caused the accident that killed him. I was drunk that night, lazy and rebellious. I didn't finish adjusting and tightening the support cables. So it was my fault that he was killed the next morning.

Daniel knows that I killed Michael. Perhaps you will understand now why he hates me and why he can't bear the sight of me. I used his hate and your love for me to keep the two of you apart. I simply couldn't stand the thought of you being married to a man I despised, to a man who despised me.

I must also apologize for encouraging you to marry a brute like Brady. I did it for his money, thinking that I could somehow get my hands on his business. Even that failed, as you know. Not only did I not get his business, but I lost ours to him.

I've ruined my life, Eirinn. My greatest regret is that I've ruined yours as well. Please forgive me and know that I've always loved you.

Ryan sat for a long time, pen in hand, considering what to write next. He wanted to tell Eirinn that he wasn't really her brother. He wanted to tell her that his love had not been simple, fraternal affection but the burning desire of a man for a woman.

But he couldn't bring himself to do it. Eirinn didn't love him in that way. She never had. Her sisterly love for him was the only tie they had. If he destroyed that, there would be no bond between them.

So he simply signed the letter, folded it carefully and laid it on the table. As an afterthought, he picked the paper up and pressed it to his lips, then laid it down again.

He walked to the dresser in the opposite corner of the room and opened the bottom drawer. With great ceremony he lifted out a wooden cigar box and carried it to his bed.

From the box he pulled a pipe, a box of matches and a purple velvet bag filled with a black, tarry powder. He hefted the bag in his hand. It was enough.

He hadn't gone to hell after all, Ryan thought with relief. This was heaven. For some reason God had forgiven him and allowed him into Paradise.

Floating above the earth, above the guilt and fear, he felt the sun's rays shining warm on his face.

And Eirinn was there. That was how he knew it was heaven.

He called her name and she turned to him. In her hand was his letter. She had read it and forgiven him. When she held out her arms to him, he knew that she realized what a sacrifice he had made for her.

He ran to her, took her in his arms and crushed her to him. She wanted him as much as he wanted her, not as a sister, as a lover.

She lifted her face to his and he kissed her. Her lips were softer than he had ever imagined, and they answered his passion, a mirror image of his own desire.

She was his for the taking. Finally. Not Sean's or Padraic's or even Daniel's, but his.

But then a dark cloud slid across the sun, blotting out the warm light. A cold darkness closed around him. Suddenly he couldn't feel the warmth of her body against his. In the blackness that enveloped him he couldn't see her beautiful face.

She was gone.

And he was alone.

Forever.

And Ryan realized . . . this was hell after all.

Chapter Twenty-six

Eirinn was halfway down the stairs with a carpet bag in her hand when she heard the heavy knock on her front door. Her heart leaped into her throat, and what little strength she had in her legs drained away.

She clung to the rail for support as she hurried down the stairs. In the entry hall she threw the bag beneath a small table and made certain that the fringed tablecloth hid it.

Smoothing her hair with her trembling hands, she took a deep breath and opened the door. An enormous policeman stood there, filling the doorway with his imposing presence.

A feeling of inevitability settled over Eirinn. She should have known that she could never get away with murder.

"Good evening, sir," she heard herself saying. "May I help you?"

Quickly removing his hat and bowing his blond head, he said, "Good evening to you, ma'am. Would you be Mrs. Brady?" His voice had a gentle Irish lilt that reminded Eirinn of her father. But that did little to ease her anxiety.

"I am."

"I'm Sergeant Denis Riley. I'd like to speak to you for a moment. May I come inside?"

She opened the door and motioned for him to enter. "Yes, of course. May I get you a cup of hot tea or coffee? It's a cold night out there."

"A cold night, indeed. And a cup of coffee would be lovely, but I'm afraid I have no time for that now." He stared down at the oriental carpet and cleared his throat. "Ma'am, there's something I must tell you."

Eirinn led him into the parlor, and they both sat on the sofa. Something was terribly wrong. She could see it in his bright blue eyes that wouldn't meet hers. But his manner toward her was gentle, not that of a policeman about to make an arrest.

"What is it, Sergeant Riley?" she asked, steeling herself for whatever news he had to deliver.

"You must brace yourself, ma'am. It's about your husband. . ." he began. He reached out and covered her hand with his in a comforting gesture. "I'm sorry to be telling you that he's . . . deceased."

Eirinn stared at him, overwhelmed, not with shock as he seemed to expect, but with confusion. Why was he telling her this? Didn't he suspect her?

"Padraic? Dead?" she managed to say.

"Yes. I'm afraid he's quite . . . deceased."

"Dear God," she murmured, her mind spinning. How should a wife react at a time like this? What should she say next? "How did it happen?" she asked. Surely that was the logical question.

The policeman's eyes brimmed with compassion and his hand tightened around hers. "That's the double tragedy of it," he said. "It seems your brother, Ryan McKevett, took it upon himself to do the deed."

"*Ryan* did it?" Her thoughts froze. None of this made any sense.

"Yes, and then . . ." He cleared his throat

310

again. "Then your brother took his own life. I'm so sorry to have to tell a fine lady such as yourself so much awful news at one time. It's a heavy burden for you to bear, I know. But I couldn't think of any nice way to say such a thing and . . ."

Eirinn was no longer listening to him. It was too much for her mind to take in at once. Ryan, dead? It couldn't be.

"But how?" she asked.

"He did it with a woodcarving tool, I believe. A long, sharp thing of some sort."

"No, I mean how did Ryan . . . kill himself," she asked, nearly choking on the words.

"Oh. Well, he'd been smoking some stuff. Opium, I believe. That black powder the Chinese bring over here."

Eirinn's mind flashed back on the night she had found Ryan and Bernadette at the hotel, nearly unconscious from the drug. Somehow, in a remote part of her heart, she had known that he would die this way. It was as though this whole scene had been set in time long ago.

"He left a note for you," the sergeant was saying as he pulled a letter from the breastpocket of his jacket. "We had to read it. I'm sorry."

"Yes, of course." She took the letter from him and unfolded it on her lap. "Thank you."

Sergeant Riley rose from the sofa and walked over to the window, where he stood with his broad back to her, providing her with a measure of privacy as she read.

One by one, she read Ryan's confessions. Each admission stunned her mind, but merely confirmed what her heart had always known.

Unable to read any further, she let the paper

311

drop from her hand to the floor, and she burst
into tears. Tears of grief, but, to her surprise,
tears of relief as well. It was over. The long nightmare was finally over. And she finally understood
it all.

"Ma'am . . ." The policeman was suddenly
kneeling on the floor beside her, his big hand held
out to her. "Is there anything I can do for you? I
can't leave you here alone like this with your grief.
I'll go get someone to be with you if you'll just
tell me who."

Eirinn thought of Daniel. Then she thought of
the way she had treated him over the years. She
thought of the lady he had handed into the cab.
No, she had no right to ask for Danny now.

"No, there's no one," she said.

Sergeant Riley looked at her doubtfully. "Surely
there's someone."

"No. No one at all. They're all dead now."

" 'Tis all so hard to believe, sergeant," Daniel
said, reeling from the news he had just heard.

He stood at the bar of his neighborhood tavern,
Noonan's Pub, his fingers gripping a mug of ale.
Beside him stood the tall, blond policeman who
looked tired . . . and relieved.

"Then you'll go see the lady?" the officer asked.

"I will, straightaway," Daniel assured him. "And
it's thankful I am to you for tracking me down
this way. However did you know to come to me?"

"Well, it wasn't easy, to be sure. The lady said
there was no one she could turn to, but I didn't
believe it."

Daniel looked down into his ale and a wave of
sadness swept over his face.

"So, I went down to the local pub," Riley continued. "And when I asked around, I ran into an Italian fellow by the name of Ignacio. He said you'd want to know, and that you'd help the lady out."

"Tell me, Sergeant Riley, do ye always go to this much trouble for the people on your beat?"

Riley smiled. "Not usually," he admitted. "But there was something about that lady's big green eyes. I've never seen eyes so full of hurt and sadness."

"Yes," said Daniel as he threw some coins onto the bar and picked up his jacket. "There's something, indeed, about that lady's green eyes."

She couldn't walk away and she couldn't go inside, so, Eirinn stood in the doorway of the carousel shop and trembled as the waves of emotion flooded over her. So much of her life was contained in that shop. So much had happened between those walls.

Could she ever summon the strength to go inside again? She didn't know how.

She would do it, of course. In spite of the numbness in her spirit and the heaviness of her heart, she would rise above it somehow. She would pull her father's dream out of the ashes. Carousels, beautiful wheels carrying Princess Niva's enchanted horses, would be built in this shop again.

But knowing that gave her no joy. What was it all for? Who was it for?

Once she had labored in love, keeping the dream alive for her father and his memory. Then she had battled out of hate, trying to ruin Daniel

313

O'Brien.

Her hate was dead, as dead as Ryan and Padraic. And her love was too far out of reach to give her any strength. She felt empty, like a pitcher from which all the wine had been poured, leaving behind not even the scent of grapes.

"Let me help, Eirinn," said a voice at her shoulder, a soft voice with a gentle Irish brogue that caressed her like a lover's familiar touch.

She turned and saw Daniel standing there, his chestnut hair glowing in the light of the street lantern.

"Danny," she said. She followed her heart and held her arms out to him. In an instant he had folded her to him. "They're dead," she whispered, her face against his hard chest. "Ryan and Padraic are dead."

"I know," he said. "That's why I came. I thought ye might need a friend."

"I killed him, Danny," she said, the confession tumbling out of her. "I murdered my own husband."

"You? But I thought Ryan—"

"That's what the police thought, too. But I did it. I stabbed him to death here in the shop with a chisel."

Daniel's eyes searched her face for a long time before he spoke. "Why, darlin'? I know that ol' Brady was a bit of a devil, but . . ."

Her throat began to close up and she could hardly speak the words. "Because he beat me. He's been beating me, Danny, all along. He was going to kill me. So I killed him first."

Daniel's eyes blazed, the eyes of a soldier, the eyes of a man who had himself committed murder. "It's glad I am you kilt him. I'd have done

314

the deed long ago if I'd known."

"Padraic was robbing me, Danny," she continued, encouraged by his understanding. "He was scheming to steal Da's business away from me completely. And Ryan was helping him."

Anger flared again in Daniel's eyes. He took a deep breath and said, "Aye, well . . . there's something I must tell ye about Ryan, darlin'. Ye don't really owe Ryan yer loyalty like you think you do. You see, he wasn't really yer—"

"Wait." She held up one hand to stop the flow of his words. "Before you say anything bad about Ryan, I want to tell you what he did for me." She swallowed the sob that kept welling up from her throat. "I don't know how he knew that I killed Padraic. Maybe he saw me do it. Anyway, he took Padraic's body to his room and wrote a suicide confession note saying that he murdered Padraic and then killed himself. He did it for me, Danny, to save me."

She watched the emotions war across Daniel's face. Hatred versus grudging respect and gratitude. Finally he seemed to come to a decision. "Well, I guess I won't say what I intended to about Ryan McKevett. If he saved you from the gallows, I owe him something. But ye must understand why I hated the man. Why I couldn't bear the sight of him. Why I beat him senseless that night in my room. He had just told me that he had kilt Michael and I couldn't stop meself."

"Oh, Danny." Suddenly, it all made sense. Every question she had asked again and again over the years was finally answered. Daniel did love her after all. That was why he had protected her, holding back truths that would have explained his actions. He had loved her all along.

"I hated him, Eirinn. But I loved you. Don't ye know how much I loved ye? How much I needed you? Didn't you love me too, lass? Didn't you need me even a little?"

"Of course I loved and needed you, Danny," she said, burrowing against him.

"I knew you did," he murmured with his lips pressed to her hair. "Even though you said you hated me, I knew 'twasn't true. You need me. And now ye've got me, for as long as ye want me."

She pulled back and looked up into his eyes. "Don't say that unless you mean it. I might want you for a very long time."

He smiled down at her. "I'm hopin' that's so. And what is it ye want me to help ye do?"

She looked around the shop, and his eyes followed hers. "I want you to help me build carousels. Big, glorious carousels that my father would have been proud of. Will you do it?"

"Ah, love," he said with a smile that took her breath away. "I could never say no to a green-eyed lassie."

"Thank you, Danny," Eirinn said as she watched the glittering wheel turn around and around. Children, from eight to eighty, clung to the backs of the majestic beasts as they rode to the Land of the Ever Young. "I couldn't have done it without you."

" 'Tis true," he said with a teasing grin as he slipped his arm around her waist and led her out of the arcade. "But I couldn't have done the deed without *you* either. So, 'tis as broad as it's long, I suppose, and we come up equal."

They walked down the boardwalk toward the moonlit beach.

When they reached the water's edge he pulled her into his arms. Slowly his lips moved over hers, warm, firm, and insistent. She melted against him, reveling in the hardness of his body pressed against hers.

"So, now that I've helped you build yer father's carousel," he said, his mouth only an inch from hers, "I suppose ye'll not be needin' me anymore."

He was teasing her; she could see the moonlight twinkling in his eyes.

"I need you, Danny."

"What? Yer after buildin' another one so soon?"

She laughed. "And another and another." Then a serious look took the place of her smile. "But that's not what I need you for."

His hand moved over her back and hips in an intimate caress. "What is it yer in need of, lass?" he said in a husky voice. "And be careful what ye ask for. Ye might get it."

"I need you to love me. I need you to tell me you'll never leave me again, Danny."

"I love ye dearly," he said. "And I'll never leave ye. I'll stand in front of a priest and swear it if that's what ye want."

Eirinn looked up at him and knew that he was the only man she had ever loved. His heart was in his eyes. And it was hers for the taking.

"That's what I want," she said. "I want us to spend our days and nights making love, and children, and more carousels."

He laughed and kissed the tip of her nose. "We will indeed, lass. We'll do all of that and more. Does that make you happy, darlin'?"

"It does." She threw back her head and breathed in the fresh saline air. "I *am* happy. And I think Da is too, wherever he is tonight."

Daniel laughed. "I know where yer father is. He's out there somewhere . . . ," Daniel waved his arm toward the moonlit horizon where the sky met the sea, "riding one of those enchanted horses of his. Michael would never waste a night so lovely as this one."

Pulling her even more tightly against him, he added, "And I don't think we should waste the night either. Come to meself, lass. I've a desperate need to tell ye just how much I love ye."

WIVES, LIES AND DOUBLE LIVES

MISTRESSES ($4.50, 17-109)
By Trevor Meldal-Johnsen
Kept women. Pampered females who have everything: designer clothes, jewels, furs, lavish homes. They are the beautiful mistresses of powerful, wealthy men. A mistress is a man's escape from the real world, always at his beck and call. There is only one cardinal rule: *do not fall in love*. Meet three mistresses who live in the fast lane of passion and money, and who know that one wrong move can cost them everything.

ROYAL POINCIANA ($4.50, 17-179)
By Thea Coy Douglass
By day she was Mrs. Madeline Memory, head housekeeper at the fabulous Royal Poinciana. Dressed in black, she was a respectable widow and the picture of virtue. By night she the French speaking "Madame Memphis", dressed in silks and sipping champagne with con man Harrison St. John Loring. She never intended the game to turn into true love . . .

WIVES AND MISTRESSES ($4.95, 17-120)
By Suzanne Morris
Four extraordinary women are locked within the bitterness of a century old rivalry between two prominent Texas families. These heroines struggle against lies and deceptions to unlock the mysteries of the past and free themselves from the dark secrets that threaten to destroy both families.

Available wherever paperbacks are sold, or order direct from the Publisher. Send cover price plus 50¢ per copy for mailing and handling to Pinnacle Books, Dept. 17-363, 475 Park Avenue South, New York, N.Y. 10016. Residents of New York, New Jersey and Pennsylvania must include sales tax. DO NOT SEND CASH.